BLOOD
LIKE MINE

BOOKS BY STUART NEVILLE

The Ghosts of Belfast
Collusion
Stolen Souls
The Final Silence
Those We Left Behind
So Say the Fallen

Ratlines
The Traveller and Other Stories
The House of Ashes
Blood Like Mine

BLOOD
LIKE
MINE

STUART
NEVILLE

Published by Hell's Hundred
an imprint of Soho Press
227 W 17th Street
New York, NY 10011

Library of Congress Cataloging-in-Publication Data

Names: Neville, Stuart, author.
Title: Blood like mine / Stuart Neville.
Description: New York, NY : Soho Crime, 2024.
Identifiers: LCCN 2023029776

ISBN 978-1-64129-541-3
eISBN 978-1-64129-542-0

Subjects: LCGFT: Thrillers (Fiction) | Detective and mystery fiction. | Novels.
Classification: LCC PR6114.E943 B56 2024
DDC 823'.92—dc23/eng/20230710
LC record available at https://lccn.loc.gov/2023029776

Interior design by Janine Agro

Printed in the United States of America

10 9 8 7 6 5 4 3 2 1

For Janet. Sorry, I mean Katherine.

BLOOD
LIKE MINE

I

Rebecca Carter saw the first flakes of new snow fall from the night sky and settle on the windshield. The road ahead was dark, twisting down through the hills, the headlights catching scrub and rock peering through the drifts of white.

Golden City lay below; she had caught occasional glimpses of its lights through the trees. She had planned this route several days in advance. Boulder lay to the north, and Superior south of that, then Golden at the edge of the Denver metro area. She would head south from there, skirting the mountains, then down to New Mexico, or maybe west toward Utah, driving until the fatigue got too much to carry. West or south, didn't matter, but she needed to put some distance between here and there.

"Try to get some sleep," Rebecca said. "Go on, get in back."

"Not yet," Moonflower said.

She had been christened Monica, but not long after, Rebecca had taken to calling her Moonflower. For the blossoms her own mother grew in the greenhouse behind their home in Madison, Wisconsin. They bloomed at night, pale white faces in the darkness. A thread that still connected Moonflower to her grandmother, causing an ache in Rebecca every time the memory surfaced.

"Come on," Rebecca said. "You're tired. I can tell. You've been doing that thing you do."

She rubbed her nose with the heel of her hand, mimicking the gesture Moonflower had made all her life when sleep wanted her.

"Have not," Moonflower said.

"Have too. Now, come on. Listen to your mother."

"Don't talk to me like I'm a baby."

Moonflower teased at her coal-black hair, twining it around her fingers, a crease in her brow.

"No, we're not doing this. It's been too long a night and I don't have the patience for your attitude. You hear—"

"Mom!"

The beast filled her vision, hulking across the road, snow dusting its back. The elk froze as Rebecca wrenched at the wheel, the van swerving left then right. The passenger side wheels mounted the shoulder, losing grip, throwing the van back across the asphalt. Moonflower cried out as her head bounced off the door. Rebecca felt the rear of the vehicle fishtail, and she eased off the gas, moved her foot to the brake pedal, resisting the urge to stamp down on it and risk losing all control. The van mounted the shoulder on the opposite side of the road and now all Rebecca could see was a white mound of snow, reflecting the glare of the headlights. A dull thump, and she was thrown forward as the van slowed with a lurch, the seatbelt grabbing her chest and waist. Now she depressed the brake, and the van finally halted, its nose buried in snow. The engine fought for a few seconds then stalled. All was still and quiet now, save for the wind and Moonflower's jagged breathing. Rebecca reached for her daughter.

"Are you okay? Are you hurt?"

"Yeah, no," Moonflower said. "I'm fine. I hit my head, but it's all right."

"Let me see."

"It's fine, Mom."

"Let me see."

She turned her daughter's head, examined the skin. A red mark at the corner of her eye, that was all, no blood. No open wound.

"Okay," Rebecca said. And to herself, "Okay."

She pulled the handle and pushed the door open, fighting against the bank of snow outside. Enough of a gap to squeeze through, she told Moonflower to stay put, then climbed out, her feet sinking into the white. She struggled to the rear of the van and looked back along the road. Thirty yards away, the elk looked back at her. Still and impassive, its breath misting. Eventually, it huffed, lowered its antlered head to sniff at the road, then moved off toward the treeline.

It didn't care. It had almost caused a serious accident, and it didn't give a damn. A creature whose only concern was its own survival. All else was background noise. Like most animals.

Rebecca cursed then made her way along the passenger side of the van, the snow deepening as she went. When she reached the front, she shoveled snow away with her bare cupped hands, ignoring the stinging cold. No damage that she could see, thank God. Could've been far worse. Plenty of stretches of this road had sheer drops on one side or the other, thirty, forty feet down onto the rocks below.

Rebecca thanked the universe for small blessings. Maybe she could just back out of the drift and move on. As she turned to head back around the van, a sound stopped her. A hard and artificial noise washing through the wind and the rustling pines. An engine. A vehicle approaching.

She slapped the passenger window with her palm. Moonflower looked back at her, shaking her head, mouthing, What?

"Get in the back," Rebecca shouted.

Moonflower shook her head again, confused. "Why?"

"Someone's coming. Get in the back."

Moonflower peered through the windshield, then in the side mirror, trying to see who approached. Rebecca slapped the window again.

"Just go, now!"

Moonflower made a show of sighing and rolling her eyes, but she did as she was told, climbing around the passenger seat and beneath the heavy blanket that separated the cabin and the load bay. Rebecca strained to hear which direction the swelling growl came from. Before she could figure it out, lights glared against the front of the van. There, coming up the incline, a pickup, glowing lamps fixed to its roof, headlights filling the world with violent white. She couldn't help but raise her forearm to shield her eyes.

The truck slowed as it neared, brakes whining, until it halted alongside the van. The passenger window rolled down, and a dog of medium size and indeterminate breed barked as it placed its paws on the edge. A man peered out at her from the driver's seat. Middle-aged, bright and watchful eyes, lined and rugged country skin. He scratched the dog behind its ears, and it dropped back down onto the passenger seat.

"You all right, ma'am?" the man called. "Need any help?"

Rebecca swallowed before she answered, dragging the fear down into her stomach.

"Yeah, I'm fine." She pointed back up the slope. "There was an elk or a moose or something in the road. I had to swerve around it, and I wound up here. But it's okay, there's no damage."

He leaned toward the window, examining the van and the bank of snow it had lodged in.

"I can tow you out of there."

"No need, thank you. It's not that bad, honestly. I can just reverse out."

"I've got a chain in back," he said. "Won't take two minutes, no trouble at all."

"Really, there's no need, thank you."

He considered for a moment, studying the van and the snow. Studying her.

"Ma'am, I won't sleep tonight if I don't know you got out of there. Now, if you're concerned for your safety, being out here on your own and all, I'll move on up the way a little. I'll just keep a watch for a minute, make sure you get yourself back on the road. How would that be for you?"

Not good, Rebecca thought. She wanted him gone, but there was no sense in arguing. It was bad enough he'd seen her out here. Arguing with a decent man because he'd offered assistance to a stranded woman could only make things worse. For everyone.

"Okay," she said. "Thank you."

He dipped his head in agreement, put the truck in gear, and moved off, his wheels spinning before catching grip. Rebecca watched as he made his slow way up the slope. He stopped at the same spot where the elk had stood a few minutes before. Through the cabin's rear window, she saw his silhouette as he turned to watch her.

Better move, Rebecca told herself.

She made her way around the van, high-stepping through the snow, leaning on the side for balance until she found the driver's door. It remained open, snow spilling into the footwell and onto the driver's seat. She swept it out with her hand and climbed in, pulling the door closed behind her, only to drag more snow inside.

"Shit," she said.

Moonflower giggled somewhere behind her.

"It's not funny," Rebecca said, her voice like flint.

Moonflower whispered, Sorry.

"Just stay quiet and keep out of sight."

Silence from the back, and Rebecca felt a sharp bite of regret. No need to vent her anger at the child. Didn't matter. They had to get out of here. She turned the key in the ignition, and the engine coughed. For a moment she feared it might not catch, but it did, a pleasing rumble that thrummed and rattled through the cabin. She placed her hand on the dashboard.

"Good girl," she said.

And it *had* been a good van. Best she'd had in years. Almost always started first time, rarely stalled, and the AC still worked. Warm in the cold places, cool in the hot.

What more could they want? But now it might have to go. She might have to get something else.

"Goddammit," she spat.

"What's wrong?" Moonflower asked, fear creeping into her voice.

"Nothing, honey," Rebecca said, smoothing her tone. "Just stay quiet back there, okay?"

"Okay."

She put the van into reverse and dabbed at the gas pedal, felt the wheels spin beneath her, barely rocking the suspension. In the side mirror, she saw the truck idling, the man's silhouette, watching.

"Please," she whispered.

A touch of pressure from her right foot, barely enough for the tachometer's needle to rise, then a little more. An inch of movement, then another.

"Thank—"

Then a lurch, the wheels spinning again.

Rebecca eased off the gas, pressed down on the brake, grasped the wheel between her cold-bitten fingers. Closed her eyes and offered a prayer to the god who'd abandoned her decades ago. She toed the gas pedal once more, feeling as she pressed down, listening with her body to the engine, the wheels, the chassis, seeking the sweet spot. The van moved, crawled, slow as spit on glass.

Hold it there, she thought. Hold it.

Back and back and back, still going, thank God, still going until the rear wheels met the road, the front wheels following, and she could feel the asphalt beneath. She rested her head against the steering wheel.

"God," she said. "Thank you, God."

She looked up into the side mirror. The truck still idling, the driver watching. She lowered her window, waved back at him. His hand, a thin black silhouette, returned the gesture, then he turned away. His exhaust belched, and the truck climbed the slope and rounded the bend, out of her sight.

Rebecca began to tremble, pent up adrenaline charging through her, seeking escape.

"Jesus," she said. "Jesus, fuck. Fuck me."

She had long since stopped worrying about swearing in front of her daughter. What was the point?

"You okay?" Moonflower asked.

The blanket lifted, her pale face appearing from underneath, and again Rebecca remembered why she'd called her daughter that all those years ago. Like the flowers in the old greenhouse. The memory of her own mother tending them, and the ache that came with it.

"Yeah," Rebecca said. "You need to sleep. Get back there."

She put the van into drive and moved off, slow, feeling the road through the steering wheel. Be careful. No more mistakes.

That man would remember her. And the van. The make, the model, the color. Maybe the registration, not that it mattered. And he'd remember her, describe her if he was asked to. Rebecca cursed under her breath, made a fist, bit her knuckle to keep from shouting out her anger. Breathe. Deep in, from the belly, then out, long and slow. Calm.

When she'd found her balance, she said, "Love you, Moonflower."

From the back, her daughter's voice heavy and weary, "Love you, Mom."

2

Special Agent Marc Donner was met by a Jefferson County Sheriff's Deputy at Denver International Airport. It occurred to Donner as he followed the deputy to the parking lot that he'd bounced through Denver countless times on his way to somewhere else but never actually left the airport. At least this was a first.

Foster was the deputy's name, a brawny young man, buzz cut hair and thick forearms. Probably polished his service weapon more than he needed to. He steered the cruiser, a Ford Interceptor SUV, out through the crisscrossing lanes, away from the terminal, and onto a wide road with nothing but stretches of dry eternity on either side. Then, suddenly, a towering dark horse, rearing toward the sky, its eyes blazing red. Like the devil's own steed bucking against its rider.

"What the hell is that?" Donner asked, pointing at the sculpture as they passed.

"Blucifer," Foster said. "Blue Mustang, to give it its

proper name. You remember that Osmonds song? Crazy Horses, waaah, waaah!" He splayed out his fingers as he wailed, wobbling his jaw, then gave a bellowing laugh. "You know, the guy who made that thing? It fucking killed him. I shit you not."

Donner looked back over his shoulder at the sculpture. "No kidding. How?"

"Damn thing fell on him. Killed him dead."

"Jesus," Donner said.

The road straightened, more wilderness spreading out on either side of the road. Flat as a plate and rough as sand. The suggestion of buildings on the horizon, settlements, industry, life in the far distance. So much space made Donner's skin crawl. The isolation of it. He was used to walls, high and tall, all around. The sky a punctuation between buildings, not this great blue blanket that hung over all creation. Nature was for parks and playgrounds, not growing wild and free in places like this. He pulled his coat tight around him.

The deputy cleared his throat.

"You're here to look at the body, right?"

"Yeah," Donner said.

"Why?"

"Why what?"

"Why's a fed want to look at this particular corpse?"

Donner fussed at his shirt collar. "I don't know, maybe it's relevant to my interests, something like that."

Foster stared at him, hard, then looked back to the road. "It's a serial, right?"

Donner didn't answer.

"Right?"

Donner raised his hands in a noncommittal gesture. "I don't know. Could be."

"Holy shit," the deputy said, rubbing his fingers across his smiling mouth. "A fucking serial killer. Goddamn."

"Maybe," Donner said. "Probably not. Probably just some random shit that went down, some poor bastard got his throat cut for no good reason, but I gotta look at it. I gotta see."

"Holy shit," Foster said again. "So, it's just you? I thought maybe they'd send down a whole team for something like this. Like forensics and psychologists, all that. Like Jodie Foster in her brown suit and flat shoes and shit."

"No, just me," Donner said. "I gotta look at it first, try to figure out what it is. Then, maybe after, we send for Jodie Foster. Her and Hannibal Lecter tied to a hand truck."

Foster laughed.

"Tell you what," he said. "You need anything while you're here? You need a ride someplace, or some local intelligence, whatever. Just call. Night or day. I'll see you right."

Donner nudged his shoulder. "Thanks, man."

He was good at that. Making friends.

Avista Adventist Hospital stood on the hinterland of housing developments and strip malls between the city of Boulder and the town of Superior, a squat complex of buildings covering acres of ground. Trees and shrubbery lined every path throughout, graying drifts of old snow piled at the edges.

So much space, Donner thought. Drive him crazy.

The mortuary was a level down. Doctor Leitch from the

county coroner's office met him there, the body already laid out for inspection, covered by a plastic sheet. Donner was relieved when Leitch peeled it tastefully back rather than whipping it away with a flourish. It meant he'd dealt with murders before; they'd become mundane to him, not cause for fuss and drama.

Frost dusted the eyelashes of the dead man, and the ends of his hair. A Y-shaped incision on his chest had been neatly stitched, as had the one that circled his scalp.

"Pretty straightforward, at least on the face of it," Leitch said, pointing to the obvious wound in the cadaver's throat. "Large cut here, severing pretty much everything that matters, leading to massive blood loss. He died within seconds. But then you look closer."

The pathologist leaned down, staring into the open wound. He prodded two gloved fingers into the florid maw.

"A blade inserted here, most likely a hunting knife, pushed right through, between the C3 and C4 cervical vertebrae, cutting the spinal cord. If he wasn't dead from blood loss, he was dead from this. No blood at the scene, though."

"So, he was moved after the fact."

"Yup," Leitch said. "Strikes me as unusually thorough. Somebody went to a lot of trouble to first make absolutely sure he was dead and then prevent his discovery. But I guess that's why you're here."

"Yeah," Donner said. "Tell me about where he was found."

"Up in the foothills," Leitch said. "In the trees, way out in the sticks. My guess is whoever dumped him there reckoned he wouldn't be found till the thaw, maybe March or April. By that time, coyotes would've taken most of him. We'd have had a job identifying him, I can tell you that. But a man named Johnny Colfax found him first. His dog sniffed the body out, I believe."

"Have you spoken with Mr. Colfax?"

"Only briefly. The Jefferson Sheriff's Office and the Golden Police Department have both had their way with him, but neither made much of it. Between you and me, I think they're out of their depth. They're arguing about jurisdiction, both sides wanting it out of their hands. I believe you coming along is the answer to their prayers. Let the G-man take care of it. Especially when they found out he had a record."

Donner had received the email yesterday afternoon, pinged by the National Crime Information Center when Golden PD had uploaded the data. The body had been found almost a week ago, but it had taken a few days to ID him: Bryan Shields, aged thirty-seven, had bought himself a lifelong membership to the National Sex Offenders Registry when his credit card details were found in the payment records of a child pornography website. Probably shunned by friends and family for what he'd done, so no one to miss him when he disappeared. The first box ticked on Donner's checklist. That, the open throat, the body dumped in the asshole of nowhere. It all fit the pattern, and Donner's supervisor had begrudgingly given him permission to check it out.

And here he was, Bryan Shields, dead as dead can be, one more crumb on a trail that Donner had been following for nearly two years.

"What now?" Leitch asked.

"I gotta make a call," Donner said. "Excuse me."

He exited the mortuary into a tiled corridor and took his cell phone from his pocket. McGrath answered on the second ring.

"Well?" she asked.

"It's our guy," Donner said, "no question. Everything fits."

"Shit," McGrath said. "You want me to fly out?"

"No, there's nothing you can do here. Just try to keep Holstein off my back while I dig around a little. There's a guy I need to speak with, the one who found the body."

He listened to McGrath breathe, his partner biting back a question, until he could stand it no more.

"Say it."

"Shit," she said again. "Are you sure you want to do this to yourself? I mean, who cares if some sick fuck gets killed and dumped in the woods? It's one less creep for us to worry about."

"I care," Donner said. "It's *my* job to put these bastards away. Mine. Not some goddamn crazy with a hunting knife."

"All right," McGrath said. "I'll do what I can at this end. Call me if you need anything, day or night."

"Thanks," Donner said, meaning it.

"Yeah."

McGrath hung up.

3

Her mother's cry took Moonflower's attention from the game. Super Mario Bros on the Nintendo DS. Mom had bought it for her from a pawn shop in Bakersfield. She couldn't count how many times she'd played through the game, every beat of it committed to her memory, every button press, every move. There were so many hours to fill out here in the big wide nowhere.

She dropped the Nintendo and scrambled to Mom's side.

"Jesus Christ," Mom said through gritted teeth. "Goddamn altitude."

Cramps in her calves. She always woke with cramps when they were way up high in the mountains. Mom hissed through her teeth and writhed, her eyes screwed shut. Moonflower unzipped the sleeping bag and reached inside, massaging the calf of her mother's right leg, pulling and stretching at the knotted muscle, like steel balls beneath the skin, getting the blood flowing. Mom groaned, her legs forced straight by the pain.

"We need to get down from the mountains," Moon-flower said. "Go south, go somewhere warm, like Scottsdale. You like Scottsdale."

"Not yet," Mom said. "Not until I'm sure it's safe."

"You can't ever be sure."

Mom knew she was right. They would never be safe, not really. But Mom had said they needed to balance the risk. What if that man had said something? She'd been keeping an eye on news reports from the Denver area and no mention had been made of a woman and a van, but still, she couldn't be certain. Later that same day, Mom had stolen the plates from a Ford van outside a truck stop near Boulder, and she'd drawn no attention as they made their way through the rises and falls of the Colorado Plateau.

They'd arrived in Blanding two days ago and taken a spot in the White Mesa RV Park and Trading Spot. Forty-eight hours was too long to stay in one place, but exhaustion had been wearing on her mother, making her irritable and forgetful. She needed to rest and get her head straight or she'd get careless, make mistakes. And she always said they couldn't afford any mistakes.

Careful, she would say. Think. Don't draw attention.

Having a power supply in the parking bay meant they could keep the little portable heater going, and charge Mom's Chromebook as well as her phone. And Moon-flower's Nintendo. Maybe one more night here, but then they had to move on.

Mom gave a weary moan and raised her left leg to get her daughter's attention. Moonflower obliged and moved her hands to that bunched-up muscle, kneading it with her knuckles. Mom wriggled her thick-socked toes as the blood circulated. She let out another moan of relief.

"Okay?" Moonflower asked.

"Yeah, thank you."

Mom sat upright on the mattress and stretched her legs out in front of her, continued rubbing at the calves.

"What time is it?" she asked.

"Eleven," Moonflower said.

"Shit. I didn't mean to sleep so late."

"You needed it. It's good for you."

"Did you sleep?"

"A little," Moonflower said, dipping her head as she spoke, betraying the lie. She had lain awake through the last hours of the night, into the morning, the Nintendo's volume turned down low so as not to disturb her mother.

"Maybe try to get some now," Mom said. "I'm thinking we could stay here another day."

"Maybe."

She dipped her head again.

"I need to eat something." Mom reached for her boots, pulled them on, then shrugged on her winter coat. "I won't be long."

She crawled to the back of the van and pulled the release, the door opening out, light streaming in. It didn't reach as far as Moonflower. Mom climbed out and buttoned up the coat. Her breath misted in the hard, thin air.

"I can check if they have any new magazines," she said. "Maybe a paperback?"

Moonflower gave a smile, humored her. "Yeah, sure."

As Mom went to close the door, Moonflower said, "No. Can you leave it open? I like the view."

Mom turned and saw what she meant. Endless blue sky. Snowy mountaintops in the far distance. She pondered for a moment then shook her head.

"It's cold, honey."

"I've got my coat and my sleeping bag." She gathered them around her, even though the cold didn't bother her. "I can wrap up."

Mom regarded her, her face drawn tight with worry.

"You stay right there," she said. "You don't talk to anyone, even if they talk to you."

"I won't," Moonflower said.

"Okay. I'll be right back."

She lingered a moment, like a leaf unsure of the breeze, before walking away in the direction of the store.

Moonflower pulled on her coat, too big for her, but warm and pillowy. Roomy enough for her to draw up her knees to her chest, her chin tucked down inside the collar. Huddled against the blaket that separated the van's cabin from the rear, too far back from the open doors for the light to touch her, she studied the rise and fall of the mountains. Like white elephants. She had read that description somewhere, and she had to search her memory to find it: a story by Ernest Hemingway. It had been in a collection Mom had shoplifted from a used bookstore. Moonflower hadn't liked the story; it had seemed like a lot of words to say not much at all. She understood it well enough, a man and a girl—a girl, not a woman, the story had been clear—talking around her getting an abortion, but never actually saying it out loud. Moonflower was old enough to know about such things.

Like white elephants. To Moonflower, the mountains

were more like giant ocean waves, foaming with rage. It was the sky above them that she loved. So wide and blue, and she wanted to swim in it. She remembered swimming. Moonflower remembered a vacation somewhere in California, she couldn't recall where exactly, but the hotel had a pool, and she swam in it every day, her body a blade cutting the warm water. So long ago, before they had to run, but she could feel the water on her skin even now.

A girl walked across the open rear of the van, silhouetted against the blue. She glanced into the gloom as she passed, then disappeared. Moonflower held her breath, knowing she had been seen. Sure enough, the girl stepped back into view, peering into the van. Thirteen, Moonflower guessed, maybe fourteen. She wore a puffer jacket and a woolen hat with a pom-pom on top.

"Hey," the girl said.

Moonflower froze and said nothing, hoping to vanish into the shadows.

"I'm Olivia," the girl said. "Or Livvy. That's what my parents call me. What's your name?"

She waited for an answer, the silence clamoring between them.

"You here with your folks?"

Moonflower felt the cold now, creeping in beneath her coat. She became aware of the mess back here. The mattresses and the blankets and the sleeping bags. The loose piles of clothing. The little propane stove, the dented pots and pans. How her own hair hung lank and dark while this girl's curled from beneath her hat, the sun catching the golden highlights. Stud earrings and lip gloss. A dusting of eyeshadow. She wanted to tell the girl to go away but she kept her mouth tight shut.

"I'm here with mine. They're hippies. I mean, they say they're Generation X, Nirvana and all that shit, but they're totally hippies."

Go away, Moonflower thought.

She saw the hurt flit across the girl's face.

"Yeah, anyway, I'm bored out of my mind, so if you want to hang out, we're in the Jayco two spots down. Just knock on the door."

The girl forced a smile and walked away. When her footsteps had receded, Moonflower scrambled to the doors and pulled them shut, one after the other, sealing herself in the darkness.

File #: 89-49911-5
Subject: Rebecca Carter
OO: Flagstaff
Desc: Letter, Handwritten
Date: 12-25-1994

Dear You,

I don't know who "You" are.

Let's start with that. I don't know who you are or who you'll be, but I felt you move today, so I know you're real. You're not just an idea anymore, but a real, living thing. I don't know if I'm excited or terrified or both.

Today is Christmas. It used to be my favorite day of the year. I guess it still is. This year is different. It was just us, me and my parents, no one else. The house felt too quiet, and I felt a little low, thinking about what all my friends are doing, and everything I'm missing. I went and hid in my bedroom, and I cried pretty hard.

Then I felt you move, like tiny bubbles popping in my stomach. I lay very still and quiet, listening and feeling, and you moved again, so I ran and told Mom. Then she cried too, and so did I, but happy crying.

It's funny how things swing from one place to another, like a pendulum in a big old clock. One minute you want to dig your own grave, the next you want to hug and kiss the whole wide world.

It was Mom's idea to write you this letter. She said it would be as much for me as for you, to help me remember this time. And to help me process everything that's happening. I have a good mother, I know that. We do argue, and I'm mean to her sometimes, but she has been good to me these past few months. She's been supportive and kind, never angry, and I know lots of moms would be angry at their daughters for this. When I told her I'd missed my period, she looked sad for just a moment, but then she hugged me and told me everything was going to be all right. Dad too. I know he was angry, but he didn't let it show. And he wasn't angry at me, but at Christopher.

I don't want to talk about him.

They both said they'd support me no matter what, and if I didn't want to go through with it, they would help make that happen. They didn't say it, but I think they'd rather I'd gone that way. Christopher's family sure wanted me to.

There he is again, even though I said I didn't want to talk about him. He's an asshole, that's all you need to know.

Anyway, I decided to keep you. I don't know why. Things would be easier if I didn't, sure, but like Mom says, I never do anything the easy way. I just had a feeling it was right for me. I still do, for the most part, even when I'm puking my guts up. I started having doubts a few weeks ago. I guess seeing all my friends getting on with their lives, hearing them talk about college, all the things they're going to be, it made me wonder what I'm going to miss. It really started to play on my mind, and I couldn't sleep, thinking about everything I've lost. But then I felt you move today, like bubbles popping in my stomach, and I knew for sure I'd made the right choice.

And it was my choice, mine alone. Always remember that: my life, my body, my womb, my choice. No one else has a right to tell me otherwise.

Mom says I'll still get to travel. I had planned to take a year out before college, go to Europe, see what they know over there. That's gone, of course, but there's still time. And I can still go to college when I'm ready, I don't even have to leave home. Mom says she can take fewer hours at work to help watch you while I study. She keeps telling me my life isn't over, but I know that. It's just going to be different, that's all. Doesn't mean it won't be good.

Life is what happens to you when you're busy making other plans. I think it was John Lennon who said that. It's a quote worth remembering because it's true.

I've been watching this new comedy show called Friends. It's about these six people living in New York, all in their twenties, three boys, three girls. I can't decide if I like them or hate them. There's something smug about them all living in their nice apartments in the big city, like yeah, an average twenty-five-year-old can afford to do that. But I keep watching, because life keeps happening to them.

I just realized why I kind of hate them. They have the life I want, and it reminds me how far out of reach it is. Everything I ever wanted to be is gone, replaced by little popping bubbles in my stomach. But I keep watching anyway, and I keep going.

Anyway, that's all for now, I guess. I'll get to meet you in not quite four months, then I can tell you all this in person.

I hope I can give you a good life.

All my love,

Rebecca

4

Inside the store, Rebecca chose a 30 oz. bottle of water, a hot coffee, two granola bars, a *Girls' Life*, and a *J-14*. She added a day-old edition of the *Denver Post* and went to the check-out. A young man with braces and pimples rang up and bagged the items.

"Anything else I can get for you this morning?" he asked, an artificial chirp to his voice.

"A pack of Marlboros," she said.

"Sure thing," he said, reaching beneath the counter.

She dug the money out of her coat pockets, dollar bills and an array of coins, counting them out one by one. Not much left. She considered putting back the magazines and one of the granola bars, but decided against it.

Outside, Rebecca walked to the far side of the store, out of sight of the van. No way Moonflower could have seen her, the rear was facing the wrong way, but still. She opened the pack of cigarettes, gripped one between her teeth, then fished a disposable lighter from her coat pocket.

The beautiful taste of butane and tobacco filled her head and her lungs. Like choirs of angels singing into her. She breathed out, the smoke swept away by the wind. Her brain crackled with nicotine. Four, five a day. That was all. She and Moonflower both pretended it was a secret, lying to themselves and each other.

"What if you get cancer?" Moonflower had once asked, years ago. "You'll die and I'll be all alone."

Rebecca had promised to quit, and for two years had kept that promise. Then one night at a gas station south of Seattle, she had bought a pack of Camels and lit one, choked on it, but kept sucking the smoke in. And then another.

Moonflower had screamed at her that night, threatened to run away, and Rebecca had crushed the pack between her fingers and sworn never to buy another. But two days later, she did. They didn't talk about it anymore.

Rebecca pulled the last of the smoke from the Marlboro and stubbed it out on her heel before dropping the butt into a garbage can. Another, she thought. Why not? It'd be hours before she could sneak off again. She took her things to a picnic bench at the edge of the RV park, checking to see if it was in sight of her van. A large Winnebago stood between here and her Ford. Moonflower would have to come looking for her, and Rebecca knew she wouldn't.

She sat down, placed the coffee on one side, the pack of cigarettes on the other, with the newspaper in between. Just sit here, have a coffee and a smoke, and read the paper. Like a normal person.

Rebecca scanned the pages, barely registering the head-lines. They were still counting the cost of the Marshall fires a year ago, and they'd be rebuilding for many more. More than a thousand homes turned to ashes. That on top of recovering from the pandemic, the human and economic cost beyond counting. She had remained untouched by it all, isolation being the norm for her and her daughter before anyone had heard of COVID-19.

One headline caught her attention, and she paused, the page half turned.

POLICE CHIEF PLAYS DOWN TALK OF SERIAL KILLER

She flattened out the page, reached for the cigarettes, and read.

Division Chief Tom Johnstone of the Jefferson County Sheriff's Office last night dismissed speculation that a serial killer was operating in the area. Rumors spread amongst law enforcement personnel that an FBI special agent had flown in from Washington, DC, to aid in the investigation into the murder of Bryan Shields, a convicted sex offender who had been residing in Broomfield for several years.

Mr. Shields had moved to Broomfield after receiving a conviction for possession of child pornography in his native Omaha, Nebraska. He had lived quietly in the area ever since, working various minimum wage jobs, drawing little attention to himself from neighbors or law enforcement agencies. That is until his remains were discovered a week ago in the forested hills above Golden. Investigators believe Mr. Shields was killed elsewhere before his corpse was moved to the remote location, presumably to delay discovery until the spring.

A source within the Jefferson County Sheriff's Office said a cell phone and laptop computer removed from the victim's home were currently being examined, and that a prominent line of inquiry was that Mr. Shields had been in communication with someone posing as a minor and had arranged a meeting with what may in reality have been a vigilante.

Division Chief Johnstone refused to comment on these and other details, or on the significance of the arrival of an FBI agent. When one reporter asked about the rumor that some officers in the Sheriff's Office viewed the killing of Mr. Shields as no great loss to the area, Division Chief Johnstone said: "Whatever the circumstances of the victim's life and death, the fact remains that it is the responsibility of law enforcement and the courts to administer justice, no one else's."

The investigation is ongoing.

Rebecca read the piece again, and a third time. No mention of a woman at a roadside, a van wedged in a snowbank. No description, no make, no model.

Maybe they'd be safe for a while longer.

Maybe.

5

Liz answered on the third ring.

"Hey," she said, her tone neutral.

"Hey," Donner replied. Then the words deserted him.

He sat in the passenger seat of Deputy Foster's cruiser as they wound their way up into the hills over Golden. Donner's stomach shifted queasily inside of him with each bend in the road as they followed Johnny Colfax's pickup. They were traveling to his father's place in the woods, close to where the body had been found.

Donner listened to Liz's breath against the phone for a moment as he scrambled for what he needed to say.

"Yeah," he said eventually, "about the holidays."

"Uh-huh?"

She was distracted. At work, presumably, at her desk, shuttling numbers around a spreadsheet, adding them up. That was her great skill in life: to impose order, forcing things to make sense, whether they wanted to or not. It had broken their marriage, at least as he saw it, but perhaps could mend it again.

"I was thinking about what you said. About coming to you and the kids. I'd like to do that. If it's okay with you."

A pause, and he wondered what expression played on her face. Gladness or regret? Maybe both.

"Yes, it's okay with me. It's very okay. And the girls will be happy."

He doubted that. Emma maybe, but not Jess. She'd barely spoken to him since he'd moved out. Even when her mother handed her the phone, she'd allow him no more than a few syllables. And he understood. He'd never forgiven his own father for leaving, even though it was the best thing the stupid bastard had ever done for his family.

"Good. So, I'll come over, what, Christmas Eve?"

"Sure. But listen."

"What?" he asked, knowing the answer.

"No drinking."

He gave Foster a glance then looked the other way, as if that would render the deputy deaf.

"Not for a year," he said.

"You swear to me."

"Yeah."

"Say it."

Donner shifted in the passenger seat. "I can't really go into it right now."

Her tone hardened. "If you mean it, you'll say it."

"I swear."

Silence for a moment, then, "Okay. I'm glad."

"Me too."

Up ahead, Colfax turned on his blinker, and his brake

lights glowed red. Deputy Foster did likewise, easy on the pedal to keep control in the fresh snow.

"Listen," Donner said, "I gotta go."

He wanted to tell her he loved her, but he couldn't. He wasn't sure if Foster being there made any difference. It might have been too hard to say it anyway.

"Yeah. See you Christmas Eve."

"Yeah."

He tucked the phone away in his coat pocket as the cruiser turned onto a narrow road, barely wide enough for either vehicle.

"The coroner said it was out in the sticks. He wasn't kidding."

"Right," Foster said. "My grandpa used to go hunting with Johnny Colfax's old man. Between you and me, he's crazy as a Bessie bug. I mean, age has gotten to him these past few years, but he was a fucking whack job long before that. You'd have to be to live way out here."

"I don't know," Donner said. "I think I'm starting to see the appeal."

The pickup turned once again, left into the treeline. Foster cursed and hit the brake too hard, the cruiser losing grip on the packed snow. He managed to regain control and slowed in time to make the turn. No more than a trail between the trees, the cruiser jolting and lurching over the rough ground. Donner reached up for the grab handle as he bounced in his seat. He kept his mouth shut to let Foster concentrate on avoiding the tree trunks. He saw the pickup's brake lights up ahead before he saw the cabin. Foster pulled the cruiser up alongside the other vehicle.

Donner felt a shock of cold as he climbed out. The

temperature had dropped as they climbed up into the foothills of the Rockies, and he wished he'd brought a heavier coat, maybe even a pair of gloves.

Colfax's dog jumped out of the passenger window and ran yelping for the cabin's porch. Colfax followed it, telling it to cool its engines. The cabin's door was already open a crack, a hint of a ruddy face inside, small black eyes peering out. Colfax leaned one elbow against the frame, discussing something with the occupant. The conversation grew more heated, more animated, until eventually Colfax's father stepped out, pulling a torn and tattered coat around him. He petted the dog as he emerged, and it barked its delight. His hair stood in wild white tufts, several days of stubble on his chin and jowls.

"All right, goddammit, all right," he said as he followed his son toward them. He wore pajamas under the coat, and his boots were untied. He was short and stocky while his son was tall and slender. The dog remained at the old man's side, nuzzling his open hand.

"Mr. Colfax," Donner said, fetching his ID from his coat pocket. "I'm Special Agent Marc Donner, FBI, Cybercrime Division. I need to speak with you about what happened here last week."

His voice sounded strange to his own ears, muted by the snow all around. The old man kept his distance, his features sharp with distrust. The dog leaned against his legs.

"Cybercrime? Ain't that computers and internet and such? I don't even have a phone line out here."

"I believe this killing is connected to some others I'm investigating," Donner said. "Yes, there's an online aspect to this case, but the killing happened out here, in the real world. I just want to ask you a few questions about what you saw."

"I already told the cops everything."

"Pop," the younger Colfax said, putting a hand on his father's shoulder.

"I understand that, sir," Donner said, "but I'd appreciate it if you could go over things one more time for me. It'd really be a big help."

The old man blinked at him as more snow began to fall, cold white feathers drifting all around.

"All right. It was out back. Come on."

He trudged away to the rear of the property, boots crunching snow, and the rest followed. An ancient pickup stood behind the cabin, more rust than anything else. Donner wondered if it still went. There were enough car parts strewn around the place to build a new truck, if not for the corrosion. The snow had turned reddish-brown in places.

"Over yonder," the old man said, pointing into the trees. "I heard it first. I don't sleep so good at night, and I was just reading a murder book. Johnny gets them for me from the library. Anyway, I was sitting up reading a book, I don't recall which one, and I heard an engine. It was a diesel engine, I know the sound, and I thought, who in the hell is driving all the way out here this time of night? So, I set my book down and went to the back door. I could see the headlights way over there, where the road curves around behind my property."

He pointed again. Donner could barely make out where the trees thinned about a hundred yards away.

"It stopped around about there and I stood and watched for a time. Then I saw a couple flashlights bobbing around, going slow through the trees. It crossed my mind to holler at them, ask them what they was doing out here, but then I reconsidered. I thought it might be best just to keep quiet, not draw their attention. For all I know they could be drug cartel people. I would've got my rifle, only Johnny here tells me not to go drawing guns if I don't have to. Says I'll just get myself shot for no good reason."

Donner couldn't help but smile. "I think your son's probably right on that one."

"Hell, maybe if I'd sent a round or two over that way, I might've bagged the bastards for you, saved you a whole lot of trouble."

"Maybe," Donner said. "What time of night was this?"

"Oh, one-thirty, one-forty-five, something like that. Anyway, I went back inside and got on the radio to Johnny, says there's people sneaking around up here, and if he didn't get up here right quick and see to it, I'd get my rifle and see to it myself. He told me to stay put and he'd be here as soon as he could."

Donner addressed the younger Colfax.

"How long till you got here?"

"About an hour and a quarter, hour and a half, something like that. Whoever it was, they were long gone before I got here."

"And then you found the body?"

"No, not right away. The snow had come on pretty heavy by that time, and I didn't want to wander too far from the house. Sumbitch was kind of antsy about something out there, he kept running off into the dark, and I had to call him back. Thought maybe he'd got scent of a bear or some such."

"Sumbitch?"

"My dog."

Donner looked at the animal, still glued to the old man's legs, enjoying a scratch behind the ears from a hard-weathered hand, its tail beating out a steady rhythm against his thighs.

"Why'd you call him that?"

"Cuz he's a sumbitch," Colfax said. "Anyway, I decided I'd stay the night then go have a look in the morning. I guess I went out around eight-fifteen, something like that. There'd been a heavy fall overnight, and it was still going. I couldn't see my own tracks, and my truck was pretty well covered. As soon as he got out, Sumbitch went tear-assing over that way, didn't even stop to take a piss. Pop, how about you go back inside?"

The old man spat into the snow and said, "I heard the dead guy was some kind of pervert."

"He had a record, yes," Donner said.

"Then I guess whoever dumped him out here was doing the world a favor."

A spark of anger ignited in Donner. He wanted to tell the old man that, no, it was no favor to anyone. It was his job to go after men like Bryan Shields, to lock them away where they could harm no one. Every body found with its throat cut was a man he should have caught. Each one was his failure. Maybe it was prideful to think that way, but so be it.

"That'll be all, Mr. Colfax," Donner said. "Why don't you get out of the cold? Your son can take us from here."

The old man harrumphed and did as he was told. The dog followed him for a few yards then returned to the younger Colfax.

"I lost sight of him," he said, beckoning Donner and Foster to follow him into the trees, "then a few seconds later, he starts barking and barking, and I knew something was up. I told Pop to stay inside while I went to look. It took a few minutes to find him, but when I got there, he was digging at something in the snow."

Colfax seemed surefooted in the snow-covered terrain, stepping high with his long legs while Donner used trees to keep himself upright, feeling with his feet as he went. His toes began to ache with the cold, sending hard chills up through his calves. Donner cursed himself for not having better footwear as snow melted and seeped between his socks and the leather of his shoes. Colfax spoke as he walked, his words carried on misty breath.

"Sumbitch was pulling at branches and whatnot, and I figured maybe there was a dead coyote or something under there, like whoever was out here had hit one on the road and carried it into the trees for some stupid reason. So, I got down and pulled some of the branches out of the way, and that's when I saw it."

A loose string of yellow tape became visible in the trees ahead, off to the right, and Colfax corrected his course.

"Saw what, exactly?" Donner asked, lifting his feet high for fear of tripping on roots hidden in the snow.

"A shirt," Colfax said. "It was a plaid shirt, but not one like a working man would wear. One of those shirts you find folded up on a table in a clothes store where the salespeople look at you like you don't belong. A shirt like that. And there was blood on it. That's when I knew it wun't no dead coyote."

They arrived at the small clearing, a space no more

than ten feet square, with an unnatural hollow for a floor. Even covered in snow, it was obvious the clearing had been stripped of every twig.

"I took Sumbitch and went straight back to the house so I could radio down to the police department in Golden. Then I walked out to the main road so I could guide them in when they got here. I guess you know all the rest."

Donner had his cell phone in hand with a PDF of Colfax's statement open on the screen. He scrolled down, reading as fat snowflakes settled on the glass.

"It took you more than an hour to get here, and you live, what, eight miles away?"

"I was out cold when Pop called. I might've had a beer or two that night, so I took a while to gather myself, and then I had to lock up my place. And it was slow going that night on account of the weather. Plus, I stopped and talked to that lady, so that was another few minutes."

Donner lifted his head from his phone. "Lady? What lady?"

"I told the officer about that. Don't it say there?"

"No, it doesn't. It mentions you passed a couple people on the road, that's all. Nothing specific about a woman. Who was she?"

"I don't know who she was, but her van was stuck in a snowbank about two, three miles toward Golden. I stopped and asked if she needed any help, and she said no, she could manage. I waited up the road a ways, just to make sure she got out of there, and then we both went our separate ways."

Donner stepped closer to Colfax, stumbling before righting himself again, the biting cold forgotten.

"How was she? I mean, was she nervous, agitated, what?"

"I guess you could say she was agitated," Colfax said, nodding. "She made it pretty damn clear she didn't want any help. I put it down to her being a woman out here all on her own, and me being a man, and the way things are nowadays."

Donner turned to Foster. "Did you know about this? Why wasn't this in the reports?"

Foster held his hands up. "Shit, don't look at me, no one tells me anything."

Donner took Colfax's arms in his hands.

"Tell me about this woman."

6

By sunset, Moonflower had read both magazines cover to cover and completed the Super Mario game. Again. Mom lay bundled in her sleeping bag, engrossed in a paperback by some Scottish mystery writer. Moonflower liked the title—*The Mermaids Singing*—and Mom had promised to let her read it next. She had once said Moonflower was too young for such books, but that reasoning didn't hold up anymore.

Moonflower stretched and yawned, an exaggerated movement. Her mother noticed.

"What?" she asked, putting down her book.

"Can I go for a walk?"

"It's cold out."

"I know," Moonflower said. "I'll wrap up. It's just, I've been in here all day. Yesterday too. I just want to get some air, stretch my legs."

Mom turned her head to look at her, studying. Moonflower kept her face loose and blank, unreadable.

"Just a walk," she said. "Just for a little while. I won't go far."

"Are you hungry?" Mom asked.

Moonflower placed a hand on her belly and shook her head. It was barely a lie.

"You sure?"

"Yeah."

She felt her mother's eyes on her like searchlights.

"All right," Mom said. "Don't leave the RV park. Fifteen minutes, that's all. Don't make me come looking for you."

"I won't."

"Okay."

Mom picked up her paperback, but she kept her gaze on her daughter. Moonflower pulled on her coat, a knitted hat, and wrapped a scarf around her neck. She climbed into the cabin where her boots lay in the footwell. Once they were laced up, she opened the passenger door and climbed out.

"Fifteen minutes," Mom called from inside, "not a second more."

"I know," Moonflower said, and closed the door.

She looked up at the sky. Clear and black, no stars yet visible. The cold crept in beneath her scarf and the cuffs of her coat; she felt it through her jeans. Not that it bothered her. She opened her mouth and let out a long breath so she could watch the mist carried away on the breeze. All around, the warm pulsing hum of people, couples and families in their RVs, preparing evening meals. She sensed the mingled odors muddying the crisp mountain air like dirty probing fingers.

Moonflower walked around the front of the van and

past the empty bay beside it. A pristine new RV stood in the next spot. She heard a couple arguing inside, felt their anger and hurt, and their love. An older pair, she thought, probably retired. Tired of being together, and terrified of not.

She knew these things, picking them out of the air like a hound tracking the scent of a deer. Mom used to say it was her imagination, that she couldn't possibly feel such things, but she'd been proven right time and time again. She was an antenna, dialed into the emotions of others, hearing the true rhythm of their hearts through the static.

The Jayco RV stood in the next spot, music playing within. Not loud enough to bother anyone. Heavy guitars playing a looping riff, a stuttering drum beat, tortured vocals. The kind of music Mom liked, though she rarely played any. She kept the radio tuned to news stations, mostly, so they could stay in touch with the real world.

Olivia—Livvy—sat on one folding chair, her booted feet up on another, beneath an awning attached to the side of the RV. Her cell phone illuminated her face in the darkness, and Moonflower wondered if she was younger than she'd guessed. Moonflower stood silent, her arms loose at her sides, her mouth open. She wanted to speak but her tongue felt thick and heavy in her mouth.

Livvy's head jerked up from her phone, and she gasped. Moonflower took a step back, felt the urge to run. Then Livvy laughed and placed the phone on the small camping table beside her.

"Jesus, you scared the shit out of me."

Moonflower attempted a smile.

Livvy lifted her feet from the other chair and used them

to push it back. An invitation, Moonflower knew, that tried hard to appear nonchalant. Even so, she hesitated.

"Come on," Livvy said.

Moonflower took one step, then paused, looked back toward the van to see if Mom was watching. She wasn't.

"Jesus, sit down already, what's wrong with you?"

A realization appeared in Moonflower's mind: She thinks I don't like her. Livvy thinks I won't speak because I don't want to talk to her. She's as scared as I am, just better at hiding it.

Moonflower approached, taking careful steps as if Livvy might flee, and sat down.

"There you go," Livvy said with a crooked smile. "Didn't hurt, did it? You still didn't tell me your name."

"Monica," she said, her voice thin and metallic like tinfoil in her throat. "But everyone calls me Moonflower."

"Everyone?"

"Well, my mom."

"Your dad not around?"

Moonflower shook her head.

"Was he ever?"

"No," Moonflower said. "I've never met him."

Mom had only talked about him once that Moonflower could remember. It had been a New Year's Eve, she couldn't recall how long ago. They'd been camped at an RV park like this one, somewhere warm, and the owner had gone round every vehicle and presented the occupants with a bottle of wine. Mom had drunk the whole bottle and become weepy, talking about her life before she got pregnant. All the things she could have been. Then there was Christopher, in high school, and she loved him, she really did, thought she would marry him one day. But then she got pregnant, and Christopher and his family didn't want to know. Just like that, a whole life given up for another. Moonflower didn't like it when Mom drank. She became sad and mean when she had wine in her, then groveling with apology when she sobered up. Thankfully, it hardly ever happened. She still smoked cigarettes, and Moonflower pretended not to know. It wasn't worth the fight.

"Parents are overrated," Livvy said, casting a weary glance over her shoulder to the open window above them. A warm, sickly-sweet scent drifted out, like something unearthed from a forest floor. Livvy pinched the tips of her index finger and thumb together and brought them to her pursed lips, made a sucking sound. Moonflower smiled as if she understood, even though she didn't.

It was dark here between the RVs, and Livvy's eyes glittered in the light from the window as she giggled.

"You 'home-schooled' too?"

Livvy made rabbit ears with her fingers and bobbed them up and down as she spoke.

"Yeah," Moonflower said.

"Always, or just since the pandemic?"

"Always."

"I used to go to regular school till the COVID hit. When school started back up again, my folks decided it'd be better for me to stay home. Really, it was less hassle for them seeing as they work from home anyway. My dad's a programmer, and Mom's a copyeditor, so they can do what they want. Like head off into the middle of nowhere for no good reason. God, I'd love to go back to school. Used to think it'd be fucking great to stay home all day, but Jesus, it's driving me batshit crazy. You know, you're the first person under the age of thirty I've had an actual conversation with for weeks. I mean, I call it a conversation, but you're hardly letting me get a word in. Like, shut up already."

It took a moment for Moonflower to understand that Livvy was making fun out of kindness. She laughed and looked down at the ground.

"Sorry. I'm not very chatty, I guess. I'll go if you want."

"Why would I want you to go? I'm *too* chatty, I know. My mom says I overcompensate. Like she would know the first thing about me. How long are you staying here?"

"Not long," Moonflower said. "A day or two, maybe."

"So, what, you're boondocking around the place?"

"Something like that."

"Where do you live?"

Moonflower felt a crack of confusion. "What do you mean?"

"I mean, when you're not out on the road, where do you live? Where are you from? We're from just outside of Denver."

Moonflower clasped her hands together and thought hard.

"You have to be from somewhere," Livvy said.

"Madison," Moonflower said, flooding with relief at the memory.

"Madison? Like, Madison, Wisconsin?"

"Yeah," Moonflower said, the relief giving way to a fear she'd said something wrong.

"Jesus, that's, like, halfway across the country. In that little van? Shit. How long have you been traveling?"

Moonflower felt a sudden shame, knowing Livvy had seen how they were living. Shame and anger. Anger at Livvy for seeing and knowing, anger at Mom for making them live that way. For their safety, she had said. It had to be a van that could be sold and replaced in a hurry when they needed to.

"I don't know," she said. "A while, I guess."

"God, I thought I had it bad. How do you—"

A growl silenced her. Moonflower put a hand on her stomach.

"Holy shit, was that you?"

Moonflower nodded, heat flooding her neck and cheeks as Livvy chuckled, wide-eyed. Shame washed in anew, and something else, something deeper and darker. She felt Livvy's warmth from here, her pulsing, living warmth.

"I can get you some food," Livvy said, the laughter drifting away, replaced by stinging pity. "We got plenty. I know I rag on my mom, but she's a pretty decent cook. There's lasagna in the fridge, I think, and—"

"Monica."

Moonflower startled at the sound of Mom's voice, and her own name. Her real name. Mom almost never used it. Not unless she was upset, like now, standing near the front of the Jayco, her arms folded tight across her chest. Moonflower got to her feet, and Livvy did likewise.

"Go back to the van," Mom said.

"Hi," the other girl said. "I'm Olivia. Livvy."

"Pleased to meet you," Mom said, her face like stone. "Monica, go back to the van."

"She can stay for dinner," Livvy said. "I was just saying, we have plenty."

"Thank you, that's very kind," Mom said, "but she has to come back to the van now. *Now*, Monica."

Moonflower stepped toward her mother, turned back to Livvy, raised her hand in a small goodbye. Livvy smiled and waved back. Moonflower listened to Mom's hard footsteps behind her as she walked to the van, feeling the waves of fury wash up on her back.

This would be a long night in a lifetime of long nights.

File #: 89-49911-6
Subject: Rebecca Carter
OO: Flagstaff
Desc: Letter, Handwritten
Date: 11-24-1995

Dear Monica,

Your father came to see you this morning. That was big of him. I think it's the third time Christopher has ever met you in the eight months you've been here. He's home from CalTech for Thanksgiving. He looks good, tanned and healthy. I wish I could tell you I felt nothing but contempt, but part of me still ached at the sight of him. I caught Mom's eye while we were sitting around the living room, and I think she understood. Part of me might hate someone, might know everything that's bad and wrong with them, but another part still loves them. Both things can be true. It's not like you can turn your feelings on and off like a faucet or a light switch, is it?

Just, please God, don't let me grow into a bitter old woman. Please?

Christopher's father came with him. I saw the muscles in Dad's jaw clench when he shook his hand. He'd have punched him if he could have gotten away with it, I'm certain of that.

Your father brought presents. A teddy bear for you, along with a little outfit. A tiny denim dress with a T-shirt and booties. They're achingly cute and I will never let you wear them. The bear is already in the trash. I'm sorry, I know you would've liked it, but I couldn't watch you play with it and not think of what happened next.

Christopher's father, Adam Hanratty, your grandfather, handed my father an envelope. Just a regular legal-sized manila envelope.

"What's this?" Dad asked.

"Open it," Adam said.

So, Dad opened it, and it was a check. Twenty-five thousand dollars.

Dad looked at the check, and he looked at Adam, and he looked at the check again, I don't know how many times, over and over. Eventually, Adam got tired of it. He spoke then, and I'll do my best to repeat it word for word, but my memory might have twisted things a little. As best as I can remember, he said:

"That's a one-time payment. I think you'll agree it's most generous. You cash it, do what you want with it, though I'd like to think you'll invest it for your granddaughter. That done, there will be a total and complete severance of contact between your daughter and Christopher. Your daughter will make no attempt to claim any form of child support from my son. Not ever. If she does, we will deny parenthood. You can try to push for blood tests, DNA, whatever, but I will fight you through the courts, and believe me, I can afford better lawyers than you. We're going to leave here today and there will be no further contact, am I clear? Now, I advise you to take that check and cash it because it's the last penny you'll ever see from me or my boy."

I think I'll remember the next part for as long as I live.

Dad sat very still and very quiet. He wasn't staring

at the check so much as he was staring through it, at something hundreds of miles away. It went on for what seemed like an age, everyone getting more and more uncomfortable, until Mom said, "Jonathan?"

Dad didn't startle. He just looked up from the check to Adam. Dad smiled as if he'd just heard a favorite joke, then he took that check and he tore it into exactly eight pieces. Not angry, not in a frenzy, but like he was tearing up a letter before dropping it in the recycling. Then he let the pieces fall to the floor and spoke:

"Go fuck yourself."

I saw Mom's lips go thin as if she was holding in a laugh.

"Excuse me?" Adam said, like he was about to scold a child for backtalking him.

"I'm pretty sure you heard me," Dad said, leaning forward, his elbows on his knees. "But, for the sake of clarity, I'll say it again: go fuck yourself. And, just so we're absolutely clear on this, Christopher, you can go fuck yourself too."

I loved my father then more than ever, more than when I was little and he carried me on his shoulders so I was taller than anyone, more than when he built me a castle in the garden out of plywood and old branches, more than when I had the flu and he lay with me in my bed and held my burning body to his and whispered stories in my ear.

"Who do you think you're talking to?" Adam asked, his face turning purple.

"I think I'm talking to the man who's going to get his ass kicked up and down the street if he doesn't get the hell out of my house right this minute. Him and his dipshit son."

Adam sat there for a moment, shaking, while Christopher stared at his own feet. Then he got up, grabbed his son's arm, and dragged him upright.

"Not a penny," he said, making his way to the door, Christopher in tow. "Not a goddamn penny, you hear me?"

"I wouldn't wipe my ass with your money if there was a toilet paper drought," Dad said.

Mom opened the door for them, a smile held tight behind her lips. Cold fall air blew in. As they both trudged down the path to Adam's big, shiny car, Dad called, "Take care, now."

I hugged him then, with you nestled between us. He kissed the top of my head, held his mouth there for a time before letting me go. Then he walked to the kitchen without saying anything else. I wanted to follow him, but Mom shook her head, saying, no, let him be.

Your grandfather doesn't like confrontation. He is a quiet man. I've never seen him angry at anyone but himself. To strip Adam Hanratty down like that must have torn the heart out of him. But he did it anyway because it was the right thing to do. Your grandpa is a good man. Always remember that, cherish it, because there aren't many in the world.

You will never know your father. I hope you don't hate me for it. I hope you realize it's best for you and me both.

It's been a strange time. My parents are more excited for the holidays than I can ever remember. Because of you, of course. Having a baby in the house seems to have brought out the children in them. Sometimes it feels like I'm the adult of the family. They love you so much, and so do I. I want you to know that now and forever. You are loved, and you always will be, no matter what. There's nothing you could ever do to change that.

With all my heart,
(yes, this still feels weird to write . . .)
Mom

7

"What were you thinking?"

Rebecca slammed the rear door, felt the pressure of it in her ears as the van rocked. Moonflower crawled over her mattress to the front where she pulled her sleeping bag around her, buried her head in it as she lay down.

"Monica."

Nothing, not even the sound of her breathing. Rebecca grabbed the sleeping bag and pulled it away.

"Answer me, goddammit."

"We were just talking," Moonflower said, her face buried in her pillow.

"Why?" Rebecca asked, taking a hold of Moonflower's coat, shaking her. "Why did you do that?"

"What was I supposed to do? She spoke to me first. Was I supposed to just walk away?"

"Yes, that's exactly what you're supposed to do. That's the rule. You don't talk to strangers, ever, for any reason. How many times have I told you? We don't draw attention. Ever."

"And if I walked away, she'd think I was rude. Isn't that drawing attention?"

"You shouldn't have been out there in the first place. I shouldn't have let you. You went out there to see her, didn't you? You lied to me."

"No, I was just passing and she—"

"Goddammit, Monica. You lied to me so you could go and talk to her. And now we have to leave. I thought maybe we could stay another couple days, but not now. Not after this."

Moonflower sat upright, her eyes hateful.

"I just wanted to talk to someone, anyone, who's not you."

Rebecca felt the words like small biting teeth. Heat in her eyes, she looked away, resisting the urge to match spite for spite.

"You think this is fun for me? You think I wouldn't like to have some adult conversation for a change? Think of all the friends I left behind when we had to run."

"And I didn't?"

Rebecca softened her tone, but she knew there was no stopping the argument. "I know. I know, honey, but we had no choice. Neither of us. We still don't. We both had to leave friends behind, and neither of us can make new ones."

"It was just for tonight," Moonflower said. "Maybe tomorrow too, but that's all. Then we'd be gone."

Rebecca crawled closer, reaching for her daughter. "But she'd remember you. She'd remember the van. Anything you told her about yourself. We can't afford that. Just think what could—"

A growl from Moonflower's stomach, loud in the van, unmistakable. She couldn't hold Rebecca's gaze.

"Oh honey, you're hungry. You don't think straight when you're hungry. Imagine what could have happened."

"Nothing would've happened."

"You don't know that."

"Yes, I do. For God's sake, Mom, stop treating me like I don't know my own feelings."

"Come on," Rebecca said, reaching for Moonflower's hand, "it's not like that."

"Bullshit." Moonflower pulled her hand away. "It's exactly like that. It's always been like that. I can't move, I can't walk, I can't speak, not without your say-so. You might as well keep me in a fucking cage."

Rebecca felt a spark of anger threaten to kindle.

"Everything I've ever done, I've done it for you. To keep you safe. I gave up my life so you could live."

"But Mom," Moonflower said, tears forming, "this isn't living."

Rebecca barely slept, the night crawling by like shifting sand. She listened to Moonflower's attempts at rest punctuated by spells on her Nintendo or reading magazines. What little sleep she managed came in snatches and stutters, fragments of dreams lingering in her mind. By the time sunlight crept around the edges of the blanket that separated the van's cabin and load bay, a headache had settled behind her eyes. Somehow, as the world outside the van came awake, Rebecca slipped into a deep and dirty slumber, like quicksand taking hold and pulling her down.

It was Moonflower who woke her, stroking her hair, whispering.

"Mom? Mom. It's ten-thirty."

"Huh?"

She blinked up at her daughter, confused. Always that moment between waking and sleeping, that beautiful hinterland where everything was normal, where they had to run and hide from no one. Then the bitter realization that there was no such place. Not anymore.

Moonflower placed a hand on her shoulder.

"Don't move yet. Just wiggle your toes, get the blood moving."

Such a wise girl. She was right. Ease her legs into motion, don't force the muscles to cry out for oxygen her blood could not supply at this altitude. She moved her toes first, then her feet, then when they felt ready, dared to stretch her legs. Pins and needles, like spiders crawling over her feet and calves, but no cramps.

Rebecca reached for Moonflower's hand, grasped the fingers tight.

"You're a good girl," she said. "A sweet soul. Don't ever forget that."

"I'm sorry about last night," Moonflower said.

"Me too."

And that was that. Life, such as it was, could go on.

Rebecca sat upright. "Did you sleep?"

"A little."

A lie, like yesterday.

"We have to go soon. Help me pack up, then you can sleep on the road."

"Do we have to?"

Rebecca rubbed her neck, turned her head this way, then that way, felt the muscles and tendons grind. "Yeah, we have to. I'll go shower first. Might as well take advantage while I can."

She pulled her boots onto her feet without lacing them and scrabbled around for her washbag and a towel.

"Keep the doors closed and don't talk to anyone, even if they knock."

"I know," Moonflower said.

"Even if it's that girl."

Moonflower nodded.

Rebecca crawled to her, took her in her arms, pulled her close and tight, her face buried in her daughter's hair, shining black as crow feathers.

"I love you," she said. "Always. No matter what."

"Me too."

Rebecca pulled on her coat and opened the rear doors. Crisp, sharp air flooded in, along with a few powdery snowflakes. The sky was a heavy sheet of dim white. Snowstorm coming. Maybe they could outrun it. She grabbed the towel and toiletry bag, climbed out, and closed the doors behind her. Her coat did little to seal out the cold as she trudged to the restroom and shower block over by the 7-Eleven. She kept her head down as she went, made eye contact with no one.

Inside, she used the toilet, then went to a shower stall, locking the door behind her. Goosebumps already formed across her body at the idea of undressing. It'll only be for a few seconds, she told herself, until the hot water flows, that's all. It'll be worth it. Get the water running first.

The shower was separated from the rest of the stall by a plastic curtain and a raised step. She reached in and pulled the faucet, cursed as a jet of water soaked her sleeve. Icy cold against her fingers. She reached around and turned the faucet toward hot, then tested again. A few moments, then it was scalding. Several more adjustments until it was just right. Now she could undress in what little light reached into the stall from the fluorescent tubes above. She couldn't keep the curses from her tongue as she pulled her clothes off. Cold air swept in under the stall door, taking the breath from her as it moved over her back and shoulders, and her teeth chattered. She stepped into the shower, pulled the curtain over, and let the hot water cover her body. Relished it like the rare delicacy it was.

One of those things people took for granted, out there, in the real world. She thought of it that way. As if she and Moonflower lived—no, survived—in some other place, an unreal reality of endless roads and perpetual motion. In the real world, where they had once belonged, a moment of stillness like this was nothing special. No more than a chore, a routine, an interruption to the day's flow. But in this other place, it was a luxury in which to bask. She would sometimes take the opportunity to masturbate. Today? It was too fucking cold. She did it anyway, no real pleasure in the act. A loosening of knots, nothing more.

Those knots had gotten tighter lately. The edges of herself more frayed. Weariness in her body, yes, but more so in her mind. It seemed like months since she'd been able to stop and take a breath. Just to be still and quiet. But she was always in motion, always running. Everything had become so brittle, as if the touch of a finger could cause the entire world to splinter into millions of pieces.

Dried and dressed, Rebecca exited the block and sought out a secluded place, out of sight of the van.

There, between the block and the boundary fence, she sparked up a cigarette and drew deep, letting the hot tarry smoke fill her chest. She'd dried her hair as best she could, but it chilled against her neck. She pulled up the hood of her coat to shield her from the worst of the wind. One cigarette done, she smoked another. God knows when she'd get the chance again. She buried the pack and the lighter in her coat pocket, crushed the second butt beneath her heel, and set off back toward the van.

The 7-Eleven stood at the park exit. Maybe she could get something hot to eat. Her stomach grumbled at the notion, but no, she had already indulged herself too much this morning. They had to get moving. She'd paid in advance for two nights, no need to go back in there and waste more time. Besides, the money had dwindled to almost nothing.

As Rebecca neared the van, she heard a knocking, something hard, like a key or a ring on glass. No, she thought. Please, no.

She saw them from across the lot. That girl, Livvy she'd said, and a woman. Presumably her mother. Early forties, a heavy coat pulled over a Soundgarden shirt and baggy jeans. A foil-covered Pyrex dish in her hands. Livvy knocked on the driver's window with ringed knuckles, turned to her mother, and held her hands up.

"Is it locked?" her mother asked.

"How would I know?"

"Pull the handle and see."

"I can't do that," Livvy said.

"Course you can. It's not like we're going to steal something, is it? If it's open, I can set this on the seat and leave them be."

"It's not . . ."

"It's not what, honey?"

"I think her mom's kinda private, you know? I don't think she'd like us opening her van, that's all."

"Don't be silly. Here, I'll do it."

The mother balanced the Pyrex dish onto her right forearm and reached for the handle with her left.

Rebecca called out, "What are you doing?"

The mother looked around, seeking the voice. Livvy spotted her first.

"Oh, hey," she said. "Monica's mom."

Rebecca marched toward them, clutching her towel and toiletry bag to her chest.

"What are you doing? Get away from my van."

The mother looked to Livvy, worry on her face, then forced a smile. "Hi, I'm Patty, Livvy's mom. She's a friend of your daughter's."

Close, now. They took a step back.

"I know who she is. Why are you messing with my van?"

The forced smile cracked for a moment, then brightened. "I'm sorry, we didn't mean to intrude. It's just, Livvy saw Monica was hungry last night, and I've got all this lasagna going to waste, so I thought I'd drop some over. Actually, it was Livvy's idea. She has her moments, didn't we all at that age, but she's really thoughtful like that."

Livvy toed the ground, hunched her shoulders, and rolled her eyes.

Dozens of replies ran through Rebecca's head, none of them kind, but she steered toward polite. She cleared her throat, swallowed, then smiled.

"Yes, it's very thoughtful, thank you, but we don't need it."

"Honestly, please, it'll wind up in the trash if you don't take it. I made way too much, I always do, and I'd hate for it to go to waste. Really, you'd be doing me a favor."

Rebecca opened the driver's door and set her towel and washbag on the seat. She turned back to them.

"Thank you, you're very kind, but no. We're leaving now and I'd have no way to return the dish."

"Oh, don't worry about that, I've got more of these than I know what to do with. I mean, they're falling out of the cupboards."

Rebecca hardened her voice. "Thank you, no."

Patty and Livvy shared a glance.

"Please take it," Patty said, her smile gone, lost in pity. "For your daughter."

Rebecca's jaw clenched, her teeth grinding, feeling the cracks deepen in her exhausted mind.

"For Monica," Patty said, holding out the dish like a supplication.

"For my daughter? What about my daughter?"

"She's hungry," Patty said. "Livvy told me. Your daughter's hungry, and no child should—"

Without a conscious thought, Rebecca slapped the dish from Patty's outstretched hands. Pyrex shattered on the asphalt. Ragu and pasta sheets spread across the ground. Patty and Livvy moved back, staring, their mouths open.

Rebecca stepped toward them, Pyrex fragments crunching beneath her boots.

"You don't know shit about hunger," she said. "Now get the fuck away from me and my daughter."

8

"I don't buy it," Holstein said.

Special Agent-in-Charge Lawrence Holstein. God forbid you called him Larry.

A small office in a nondescript corner of the Hoover Building. A slit of a north-facing window allowed barely any light to enter. Stacks of file boxes left scant room to move around. Holstein sat on one side of the desk, Donner and McGrath on the other.

"What don't you buy?" Donner asked. "I laid it all out right in front of you."

A mess of pages spread across the desk, printed out from the PowerPoint presentation Donner had spent hours preparing. Holstein let his fingertips wander over them, lifting a corner here, shifting a page there.

"All right, let's say you've got a serial."

"Okay, thank you. It's a serial."

Holstein raised a hand. "I'm not saying that. But

suppose I did. What you've got here is bare-bones. Only a handful of alignments from case to case."

"What are you talking about?" Donner leaned forward, ignoring McGrath's hand on his forearm. "The victim profile, the method, the disposal of the body, it all matches."

"I'm not saying it doesn't, but—"

"But what? But the fuck what?"

Holstein slapped the table with his palm, his eyes glaring. He raised a finger to point at Donner.

"So help me, if you interrupt me one more time, I'll have you back on desk duty, trawling the internet for pederasts. Am I clear?"

Donner ran his tongue around his teeth and breathed through his nose. "Yes, sir," he said.

"So, we say it's a serial. Then what? It gets handed across to CID, they say thanks a bunch, and it winds up at the bottom of someone else's in-tray."

"It doesn't have to go to CID," Donner said. "All the victims fall under our remit. They were all grooming minors, or what they thought were minors, online. That's my field."

"That's right," Holstein said. "And you're damn good at it. You've nailed more of these motherfuckers than any other agent in the Cybercrime Division. But these guys aren't getting killed online. They're getting killed in the real world. With real weapons, leaving behind real bodies. That's CID's business, not ours."

"All right, then let CID have it, but loan me out to them. I can be a, what do you call it, a secondment. Me and McGrath."

Donner saw McGrath flinch from the corner of his eye.

She said nothing, but her shoulders straightened, her lips thinned.

"Not with something this flimsy," Holstein said.

"What about the description?"

"What about it?"

Donner tapped McGrath's arm. She cleared her throat and flattened the sheet of paper she'd been holding in her lap.

"A Caucasian woman, mid-thirties to mid-forties," McGrath said. "Medium height, slender build, dark hair cut to less than shoulder length."

She held up a Xerox of a composite that looked like no one in particular.

"Dressed in winter clothing, long puffy coat, boots. Driving a Ford van, red or tan, ten to fifteen years old. Seen approximately three miles from the location of Bryan Shields's body. When the witness offered assistance to the woman, she became agitated, bordering on hostile."

McGrath returned the pages to her lap. Holstein looked from her to Donner and back again.

"That's it?"

Donner opened his hands. "Well, it's—"

"That's fucking it?"

Donner sat back in his chair, his jaw clenching. McGrath turned her head to him, one hand raised to shield her lips as she mouthed, Don't.

"What else do you want?" Donner asked. "A string of bodies across, what, five, six states? All fitting a profile, the method all but identical. A solid lead on a suspect. What the fuck more do you need, Larry?"

Jesus, McGrath whispered, her fingertips pressing against her forehead.

Holstein trembled. Then he spoke.

"Yeah, we got a string of bodies. All men. All aged twenty-five to sixty. Every single last one of them with either convictions for sex offences, or previous investigations, most of them involving minors. Each one of them a lowlife piece of shit who didn't deserve to breathe the same air we do. Good luck convincing anyone, least of all CID, to expend one ounce of energy tracking down that killer. More likely they'll bury the investigation and wish your suspect well. Speaking of which, oh, your suspect."

Donner didn't want to answer, but Holstein waited, smiling, until he could bear it no more.

"Yeah, what about her?"

"I spoke about this with my counterpart over at CID. Do you know how rare a female serial is? Rare to the point of might as well be non-existent."

Donner was ready for this. He sat forward, raised his finger like he had a bullet-proof argument that would settle it all.

"No, no, no," he said. "I've researched this. There are plenty of cases from way back right up to now. You can't—"

"Baby killers," Holstein said, the words spat out as if they soured his tongue. "Nurses killing newborns in their cribs. Plenty of those. Or elderly patients in care homes, poisoned or suffocated after they changed their wills. There's a fair few of them. Or black widows who killed one too many husbands, or even their own children. Maybe a few who came over all Bonnie-and-Clyde and went on a spree with their significant others, or offed some unfortunate people as part of some goddamn cult. Yeah, you look back, you'll find plenty of those. But honest-to-God serial killers like Ed Gein or Ted Bundy? I'd say you could count them on one hand, but you wouldn't get past your damn thumb. Don't come at me with this bullshit, Donner."

Holstein leaned his elbows on his desk and clasped one fist inside the other.

"I've been indulging you on this for far too long. I did it because you're a good agent and you've helped put away more internet creeps than anyone else in the division. Now, you've been chasing your tail on this for two years, and there's a backlog forming. I can't afford to lose you to this nonsense, Marc. I just can't. And every hour you spend chasing this bullshit is an hour you're not trapping the real threats out there. Jesus Christ, Donner, get your shit together. Give me one good reason why I shouldn't order you to drop this right now. Just one."

Donner closed his eyes for a moment, then opened them again. Focused on Holstein.

"Michael Roach," he said.

"Who?"

"You wouldn't remember. No reason you would, I guess. We got him in a sting outside of Pittsburgh. Thirty-seven years old. Bit of a loner, not many friends, a nerd long before being a nerd was cool, but he did manage to get a wife and raise a child with her. The kid was twelve when he and his mother were killed in a car accident. I say accident, but the other driver had enough opiates in his system to knock out a horse. Anyway, Michael's life is ripped apart. I mean, he just falls to pieces, loses his job, his home, all the rest of it. Just a wreck. And he loved his son, and he missed him so bad he starts hanging out online with kids around that age, just so he can feel some connection back to him.

"Then one day, he strikes up a conversation with a boy called Nathan. They get to be friends, close friends, and they talk about the things boys that age talk about. Including sex. What's it like, how do you do it, all of that. They agree to meet up. Except Nathan is really me and it's a sting. We arrest Michael in a shopping mall, right in front of everybody.

"Of course, turns out, we don't have a case. Yeah, the conversations we had were maybe a little weird. But Michael never meant Nathan any harm. He wasn't a risk to anybody. He just wanted a reminder of his son. So, we let him go, no charges. But people talk, word gets around, his neighbors found out about the sting. Didn't matter that he was innocent. Michael went to the graves of his wife and son and shot himself in the heart. Died right there."

"Tragic," Holstein said. "What's your point?"

"My point is, sometimes we get it wrong," Donner said. "Not often, but sometimes, we grab some poor bastard for grooming a minor online, and it turns out he's just some lonely guy who made a mistake. Or he's someone without the mental capacity to understand the boundaries. Or maybe he just wanted to talk about *Star Wars* or Transformers with someone who cares about it as much as he does. My point is, with all our resources, with all the computers and experts and manpower we have at our disposal, sometimes we still get it wrong. Now, we got eight bodies over two years, probably more stretching back that we haven't connected yet. How many bodies haven't we found because they were hidden too well? How many of them were just lonely guys who didn't know any better?"

Holstein sat back, the muscles in his jaw bulging. He stared at Donner, then at McGrath.

"You willing to back him up?"

McGrath startled, as if her mind had been elsewhere. "Sir?"

"If I give your colleague some leeway on this and it blows up in his face, are you willing to eat shit alongside him?"

The paper creased in McGrath's hands before she flattened it against her thigh.

"Yes, sir," she said.

"Okay," Holstein said. "Go wait outside. I'll make a couple calls."

Donner stood with his back against the painted cinder blocks of the corridor wall. McGrath sat on one of the plastic chairs opposite, looking anywhere but at him. The fluorescent lighting picked out the orange glints in her short red hair.

"What?" Donner asked.

McGrath shook her head.

"Come on, don't shut me out."

She looked up at him. "I'm worried, that's all."

"About what?"

"About you," she said. "I mean, you've been doing so much better. You're in the best shape you've been in for years. You quit drinking, quit smoking, you're patching things up with Liz. I'm worried you're going to throw all that away over this thing."

He studied her, knowing there was more to it. She shifted in her seat, dropped her gaze once more. He would not ask again. She'd either tell him the truth or she wouldn't.

"Goddamn you," she said, angry now. "Are you going to make me say it out loud?"

Donner pressed his shoulders into the wall, his hands down into his pockets.

"Uh-huh," he said.

She slowly shook her head, then spoke.

"It's not just Michael Roach, is it? You're not righting some wrong you think you've done by chasing this. Not really."

"Enlighten me," Donner said.

The air between them crackled.

"It's Liz, your kids," McGrath said. "Your family. There's such a hole in your life since you left them, and you've been trying to fill it these last two years by chasing these killings. You fucked up, and I don't mean Roach. You blew your own life apart, and it's easier to pretend you can fix it by catching this killer than to admit the truth to yourself."

Donner snorted and shook his head. "You're not the only one who majored in psychology. I call bullshit."

"Call it bullshit all you want," McGrath said. "Doesn't change a damn thing."

A dozen replies passed through Donner's mind, all of them hurtful, only one of them true.

"It's not just me you're worried about, is it?" he said.

An accusation, not a question. McGrath stared back at him, hard.

"What does that mean?"

Donner took the seat beside her. "It means, you're scared if I fall, I'll take you with me."

"That's not fair. I've stuck by you every step of the way. Ever since Michael Roach, I've had your back."

"Fair or not, makes no difference if it's true."

She turned in her seat to face him, her eyes sparking. "All right, so I don't want to destroy my career over this. Is that so bad? I have a good life, you know? I've got Cara, I've got our son, our home. I don't want to lose all that over this obsession of yours. Jesus, Donner, I've done everything I can for you, and I'll keep doing everything I can. But someday, somewhere, there's going to be a line I cannot cross. And I'll have to say no to you, and you'll hate me for it. So, yeah, if that's selfish, then I'm selfish, and I'm sorry."

McGrath turned away. His anger churned in him as he watched her profile. So many things he wanted to say, so many blades with which to cut her. But what good could it do? She was the only real friend he had in the world. Why push her away? He breathed in deep, drawing cool air to the center of himself, then reached for her hand.

"It's not selfish," he said, his voice low. "It's smart. I'll never ask you for more than you're willing to give. I promise."

Her shoulders softened, and she squeezed his fingers between hers.

"You're an asshole, you know that?"

"Yeah, I know," he said.

They had come up through Quantico together. He had majored in psychology at Rutgers-New Brunswick, then spent three years at Newark PD while he earned his master's. It had mostly been desk work; he'd spent little time on the street. He didn't enjoy the company of beat cops, the hard edges they developed to shield themselves from the awfulness they dealt with day to day was too much for him. It was there that he'd met Liz. She worked in admin, and he'd found himself seeking excuses to drop off paperwork for her to process. She had finally told him if he didn't ask her on a date soon, he needn't bother at all. They were married within a year, and she'd encouraged and supported him in his recruitment to the FBI.

McGrath had been part of the same intake as him, and they had become friends almost immediately. Liz had been worried initially, but Donner had explained that Liz was more McGrath's type than he was. They followed different paths through their first years in the Bureau, but fate had brought them together six years ago when they were both assigned to a special unit within the Cybercrime Division that was tasked with catfishing online groomers and predators. Their friendship had picked up where it left off, and they wound up spending so much time together that Liz once again questioned their relationship. When McGrath brought Cara over to dinner, and they talked about their desire to have children together, that seemed to put Liz's mind at rest. Not that it mattered much, in the long run.

The door to Holstein's office opened, and he stepped through. Donner got to his feet.

"All right," Holstein said. "You can pursue this."

Donner opened his mouth to speak, but Holstein raised a hand to silence him.

"Listen, goddammit. You can put out an alert on this woman and the van. If anything shows up, you and McGrath can assemble a limited team—and I do mean limited—from the nearest local field office and law enforcement to surveil a suspect, and if appropriate, apprehend them. You keep me posted on everything you do, understood?"

"Understood," Donner said. "Thank you, sir."

"All right, now get out of here."

Holstein returned to his office, closing the door behind him.

Donner allowed himself a smile, clapped his hands together once. Then he noticed McGrath watching him. The smile dried away.

"Well done," McGrath said. "I just hope you don't end up regrettng it."

9

Moonflower woke as the van came to a halt, a falling sensation, landing on the mattress with a shock. A moment of confusion as the dream followed her into waking. Back home in Madison, in her own bed, in her own room. Then the stabbing realization of where she was, and when. She kept her eyes closed for a time, clinging to the dream, wishing it wouldn't dissolve back into memory.

Mom shut off the engine, the keys jangling as she pulled them from the ignition.

"You awake?" she asked, her voice a papery whisper.

Moonflower opened her dry eyes. The rear of the van was dim, only a sliver of tired light creeping past the blanket that separated the cabin. She pictured her mother there, on the other side, her hands on the wheel.

"Yeah," she said.

"I'm sorry about this morning," Mom said.

Moonflower dragged herself to sitting, her back against the driver's seat. She could feel Mom through it, her anger at herself, her sorrow. They had argued as they drove away from the RV park. Mom had been jittery and tearful, furious at herself for lashing out at Livvy's mother. Then she'd turned her anger on Moonflower, pointed out that her excursion the night before had brought the woman and her daughter knocking. They had bickered for miles, said hard and jagged things that still barbed even now.

"Me too," Moonflower said. "Where are we?"

"Kayenta."

"Where?"

Moonflower got to her knees and eased back the blanket. Late afternoon edging into evening, the sun weak and low, but still it hurt her eyes. It reflected burning orange on car windows and the glazed façade of the small strip mall that stood on the other side of the parking lot. Hard packed snow lay in drifts. She cupped her hands around her eyes and leaned into the cabin to take in the surroundings. Fast food outlets, and across the highway, a hotel. The sunlight couldn't touch her, but she felt it nonetheless.

"Lot of stuff for a small place," she said.

"For the tourists, I guess," Mom said. "We're close to Monument Valley."

Moonflower touched her mother's shoulder, felt the tension there.

"You okay?"

Mom didn't answer. The muscles in her jaw bunched. A tear tracked a line down her cheek to her chin.

"What's wrong?"

Mom closed her eyes, her hands gripping the steering wheel tight.

"I'm tired," she said. "In my body and my mind. I'm

exhausted. I'm getting careless, making mistakes. Like this morning. I shouldn't have done that. It was stupid, drawing attention. So stupid. If anyone comes asking, they'll remember us."

"It'll be okay," Moonflower said. "In a week, they'll have forgotten us."

"Maybe not, but it's only a matter of time. I'm going to slip up and we'll be caught."

"No, we—"

"We will. It's a miracle we've gotten this far. It can't go on forever. One of these days, it's going to go wrong."

Moonflower crawled into the cabin, took her mother in her arms. Ignored the prickling heat on her skin.

"Mom, don't."

Her mother's shoulders quivered with dry sobs.

"Promise me something."

"What?"

"When they catch us," Mom said, "you run. Don't look back. Just run, and keep running, never stop. Promise me."

"No, Mom."

She untangled herself from Moonflower's arms, gripped her shoulders.

"You promise me. You swear to me you'll run."

Mom's fingers squeezed hard, digging into Moonflower's flesh.

"No," Moonflower said. "If they take you, I'll come for you."

"You won't," Mom said. "You'll run. Promise me you'll run."

"I can't. I'll die without you."

The hands loosened, and Mom seemed to deflate,

sinking into the driver's seat. She grew old before Moonflower's eyes, withering like a fall leaf.

A cramp seized Moonflower's stomach, a tortured growl sounding from her abdomen. She couldn't help but fold in on herself.

"Goddammit," Mom said, wiping a hand across her eyes.

"I'm sorry."

"It's not your fault."

"You need to eat too," Moonflower said. She pointed one direction, then another. "There's a McDonald's, look, and a pizza place over there."

"We don't have enough money."

"But you have to eat something. We both do."

Mom sat up in the driver's seat, returned the key to the ignition.

"Then we better move," she said.

File #: 89-49911-8
Subject: Rebecca Carter
OO: Flagstaff
Desc: Letter, Handwritten
Date: 12-25-1997

Dear Monica,

I haven't written for a long time, and I'm sorry. I just didn't get around to it. But who said this had to be regular thing? Who's counting? I don't even know if I'll ever give these letters to you. They'll probably stay in the top drawer of my dresser, unread, until they get thrown out.

This time last year, everything was good and right. We had a great Christmas. You could say "Santa." You didn't understand any of it, but you were so excited, and you loved tearing the presents open. Mom and Dad were so happy. Everything was in place for me to start at University of Wisconsin-Stout in the fall, majoring in hospitality and tourism. It would've been a three hour commute each way, but I'd only have had to do it once a week or so, the rest could be done over the internet if we buy a modem for the computer. Mom would've helped take care of you.

All that's gone now.

What did I say about life happening to you? A lot of life has happened between then and now.

It was around mid-February when Dad started having difficulty swallowing. He'd been having problems with his balance for a while before that, but Dr. Gorman said it was some kind of inner ear thing. After the swallowing, after the balance, it was dropping stuff. Books, cups, the TV remote, things just slipping from his fingers. So many tests for so many months until finally, just last month, they said it was amyotrophic lateral sclerosis. Lou Gehrig's disease. But we knew that already.

I didn't go to college in the fall. I can't ask Mom to watch you while she's caring for Dad. Even if I could, how can we afford college when all these medical bills are starting to come in? Just getting the diagnosis has devoured most of their savings. And it'll only get worse from here.

That's the deepest cruelty, isn't it? My mother will nurse my father toward a slow death and suffer financial ruin in the process. What kind of a society can allow that? Where is the human decency?

He can still walk, still feed himself, still speak. All with some effort, but he can do those things. I suppose we should be grateful for that. But I'm not grateful. I'm fucking angry. I'm so goddamn angry and I don't know what to do with that.

I wish I'd written to you when everything felt like it was going to be all right. That's a lesson learned, I guess. You have to mark the good times in some way. Don't let them slip past because you don't know if there'll ever be any more.

I'm sorry things aren't better.

I love you, always.

Mom

10

Rebecca scanned the dim scrubland all around with her field glasses. The maps app on her cell phone had told her there was a rest stop a mile along the highway from Kayenta, an area shaded in green, but she had found nothing more than a patch of dirt a few yards from the road. Scorched stone circles and clusters of trash showed that others had camped there, so she parked up for the night and went in search of food.

Nothing out here.

It might have been beautiful if not for Moonflower's desperate hunger. And her own. To the north, the peaks of Monument Valley glowed red in the last light of the setting sun. To the south, the glowering darkness of the Black Mesa, dusted with snow. The weather was on the turn, a thick wall of cloud to the east. Too dry to snow here, but they would surely meet it as they moved south.

Layers of clothing kept the warmth next to her body, but she felt the cold bite at the exposed skin of her face, stinging her ears, the tip of her nose. Her breath misted, the plumes carried away on the wind that swept across the plateau. How sweet it would be to go back to Kayenta, take a room in one of those hotels. A hot bath, a warm bed, a decent meal. But they couldn't, even if they had the money. Those places wanted identification, credit cards, things Rebecca couldn't provide. So they were stuck out here, boondocking on roadsides, no matter the weather. But they would move south, head for Scottsdale, where it stayed warm all year round. A day, maybe two, and they could do without the coats and blankets. All they had to do was survive a couple more days. That's all.

Rebecca remembered that tomorrow was Christmas Eve. Not that it mattered. Holidays hadn't meant anything for a long time. Moonflower hadn't mentioned it, and Rebecca wondered if she even realized the date. The thought occurred to her that she could pick up a gift somewhere along the way, a trinket of some kind. But there wasn't enough money to spare on sentimentalities. So tomorrow, and the day after, would be like any other in the endless grind of sunsets and sunrises.

There, a movement in the scrub, barely visible in the half-light of dusk. Rebecca focused. A twitch among the branches of a bush. She didn't know what kind of bush it was, a scrawny ball of twigs and green leaves, but she knew the animal: a jackrabbit. Long legs, black-tipped ears and tail. No good. They carried too many parasites.

"Shit," she muttered, lowering the field glasses.

She'd been out here almost a half hour and still nothing. Soon it would be too dark to spot anything at all. Her own hunger didn't concern her, she could tolerate it, but not her daughter. As they'd pulled up to the rest stop, Moonflower's stomach had growled loud enough to make Rebecca wince. She had been trying to hide it, to contain it, but Rebecca could see the hunger was gnawing at her. Rebecca looked back over her shoulder to the van, picturing Moonflower inside, her hands clasped to her belly. Traffic rumbled along the highway, trucks and cars, the drivers and passengers unaware.

As Rebecca turned her eyes back to the scrub, something above caught her attention: a bird, a raptor hovering still in the sky, riding the wind. Its gaze lasered on the ground. What did it watch? She raised the field glasses once more, studied the scrub beneath the bird. There, a cottontail, maybe thirty, thirty-five feet away, exploring the bushes, seeking food.

Rebecca lowered the field glasses and lifted the bow from her shoulder. A Samick Sage recurve, a beginner's bow, but good enough for her purposes. She took an arrow from the quiver at her hip and nocked it, the cock fletching to the outside, the two hens on the inside. Fur silencers on each end of the string to dampen the sound of it slapping against the fiberglass limbs. She raised the bow, her left hand loose on the riser, her right drawing back the string until her fingertips brushed the corner of her mouth. Eyes on the target, imagining the arrow's flight, the initial rise, then the fall, and the strength of the wind, adjusting her left hand to compensate. The rabbit paused in its foraging, sat upright, its nose twitching. The raptor would strike any moment, no time to waste. Rebecca exhaled and released the string. A dulled slap, a woosh of air, and she heard the rabbit's squeal. Up above, the raptor fled.

She started walking, keeping the cottontail in view. No way she would risk losing it now. She slung the bow across her back, the field glasses hanging from the cord around her neck. As she approached the rabbit, she saw its front legs thrash, but its rear legs remained still. The arrow had pierced its hindquarters but done little damage, barely enough to incapacitate it.

Good.

Rebecca reached down and lifted the cottontail by its back legs. They remained still in her grasp as she withdrew the arrow, but its upper body writhed and bucked. She closed her mind against its screaming and set off back toward the van. It was a decent-sized animal, maybe two pounds. Enough to get them through the night. But Moonflower needed more, and soon. Rebecca couldn't hold off any longer. Tomorrow or the next day.

Moonflower waited at the rear of the van, in the shadow of the open doors. Rebecca was struck by how pretty she was. That long black hair as if painted by a Shodo artist's brush, her fine features, her skin so pale it seemed to glow white from within. Moonflower looked to the rabbit, her dark eyes wide. Her stomach growled again.

"Here," Rebecca said.

She reached out, extended the twitching cottontail to her.

Moonflower snatched it from her grasp.

11

Donner laid out his clothes on the bed. A few shirts and sweaters, jeans, underwear, socks. And his shaving kit. Some small gifts for Liz and the girls. He'd never been good at buying presents, even worse at wrapping them, so he'd asked McGrath for tips and let the jewelry store package everything up. A pair of earrings each for Emma and Jess, and a necklace for Liz. It was only when he'd left the store that he realized he wasn't sure if Emma's ears were pierced or not.

His stomach fluttered with nerves. Tomorrow night would be the first time in almost three years he'd slept under the roof he'd once shared with his family. He had left the day after New Year's, having agreed with Liz he would stay through the holidays for the girls' sake. Emma and Jess had sat at the breakfast table, each staring into their cereal as he explained that he would always love them, his leaving would never change that. He and their mom still loved each other, but they just couldn't be together anymore, and really, they might not see it now, but it was for the best. Jess had looked up from her Cheerios and said, "So why don't you just fuck off already?"

He had no illusions that going back would be easy. The idea of those long and awkward silences terrified him. Jess rolling her eyes every time he spoke. Liz talking to him like he was six. Emma staying quiet. But it would be worth it. To rebuild everything that had been broken.

He remembered back then, fantasizing about being single, doing whatever he wanted, whenever he wanted. Staying out till all hours of the night, sleeping late on the weekends. Imagining how happy he'd be without all the grinding responsibility. And when he'd packed his bags and left, found himself in this shitty Bloomingdale apartment, it didn't take long to realize the truth: he was miserable on his own. All that freedom, and he spent it commuting between this rotten place and the J. Edgar Hoover Building on Pennsylvania Avenue, occasionally stopping at a bar in between to get drunk and hit on women who looked like Liz. They all rejected him, of course, and he was thankful for vodka's ability to blot his memory. Otherwise, the shame might have unmanned him.

In three years, he'd gotten laid one time. A brief fling with an admin assistant at work. Shannon was her name. They'd slept together once, after five dates, and he felt like he was cheating on his wife. Shannon had asked him what was wrong as he struggled to reach a climax, killing any possibility of achieving that goal, and she'd cried herself to sleep. He crept out of her apartment at the first sign of dawn, and they hadn't spoken to each other since. Last he'd heard, she'd transferred over to the Department of Justice building across the street.

Donner sat on the edge of his bed. The cheapest double that IKEA had. He'd furnished the entire place in one trip in a borrowed van. A weekend of cursing at flat-pack furniture, and his new bachelor life was all set. And, oh, what a shitty life it had been. He buried his face in his hands and thanked God and Jesus that he had been given a chance to put things right. There would be a mountain of shit to eat, of course, but he was prepared to do that. Anything to get his old life back.

Quitting the booze had been the first step. Hadn't been that hard. He'd never considered himself an alcoholic, had never hidden bottles around the house, nor kept a flask in his desk drawer to sip at through the working day like so many of his colleagues did. Going without didn't leave him with the shakes or screaming nightmares. It simply bored him. God knows, he had enough boredom in his life. A little more wouldn't hurt. And it pleased Liz, so the choice was simple.

Maybe he should call her. Donner lifted his cell phone from the nightstand. He had nothing in particular to say, but to hear her voice would soothe the worry that nagged at him. A feeling in his gut that this would not go how he planned. That no matter how hard he tried, things would never be right again.

He thought of what McGrath had said: that his obsession with finding this killer was more to fill some void left by his family than to atone for the death of Michael Roach. She was wrong, he was sure of it. Just cheap psychobabble, the kind of behavioral bullshit the Bureau thrived on. What was he, Captain Ahab hunting a white whale?

"Full of shit," he said to the phone's blank screen.

No, he wouldn't call Liz. The most he could hope for would be a few awkward niceties. He returned the cell to the nightstand.

Donner got to his feet and walked to the living area. If you could call it that. Two armchairs and the cheapest coffee table IKEA had to offer. Twelve bucks from the clearance section because it had a dent in the top. No TV in the corner. He could recite from memory the exact contents of his refrigerator. The closest he came to cooking was reheating takeout in the microwave. He couldn't recall when he'd last used the oven or the stove.

The loneliness reached into him, its fist squeezing his heart and lungs. He walked back to the bedroom, heading for the nightstand and his cell phone. It vibrated as he reached for it, startling him. Liz calling. He lifted the phone and brought it to his ear.

"Hey," he said, as if he hadn't spent the last hour thinking about her, about being back in her arms, in her bed. In *their* bed.

"Hey," she said. "You okay?"

"Yeah, I was just, uh . . ."

Thinking about you.

"Just packing a few things for tomorrow."

"Good. We're looking forward to it. What time will you get here?"

"Around twelve, maybe twelve-thirty, depending on the traffic."

"In time to help us dress the tree."

"Yeah, that's what I'm aiming for."

She gave a small laugh, and a breathy sigh. The sound she used to make when he'd pleased her in some small way. It made him ache inside.

"Listen," she said, "don't bring any gifts, okay?"

"No?"

"No, it's just, we don't have anything for you, and it'll be awkward if you give us anything. Okay?"

"Uh, yeah, I guess."

"You haven't bought anything, have you?"

He looked at the row of three green boxes resting by his duffel bag.

"No," he said.

"Good," she said. "I'll see you tomorrow."

"Yeah. See you then."

He hung up and dropped the phone onto the bed. He reached down and lifted the three boxes, carried them to the kitchenette, and tossed them in the garbage can by the sink.

12

Moonflower was woken once more by the van halting, the shudder through the chassis as the engine died. She had been dreaming of the before times again, of having a bed of her own, a room of her own, a home of her own. Of staying in one place. Of never being hungry.

Her stomach cramped at the thought, and she bit on her lower lip to keep from crying out. Mom was worried enough, no need to make it worse. But she couldn't silence the growl that came from deep inside her abdomen. The cottontail had staved off the hunger for a night, but it wasn't enough. She needed more.

"You okay?" Mom asked from the other side of the curtain.

"Yeah," Moonflower said.

They both knew it was a lie. Still dark outside, no light showing at the borders of the curtain.

"Where are we?"

"Gas station," Mom said. "North of Flagstaff. It should open soon."

Moonflower crawled through to the cabin and into the passenger seat. The effort caused an aching in her arms and legs. She allowed no sign of it, but she couldn't disguise the shortness of breath. Mom turned to look at her in the dim artificial light from the gas station's twenty-four-hour pumps. She reached out and touched Moonflower's forehead.

"Goddammit."

"I'm sorry," Moonflower said, her voice low in her throat.

"It's not your fault," Mom said. "Never has been."

Moonflower's left leg jerked, a spasm that began in her thigh and shot down to her calf, bringing pain. She held a cry in her throat, trying to hide it, but Mom noticed. She sat quiet for a time, watching as Moonflower rubbed the heel of her hand against her thigh, trying to calm the quivering muscle.

"We can't wait any longer," Mom said. "It has to be tonight."

"I can wait. It's not that bad. I can hold off a day or two."

"No, you can't. I have a lead in Phoenix. It's not that far. Maybe I can get him to bite today, drive up here, or meet halfway."

"On Christmas Eve?"

"It's worth a shot."

Mom reached for the glove box and pulled the black fabric wallet from inside. She opened it and retrieved the cell phone. The van's cabin glowed green and blue as it powered up. It chimed once, and Mom thumbed the screen, working through menus. After a while, her head dropped, and she said, "Shit."

"What's wrong?"

"No data left," Mom said. "Goddammit."

Mom changed SIM cards every few weeks, never keeping the same number. She never called anyone, but browsed the web, using whatever free data came with them before throwing them away.

"You don't have a number to call him?"

"No. I was talking to him through Kik. I need more data."

Mom pulled a few crumpled bills from the wallet, counted them out. Less than thirty dollars. She cursed again.

"Not enough?" Moonflower asked, knowing the answer.

"Not if I want to get gas anytime soon. Or food and water."

They fell silent, both watching the dimly illuminated windows of the gas station's convenience store. Lights flickered within, shapes moving behind the signs advertising cigarettes and lotto tickets. Close to 6 A.M., they'd be getting ready to open.

"I'll see what I can get in the store," Mom said, powering off the phone. She returned it to the wallet and pocketed the cash. "Hey, maybe I'll get lucky."

"How?"

"I don't know."

Mom gripped the steering wheel tight, her jaw clenched. Then she spoke again.

"We might have to do it the old way."

"No," Moonflower said before the idea had a chance to take hold.

"We might not have a choice."

"I don't want to. I'd rather go hungry."

"It's a risk, but it's more dangerous if the hunger takes you."

"I can control it," Moonflower said.

"But what if you can't?"

"I can."

"What if you can't?" Mom spat the words from her mouth as if they were poison. "You know what could happen. How bad it could get. What if I lost you? I couldn't bear that." She reached out and took Moonflower's hand, squeezed it tight. "I can't lose you again. I won't let you take that risk."

Moonflower felt herself deflate, the resistance leaving her body, tired acceptance taking its place.

"So, what do we do?"

Mom watched the convenience store, thinking, its lights reflected in her eyes. Beyond the van's windshield, snow began to fall, fat flakes drifting in the breeze to settle on the dry ground.

"There's a shopping mall in Flagstaff," she said. "We can try the food court there. There'll be cameras, but we can work around that. We've done it before."

"What if it goes wrong?" Moonflower asked.

"Then we'll deal with it," Mom said, her voice too sure.

As if it hadn't gone wrong the last time. They had barely gotten away. Moonflower remembered the security guard's hand on her wrist, the hard grip, his cry of pain and shock when she snapped the bones in his fingers.

"It might not come to that," Mom said. "If I can get what I need here, and if I can get that lead in Phoenix to bite. Two big ifs, I guess, but I have to try. They're opening."

A stout man unlocked the door of the convenience store and flipped a sign to say they were open for business.

"I won't be long," Mom said, climbing out of the van.

File #: 89-49911-11
Subject: Rebecca Carter
OO: Flagstaff
Desc: Letter, Handwritten
Date: 12-25-1999

Dear Monica,

Two years since I wrote you last. So that makes it a biannual letter. Or is it biennial? Yes, I think it's biennial.

Today was a good day, all things considered. Uncle Grant and Aunt Jean came for Christmas. And to see Dad. Uncle Grant looks a lot like him, or like he did before the ALS. When they arrived this morning, I couldn't stop staring. It was like Dad had come back from wherever he's been these last two years with just a little more gray in his hair than he'd left with.

I guess you don't remember Dad before the sickness. He was tall and handsome with that shock of black hair you inherited. It was always wild, always sticking out someplace. Like yours. It's thinned out now. There's less of it, like there's less of him. You don't remember how he carried you on his shoulders like he carried me. Or how brave and strong he was. How he told your father and his father to go fuck themselves rather than take their dirty money.

I guess you'll remember him as he is now, sitting in his wheelchair, looking out on the garden. Still and quiet, for the most part, listening to the radio, or maybe one of those books on CD that Mom buys for him. Sometimes he gets upset. If he can't tell us what he needs, if Mom doesn't come quick enough, or misunderstands him. He cries in frustration, then Mom cries, and she gets angry, and he gets angry, then she shouts, and he screams at her from the back of his throat because he has no words.

Anger is the correct emotion. If I was him, I would burn so hot with rage that the air around me would catch fire. How God could treat him that way. A good and decent man made to waste away in front of the people who love him. Why would any god do that to a good man? Maybe God just doesn't care. Another ant crushed beneath his foot, that's all.

I heard your father, Christopher, who never wanted to know you, got a great job in San Francisco, designing database search engines. Melissa Krantz, my old friend from junior high, met him there. He has a beautiful apartment and drives a Mercedes. His parents are fit and healthy and visit him regularly. I work nights at a hotel for barely more than minimum wage, drive a nine-year-old Hyundai, and live with my parents, one of whom is dying from a wasting disease.

Where's the justice in that? What's fair about it? How come a shitty person like your father gets to live a great life in an exciting city while I barely get by in fucking Madison, Wisconsin, where nothing ever happens, and the wind off the lakes could slice you in two?

But I have you, and you know what? That's enough.

I could've made different choices. I could've taken a different path at seventeen and had the life I wanted, the career, the travel. All the places I could've seen, all the food I could've tasted, all those starlit skies I could've stood beneath. I could've had all that, but I chose not to, and I don't regret it at all.

When you came downstairs this morning, all sleepy-eyed, and your black hair standing up every which way, I think you'd forgotten what day it was. Then you walked into the living room, yawning, and you saw the tree and you remembered. And you saw the gifts all laid out and wrapped for you, and your eyes and mouth went so wide, and you squealed and started tearing the paper, giggling among the shreds of red and green and gold.

And Dad watching from his wheelchair, laughing and laughing, tears in his eyes. I wept then because I realized how happy I was and how having you was the best choice I will ever make as long as I live. You are the center of everything, the beginning and end of all things. I know there will be times I forget that, times I question that choice I made more than five years ago, but I will make myself remember Dad laughing as you tore the paper.

The house is quiet now. Uncle Grant and Aunt Jean left around nine, and Mom and Dad went to bed not long after. Jean helped Mom in the kitchen, and I know they cried together in there. I know because I saw their eyes when they brought out the food. Just like Uncle Grant cried when he saw Dad for the first time in more than a year.

I guess we all cried today. Even you when you got tired and cranky and too full of sugar. You probably won't remember this by the time you read these letters, if you ever do, but I lay with you on your bed for a while. You and me holding each other while you drifted off to sleep. There will come a day when you're too old for that sort of thing, and that'll make me sad, but for now I treasure it because it's precious.

Today was a good day. There has been joy. There will be joy again.

Love, always.

Mom

13

An electronic chime sounded as Rebecca entered the store. She looked toward the checkout. A large bespectacled man with thinning hair stood there behind a plexiglass screen, a pricing gun in his hand, working his way through a box of air fresheners, click-clack, click-clack. He raised his head from his labor, smiled at her, and nodded. Rebecca returned the gesture.

She studied the store's interior. Typical gas station. Rows of snacks and drinks. Car accessories: windshield wipers, washer fluid, de-icer. One wall taken up entirely by coolers filled with ice cream and beer. A rotating display of cheap plastic toys, superheroes who'd never seen the inside of a comic book, and knock-off Barbies.

Rebecca hated this place. She hated the large man behind the counter, even though she had never seen him before. Deep down, she knew why: guilt. She felt guilty because she planned to steal from him. And shame. By the time the guilt and shame reached the surface of her emotions they had turned to resentment. It made no sense, but still, it was the truth.

And it wasn't as if stealing was beneath her. She'd done it plenty. Ever since they'd had to run, theft had become a regular necessity, like doing laundry or hunting cotton-tails. Shoplifting was the easiest, especially at stores like this. Uninterested staff, doors within a few seconds' dash, goods just lying all around, waiting to be taken. Had she been after a Snickers or a bag of potato chips, it would have been easy pickings.

Rebecca had become attuned to opportunity wherever it presented itself. A cash drawer left open, a half-unpacked crate set too close to an open door, or a customer's credit card placed on a counter. It only took that customer to look away for a moment, and Rebecca could make it gone. Often as not, the customer wouldn't even notice, would assume they had put it away already. With any luck, it would be hours before they realized the card was missing, by which time Rebecca could have visited a dozen or more stores, making small contactless purchases in each. A few groceries here, a couple of paperbacks there, maybe a pack of cigarettes if she felt like indulging herself. One time, a card had continued working for three days without being declined. Rebecca had wound up throwing it away, convinced she was being set up in some kind of sting operation.

Today, Rebecca was not after groceries or cards. Not even a pack of smokes. She walked the length of all three aisles before she found what she wanted: a pegboard bearing rows of cell phones. All of them cheap, all of them with prepaid calls and data. She browsed the lowest-priced smartphones, sealed in blister packs, gaudy colors advertising an abundance of bundled minutes and gigabytes. This one, green and blue wrapping, came with two gigabytes ready to go, right out of the box. Rebecca noted its position on the rack, the distance between here and the checkout, between here and the door.

"Snow's coming in."

The man's voice startled her. For a heart-shaking second, she thought he stood behind her, looking over her shoulder. But he had not moved. He remained where she'd last seen him, behind the counter, pricing air fresheners. Click-clack, click-clack. He smiled at her, a direct line of sight between where they each stood.

"I said, snow's coming in. Gonna be heavy."

Rebecca looked toward the windows, obscured as they were by posters. In the few spaces, she saw the fat flakes drifting.

"Looks that way," she offered, smiling.

"You need a cell phone?" he asked.

"Maybe," she said. "Late Christmas present, you know? For my daughter."

"Yeah? Maybe I could help you with that."

He placed the pricing gun on the counter and bent down, pulled a box from underneath, grunting at the weight of it. It thunked on the counter, the contents rattling. He picked one item from the box, examined it.

"How about an iPhone XR? Clean as a whistle."

Rebecca took one step closer. There was a six-inch gap between the plexiglass and the countertop.

"You mean, used?"

"Refurbished," the stout man said. "There's a repair guy

in town, he gets these from wherever, replaces the glass, replaces the batteries, they're practically brand new. Look here, I got Samsung Galaxy S8s, S9s, I got iPhone 8s, XRs, SEs, 11s, 13s. Some of them even boxed with chargers and everything."

Rebecca took another step.

"Boxed? Like a new phone?"

The man grinned. "Yeah, look at this. iPhone SE, second generation, boxed, sixty-four gig, looks like you just walked out of that fancy Apple store in Scottsdale. One of those cheap phones on display, a halfway decent one is, what, seventy, eighty bucks? I can give you this for one seventy-five."

Another step.

"A hundred and seventy-five dollars?"

He ducked his head and smiled, clutched the phone's box between his meaty hands.

"You know what? It's Christmas, and you seem like a nice lady. I could do one sixty-five for your daughter, how's that?"

The counter was close now. Rebecca could see her reflection in the plexiglass screen.

"It's not stolen, is it?"

His shoulders slumped, and his head tilted.

"Lady, why would you ask me that? Here I am, I'm trying to do a nice thing for you and your daughter, and you ask me that? Come on. I mean, if you're not interested, that's fine."

He dropped the phone back into the larger box and went to hoist it up, ready to return it to its hiding place.

"No, I'm interested," Rebecca said, crossing the remaining distance between them.

The stout man placed the box back on the counter and retrieved the iPhone. Its own box was small and rectangular. He removed the lid, revealing the phone within, glistening in the store's fluorescent lights.

"Look, it's a beauty, isn't it? I mean, it's an older model, but it's not an antique, you know? Believe me, unless your daughter is a total brat, she'll be happy to find this under the tree tomorrow morning."

Rebecca's breath misted on the plexiglass. He held the phone up for her to see better.

"How do I know it'll work?" she asked.

"Oh, I promise you, it works," he said, his smile widening.

"Well, you say that . . ."

She made a show of checking out his name tag.

". . . Martin, and I don't mean to be rude, but what kind of warranty can you give me? I mean, you're selling these phones out of a cardboard box underneath the counter of a gas station. How do I know my daughter won't switch this thing on in the morning and find out Santa left her a dud?"

Martin laughed.

"Okay, you want a demonstration? I can give you a demonstration. Look, I got a SIM card right here for exactly this circumstance. Just give me a minute."

He pulled the phone from its packaging, poked at the side with a small metal implement, and a tiny drawer popped out. Having placed a SIM in it, he pushed it back in, and powered up the phone.

"Should be enough charge in it for our purposes."

Martin leaned in, his head on one side of the plexiglass, Rebecca's on the other, both of them peering down at the screen as it turned from black to white, and the word "Hola!" appeared. He held it in the gap between the plexiglass and the counter.

"I'm not going through the whole setup process, but look, it's showing a signal, we have data, everything's good to go. So, what do you say?"

Each of them stood back from the partition. Rebecca glanced over his shoulder. Martin turned his head to see what she was looking at.

"One sixty, you said?"

He gave her a wounded look.

"Come on, what are you doing to me? It's Christmas and you're trying to rob me?"

Rebecca gave him her warmest smile and looked over his shoulder once more.

"Okay, one sixty-five and you throw in a pack of Marlboros."

He put the phone flat on the counter, a few inches from the gap, his hairy-knuckled hand on top of it. "Really?"

"Really," Rebecca said, giving him a wink. "I'll need a cigarette after this."

"Shit," he said, a laugh rising up from his belly. "All right. But only because it's Christmas."

He turned, his hand lifting from the phone, leaving it on the counter. He might have reached for the Marlboros, Rebecca wouldn't know, because by the time he'd fetched them from the display, she'd grabbed the phone and was running for the exit.

14

The call came as Donner was crossing the Potomac, heading south, on his way out of DC, entering Virginia. The traffic wasn't as bad as he'd feared. He could make it home—he still considered it home—in less than two hours. Sleep had been hard to come by the night before, his mind racing as the clock crawled. Like a kid waiting for Christmas morning.

The Chevrolet's touchscreen showed it was McGrath calling. He considered not answering; he could always call her back when he got to Richmond. But she wouldn't call on Christmas Eve unless it was something important. All the more reason not to pick up, but he did it anyway.

"Yeah."

"Hey," she said. "Where are you?"

"Driving," he said. "Just crossed the river, about to salute our friends at the Pentagon."

"You're close to the airport, then."

He looked south, saw a jet descending from the winter-gray sky into Reagan. His stomach turned cold.

"Yeah. Why?"

"We got an alert from Flagstaff, Arizona. An attempted theft from a gas station north of the city. A woman aged around forty-ish in a van. Everything matches. We have license plates, security video, everything."

"Shit," he said, changing lanes, heading for the exit. "Gimme a minute."

Horns blared around him as he forced his way across. He barely made the exit, signed for Reagan and the George Washington Parkway, forcing a Subaru pickup to brake hard to avoid a collision. The road swept around in a wide arc before merging with the southbound Parkway. He passed under two bridges before finding a turnout beneath a third. His tires skidded on the concrete.

"What time?"

"About six A.M., local."

He checked the clock on his display.

"So, ninety minutes ago. Did the witness see which direction she headed?"

"There was an altercation, then she took off toward Flagstaff. All local law enforcement are instructed to keep an eye out for the van. They'll ping us if they spot it. But listen, Marc."

She used his first name. She never used his first name.

"What?"

"You don't have to go."

"Yes, I—"

"Listen to me, for Christ's sake. There are local Bureau people there, they've got a police department and state troopers. They can deal with it."

"No," Donner said. "They don't know her methods like I do. They'll lose her. Flagstaff's in the mountains, right? Surrounded by forests. It's the kind of terrain she works best in. They don't know that. They don't know how she operates. I do. That's why I have to be there."

"What about Liz? Your family is more important."

"She'll understand."

"You sure about that?"

"Yeah, I'm sure," he said, even though he wasn't. Not at all.

"Don't use this as an excuse just because you're scared to face her. Don't chicken out."

"Fuck you."

He regretted it the moment he spoke. Truth angers, he knew that as well as anyone.

"Sorry," he said.

"Okay," she said, but the stiffness in her tone didn't sound much like forgiveness. "Look, it's your decision. Just be sure you're making it for the right reasons."

"We can't miss this opportunity," he said. "We can finish this."

McGrath didn't argue. She said nothing at all, the silence stretching out like a thread until Donner could stand it no longer.

"Say it."

He heard her exhale into her phone's mouthpiece.

"Say it, goddammit."

"I can't go with you," she said at last. "I just can't. It's Matthew's first Christmas with us. We went through so much to make the adoption happen, and Cara would never forgive me if I—"

"It's all right," Donner said.

"—skipped out on her. She's already pissed at me for being in the office today. There's no—"

"Sarah, stop."

Her first name silenced her. First names were for serious business only. Personal business.

"It's okay," he said. "Just find me a flight, get me on it."

He heard the clacking of a keyboard, her breath against the mouthpiece.

"All right, American Airlines, flying into Phoenix, leaves in fifty minutes. I'll have you pre-cleared and get a local agent to meet you at the other side. It's a two-and-a-half-hour drive to Flagstaff, unless you can get there by some other way. You'll be there by five, give or take."

"Shit," he said. "Nine hours after the incident. It's too long. She could be anywhere by then."

"Your call," McGrath said.

Donner leaned forward, rested his forehead against the wheel. If the woman had any sense, she'd get as far away from Flagstaff as she possibly could. By the time he got there, she'd be long gone. But only if the local cops didn't find her first. Would Liz forgive him? She'd have to understand he couldn't let this chance slide by. But what about the chance to patch things up with her? And what if the woman got away? How many more might she kill before he caught up to her again?

"Goddamn it," he said.

"Marc, you have to decide. Now."

Donner thought about his wife and his daughters. About the warmth of his home. And the body of a man, his throat ripped open, bled dry.

He raised his head and said, "Get me on that flight."

15

Moonflower listened from the rear of the van as her mother paced outside, cursing, kicking at the earth. Stones pinged and clattered on the metalwork. Mom had smoked at least three cigarettes. Moonflower could smell them, but she would say nothing.

Mom had steered onto a narrow trail between the trees, past a scattering of homes, deeper into the forest, until the trail lost its surface and the van had juddered so much it felt like it might fall to pieces. She had shut off the engine and sat still and quiet for what seemed like a lifetime, staring into the shadows below and between the pines. Her nostrils flaring, her hands shaking on the wheel. Eventually, she said fuck, and got out of the van. Moonflower had watched her until the sun rose high enough behind the thick cloud to hurt her eyes, then she crawled into the back where she lay in the dark with her hands clasped to her stomach, as if she could calm the growling hunger by touch alone.

My fault, she thought. All my fault.

Moonflower didn't know how long Mom had been in the convenience store. Time had become a slippery notion to her, and she sometimes struggled to understand the difference between a minute and an hour, a day and a week, a month and a year. But it had seemed like she'd been gone longer than she should. Moonflower had peered through the windshield and the fat drifting snowflakes, but the posters over the windows obscured the inside of the store.

Her mind had wandered as she watched the snow, each flake glowing in the bright lights above the gas pumps. Like damned angels falling to earth. It crossed her mind to get out of the van and stand with her face to the heavens, her mouth open, her tongue out to catch the flakes. Like she used to do when she was little, back in Madison, in the yard behind their house. She remembered the feel of it, the cold on her skin, the tingle as one landed on her tongue and melted away.

The memory brought an ache with it, like touching a bruise. And you touch it anyway because you like how it hurts.

A slam and a rattle had pulled her attention back to the store, and she saw the door swing open hard, Mom throwing herself out into the early morning cold. Arms and legs churning, something held tight in her right hand. Her eyes wide, her mouth open, shouting. Even if she hadn't been able to make out the words, Moonflower would have known what Mom was saying. She reached for the lock button on the driver's side, heard the mechanism clunk, grabbed the handle, and pushed the door open. Mom sprinting, reaching, left hand outstretched.

A man came after her. Heavyset, but long-legged and quick on his feet. Fury on his face. Hardly any distance between them. But it was too much. He would never catch her. Not ever.

Mom tried to slow as she neared the van, but her feet slid on the fresh snow that melted to slush on the salted pavement. Moonflower saw her eyes flash as she went down, heard her cry out first in shock, then in pain as she slammed into the frame of the open door.

The man came fast behind, carried by his own momentum, stumbling over Mom, his chest landing on the driver's seat. He registered Moonflower for no more than a moment before gathering himself and crouching down beside the van, grappling with Mom, grunting as she fought back.

"Give me the fucking phone," he shouted, spit flying from his lips.

Mom reached up, clawed at his face. He pulled his head back but kept hold of her.

"Gimme it," he shouted again.

"I don't have it," Mom said, her voice thin and breathless. "I dropped it. It went under the van. Let me go and I'll get it."

"No way," he said, leaning down till Moonflower could barely see him beyond the base of the driver's seat. "You just stay right there."

He raised his head, looked back to the store.

"Marcy? Marcy, get out here! Marcy, goddammit!"

Mom's hand swiped at his face and neck, over and over, until he slapped it away. He leaned down, putting his weight on her.

"Let her go," Moonflower said.

The man did not hear, too busy wrestling with her mother.

"Get off her," Moonflower said, louder. "Let her go."

He glanced up at her, then away, then back again, his stare lingering now, seeming to notice her for the first time.

"It's all right, sweetheart," he said, breathless. "We're going to get this all straightened out, don't you worry."

Moonflower crawled across to the driver's seat until she could see Mom on the snow-wet ground, struggling against the man's big hands and heavy arms. She looked up at Moonflower, quiet for a moment, and shook her head, no.

"Get off her," Moonflower said, her eyes level with the man's.

He looked back, saw the animal in her. She saw the flash of fear in him. She heard Mom say, Baby, no. But it was too late. He had loosened his grip, barely half a second, but it was enough.

Her legs like pistons, like coiled steel, launching her forward. Her body slammed into his, and she felt the softness of him, like putty wrapped around bone. She felt something break in him, a wet snap like green wood, and he would have gasped if she hadn't forced the air from his chest. They landed hard in a tangle of arms and legs, hers thin and wiry, his thick and fleshy. The back of his head bounced on the asphalt and she smelled the copper, the iron, and her stomach rolled and turned.

Moonflower straddled him as he groaned, blinking at the dark sky, his gaze a thousand miles away. She reached for his shirt collar, pulled at it, buttons popping.

The hunger. Oh God, the hunger.

"Baby, no."

Mom's voice. Pained and thin. But insistent.

"Not now. Not here."

Moonflower's stomach lurched, turned itself inside out, a roaring beast at the core of her. She lifted the man up by his collar, his head rolling as he muttered something meaningless. Then he came back to himself, looked up at her, his eyes focusing. Fear in them, in him. He screamed. So did she.

Mom's hands on her shoulders, pulling her back, then arms snaking around her, binding her. Lips against her ear, warm whispering blades.

Baby, no, please no.

Moonflower released her grip on his collar, let his head drop back to the asphalt. It connected with a dull thud, and his eyes rolled back. Moonflower roared, her voice ripping out of her throat, her chest, her stomach. It rolled across the plain to the mountain peaks on the horizon.

She fell, her body weak with hunger, her strength spent. Mom gathered her up, carried her back to the van, bundled her inside. As they sped away from the gas station, Moonflower blacked out, returning to herself as the van sped along some back road, nothing but trees all around.

Now Moonflower listened to Mom's pacing in circles around the van. Her cursing and kicking. Fuck, shit, goddammit. Sprays of pebbles and stones.

Then silence.

Not even a bird in the trees, not a branch disturbed by the wind.

Moonflower sat upright, looking first to the front of the van, to the blanket that separated the cabin. Then to the rear, the closed double doors. It was those that opened, letting in the light and the cold. Moonflower retreated as far as she could, her comforter pulled tight around her. Mom stood there, her face impassive.

"It has to be today," she said. "It has to be here. We can't hold off any longer."

Moonflower wanted to argue, to say no, she could hold out. But she knew that would be a lie. As if in agreement, her stomach shifted and groaned. She pulled her knees up to her chest, wrapped her arms around her shins, pressed her nose and mouth against her thighs.

"Okay," she said.

File #: 89-49911-15
Subject: Rebecca Carter
OO: Flagstaff
Desc: Letter, Handwritten
Date: 12-25-2001

Dear Moonflower,

I don't know what to write you this year. I couldn't last year. There was too much—well, too much. Dad was fading. We could see him winding down, and I know Mom would never admit this, but we were counting the days, wishing for him to go. That seems terrible when I see it written down, wishing for my father to die, but it's true. It was hellish, watching him cling on. And what for? What kind of life did he have those last months? I know his mind was still there, but the rest of him?

Exactly one year ago today, I brought you into his old den to say goodnight to him. You were scared, and I don't blame you. This sliver of a man on a hospital bed, tied to those machines. Before we went in, you made me promise not to ask you to kiss him. Then you did it anyway, and I felt my heart tear open inside of me.

After I'd put you to bed, I sat alone with him for a while. I read to him for a bit, then I just talked. Talked about you, about me, about Mom. I told him how my job was going pretty good, how I'm an assistant manager at the hotel now. The pay's still shit, but I like my job, and I'm good at it. Then I told him about Mom, how much she loves him, and misses him, and that I would look after her when he's gone, and she would look after me.

I said something to him then, and ever since I've wondered if I regret it, but I don't think I do. I told him he didn't have to hang on. Not for us. He could go if he wanted to. Go and find some peace.

I half expected him to pass that night. But he didn't. He lasted until the early hours of New Year's Eve. Mom found him at five A.M. and sat with him for an hour before she came and woke me. We both wept, of course, but I think by that stage, we'd done our grieving. You cried too, but I think it was for Mom and me, not for my father. You never really knew him, only the shadow of him.

I missed him today. Mom did too. She tried to make the brussels sprouts like he used to, fried with butter and bacon, but they didn't come out right, and she threw them in the trash and cried big ugly sobs alone in the corner. As you opened your presents under the tree, I kept looking to his chair, expecting to see him giggling along with you.

Uncle Grant and Aunt Jean had promised to come visit this year, but they didn't, so it was just the three of us. The Carter girls, Mom says, like we're some awful group that sings old-timey gospel songs at revival meetings in the middle of nowhere.

You and she have gotten so close this last year. There were times when I thought she might have wished I'd made a different choice those years ago, times she seemed to keep you at arm's length. But I realize now it was Dad's withering that soaked up all her attention. Now he's gone, she can give all her love to you. It's small things, like how you and she hold hands while you watch old movies together. Or the way she whispers stories to you of what things were like when she was a little girl. Or how she watches as you stir the chocolate chips into the cookie mix when she's baking up a batch.

My God, do you know how loved you are? Between me and Mom, you must feel it, the weight of it. I hope you do.

It's just us three now. The Carter girls. Mom keeps at me to get out there, meet a nice man, start dating. Ugh. I've seen what "nice men" leave behind in their hotel rooms, and I'm not talking about tips for housekeeping.

No. I've got you, and that's all I need. For now, anyway. Maybe when you're a teenager and you can't stand the sight of me, and you think I'm a mortal embarrassment and the worst mom ever, maybe then I'll see what's out there.

Until then, it's just us Carter girls, and that's enough.

Love, love, love, always.

Mom

16

They waited there among the trees as the day passed. Rebecca kept watch while Moonflower slept, crying out now and then, the growl of her stomach as constant as the snowfall outside. The world turned white as the hours crawled. As much as the persistent groans of Moonflower's hunger tore at Rebecca's nerves, the quiet outside bothered her more. But still, she had to get out of the van once in a while.

Her knees complained as she climbed down from the driver's side. These years on the run had played hell with her joints. Used to be she could drive for eight hours straight without a worry. Now, more than an hour, and the aches would start. Her knees, her hips, her shoulders, her wrists.

She remembered her mother once pausing as she climbed up on a stool to reach something from a kitchen cupboard, turning to look down at her, and saying, "You know the worst thing about getting old? Everything hurts."

Rebecca had laughed at the time. Not long after Moon-flower was born. Like all young people, she fully believed she would be untouched by age. She could not conceive of losing her youth. That was for other people. Old people, mostly, and she couldn't imagine ever being one of them. Yet here she was.

Her mother, Denise, had just become a grandmother, and a young one at that. Rebecca had put her sudden feeling of age down to her new familial status. Something Rebecca herself would never experience; it played on her mind more as time inched forward, that she would never be a grandmother. How alien that idea would have seemed to her back then, standing in her mother's sun-bright kitchen. That she would have pined for a grandchild herself.

Life is what happens when you're busy making other plans.

Who had said that? Someone famous and dead, she thought, but she couldn't place the name. Didn't matter, it was true anyway.

Rebecca closed the driver's door, clasped her hands together, and stretched her arms skyward. She stood on the balls of her feet, lengthened her body, feeling the tension pull her from fingers to toes. Like she was a piece of gum stuck between a shoe and the sidewalk. The right side of her ribcage ached from slamming into the side of the van earlier that morning. She counted herself lucky not to have cracked a rib.

Her lower back was the worst. A constant pain, like the stitching was coming undone, as if something would tear and burst apart if she wasn't careful. It had, once, eighteen months ago. They'd been boondocking at some site near Austin and she'd bent over to check the tread in one of the tires. A bolt of pain had arced out from the base of her spine, and it had taken her legs from under her. She had lain on the ground, screaming, clawing at her own back, until Moonflower had rushed out into the heat to find her sprawling in the dirt, then dragged her inside. Three days she couldn't move from her mattress. Not even to piss. Once she'd recovered, she ditched the mattress at a recycling center, bought another secondhand, and moved on. One of the degradations she'd become used to.

Speaking of which.

Rebecca went to the treeline, pulled down her sweats, and squatted. She carried tissues in her coat pocket for exactly this purpose. That done, she hiked up her pants and went back to the van. She looked up to the glooming sky, checked the time on her watch, and looked up again. Twilight coming. One of the shortest days of the year.

She went to the back of the van and opened the door. The hinge cracked and groaned, waking Moonflower. She sat up, squinting, raising a hand to shield her eyes from the scant light.

"What time is it?"

"Just past four," Rebecca said, climbing in. She pulled the door closed behind her. "We have to go now. We have to be careful. No mistakes. You remember what to do, right?"

Moonflower dropped her gaze.

"Yeah, I remember. But do we have to? I can hold off another day or two, I—"

"No, you can't," Rebecca said, taking hold of her

daughter's hand. "Look what happened this morning. Look how close you came to losing control."

Moonflower's head dipped low.

"I'm sorry."

Rebecca took her daughter in her arms, pressed her lips to her ear.

"No, baby, you don't have to apologize for anything. It's not your fault. Remember that, no matter what happens. You never asked for any of this. Neither did I. It's not your fault, and it's not mine. All we can do is make the best of what we have, right?"

She took Moonflower's face in her hands, looked into her dark eyes.

"We didn't make this world. But we have to live in it."

Moonflower nodded, as if she understood, as if she knew her innocence, but Rebecca suspected she didn't. She let her go, moved to the other side of the van.

"You know what to do, right?"

Moonflower raised her bony shoulders, a half-hearted shrug.

"I guess. It's been a while."

Rebecca nodded. "Yeah, it's been a while. It's been a long, long time. But we don't have a choice. This is the way it has to be. Like we used to do it."

Moonflower's head dropped between her knees, her body's weakness betraying her hunger.

"Do we have to?"

"I know you hate it. So do I. But yeah, we have to."

Moonflower looked up at her, her eyes dark.

"What if it goes bad? What if we get caught?"

"We won't," Rebecca said, gathering her close, bundling

her in her arms. "Don't say that. Don't even think that. It won't go wrong. It can't. And even if it did, I would save you. You know that, right? I would save you."

"You promise?"

"Of course. I promise, if it goes wrong, if someone has you, I will come for you. Nothing will stop me. I will save you."

"Me too," Moonflower said. She pulled herself away enough to look up at Rebecca. "If it goes wrong, if someone gets you and takes you away, I'll come for you. I'll rescue you. I promise I will."

"Me too," Rebecca said, pulling her tight again. "I promise. I swear to all the gods that ever were."

"I promise," Moonflower said, her breath warm on the skin of Rebecca's neck. "I swear to all the gods that ever were and ever will be."

Rebecca kissed Moonflower's cheek then untangled herself from her.

"It's time to go. Are you ready?"

"Yeah," Moonflower said. "I'm ready."

17

Donner leaned over and retched, his eyes watering, spitting into the snow. He had vomited twice on the Cessna TTx that flew him from Phoenix Sky Harbor to Flagstaff's Pulliam Airport and his stomach had nothing left to give. Special Agent Rollins slapped him on the back, offering encouragement. Donner wished his hands had been so steady on the aircraft's controls.

The Flagstaff's FBI field office stood less than a five-minute walk from the terminal, and Donner was grateful for the late afternoon's cold air. He'd learned his lesson from the few days he'd spent in Golden on the outskirts of Denver, and he'd dressed for the weather, but the heat of the Cessna's interior had done nothing to settle his stomach. The latest wave of nausea passed, and he wiped his mouth as he stood upright.

"Almost there," Rollins said with far more cheer than the circumstances called for. "Come on."

Donner had taken a dislike to Rollins, and not entirely

based on his skills as a pilot. Rollins was a tall man with strawberry blond hair slicked back on his scalp. He chewed gum and looked past Donner when he spoke as if he had better things to do. His conversation during the flight from Phoenix had done little to improve things.

"Cybercrime, huh?" Rollins had said, his voice crackling in the headphones that covered Donner's ears.

"That's right," Donner said.

"So, what, you sit at a computer all day?"

"Not all day."

"Must be tough," Rollins said, giving Donner a sideways glance. "On your ass, I mean."

Donner hadn't responded. Now he followed Rollins across the road to a bland single story building that stood behind a metal fence. If not for the bars on the windows it could have passed for a kindergarten or a law practice. They walked around to a small parking lot and the main entrance, which Rollins unlocked by typing a PIN into a keypad. He held the door open in an ostentatious gesture of welcome.

"After you."

Donner stepped into the reception area, the desk unmanned. He heard a murmur of voices farther inside the building.

"You need a minute to freshen up or do you want to meet the troops?"

"No, I'm good."

Rollins led him along a short corridor, pausing as his cell phone hummed in his pocket. He fished it out, checked the screen, looked back at Donner, then opened a door signed MEETING ROOM 1. A group of nine people waited inside, some seated, some standing. Five of them wore uniforms. Three shoulder insignias read FLAGSTAFF POLICE DEPARTMENT, two said ARIZONA STATE TROOPERS. The rest wore plain clothes; feds, Donner assumed. One of them lifted a phone away from his ear and addressed Rollins.

"I was just calling you. Flagstaff PD patrol spotted the van over at the mall."

Donner stepped around Rollins. "Where?"

"Flagstaff Mall, about twenty minutes from here. Agent Donner, I assume? Agent Chin."

He extended his right hand. Donner shook it.

"They said the van's in the parking lot, empty. Your target is presumably inside the mall somewhere. I've told them to go inside, have a look around, act like they're just getting a coffee or something. They have the description. If they spot her, they'll let us know. Have you seen the CCTV from the gas station?"

"Not yet."

"Well, you should. Sergeant Todacheene?"

One of the PD officers stepped forward, a closed laptop in her hand. She set it on a desk, opened it, and tapped at a few keys before turning it to let Donner see the screen. A van at a gas station, the harsh lighting not quite reaching it. Fat snowflakes falling across the camera lens, lit up like slow comets.

"Watch," Chin said.

Nothing for a few moments, then a woman, running hard. A heavyset man coming after. She falls, slides, hitting the sill of the open driver's door. It looks painful. The man is on her, trying to pry something from her hands. They become a tangle of light and shadow, one limb blurring into another.

Then he is thrown back, ten feet, maybe fifteen. Someone is on him. Someone small. Their features are indistinguishable, seeming to glow and flare, flooding the image with burning light.

"Holy shit," Donner said. "Is that a kid?"

"We think so," Chin said. "It's hard to be sure with so much glare."

The woman gets to her feet, scrambles to them, pulls the child away. Drags it back to the van, looking like she carries a ball of burning phosphate, and bundles it inside. The van speeds away as another woman comes into the frame and crouches by the man still sprawling on the ground.

"What happened there?" Donner asked.

He'd heard little since McGrath had called him that morning, only what Rollins knew, which wasn't much at all.

"I attended the scene," Sergeant Todacheene said. She looked weary, like she'd had a longer day than anyone else in the room. "The gas station clerk wasn't exactly cooperative. It seems he was hawking cell phones under the counter, but he was a little vague about where he got them from. We had no reason to take the phones as evidence, but I'd bet my ass they're stolen, and they won't be there when I follow up. As far as I can tell, the woman snatched one and ran. He chased her. Then the altercation you see in the video."

"Did he give a description? Was she calm, agitated, what?"

"He gave me almost nothing. In fact, I think if the other

clerk hadn't called it in, we'd have heard nothing about it. He doesn't want to press charges for the attempted theft or assault. She didn't try to steal any stock from the gas station itself."

"You got the phone she tried to take, right? It'll have prints."

"Nothing useful. It lay in melted snow for a while. Between that and the salt, only a couple partials were left. Probably nothing useful. If it wasn't for the CCTV, we'd have nothing at all, not even a license plate."

"And we wouldn't all be sitting here on Christmas Eve," one of the state troopers said, the words sharpened by hostility.

"That's enough," Chin said.

Another cop spoke up despite the agent's warning. "What's this all about, anyway? Christmas Eve, I should be mopping up drunks or attending domestics, but I was told to report here for a special operation. What exactly are we doing here?"

Donner scanned their faces, all watching him, expecting an authoritative answer that would justify their presence. He cleared his throat and did his best.

"The woman in this video is a suspect in a string of homicides over several years across several states. I've been tracking her for two years now. I've seen the victims, I've seen what she can do. Believe me when I say she is extremely dangerous. I requested an interagency team to surveil and, at the appropriate time, apprehend her."

He looked around the room once more. Eleven people in total, none of whom wanted to be here except for him.

"Well," he said, "I guess this is it."

18

Moonflower sat at a table at the far edge of the food court, a milkshake in front of her that had turned from icy cold to barely cool over the last hour. She'd taken a few sips, for appearances, and had so far managed to keep the cloying liquid down. A few wet, sickly burps, that was all. She could cope with that.

The crowds had thinned to a trickle. The mall had been thronged with people when they first got here and staked the place out, last-minute Christmas shoppers seeking gifts for those they'd forgotten about, or looking for reductions on seasonal goods. But now only the stragglers remained. Earlier there had been more women than men, but now the balance shifted the other way. Guilty husbands desperate for some idea what to buy their wives, or single men who couldn't face themselves alone on such a day as this. The weak ones. They were the ones she sought.

Mom occupied a table on the opposite side of the court, watching over her long-cold coffee. She had been calm ninety minutes ago. Now her nerves trilled like a piccolo. Moonflower could hear them from all the way over there.

They made eye contact. Moonflower raised her eyebrows, tilted her head, should we go? Mom shook her head, a movement so small no one else could possibly have seen. No, stick with it, she said. There's still time.

Moonflower's stomach spoke up. A low gurgling growl that turned the heads of an elderly couple four tables away. She felt it cold and rolling in her midsection, chilled by the few sips of milkshake she'd taken. Her fingers danced along the tabletop, her feet skipping in place. Her legs wanted to move, to run, to chase. She forced them to be still and looked back to Mom.

Mom wasn't watching her. Her gaze was elsewhere, somewhere over Moonflower's shoulder, her face tight with concentration. Without looking away from whatever had her attention, she clasped her hands together, the fingers knotted, her elbows on the table. She lifted her finger a little, hardly anything at all, tilted toward the corner behind Moonflower.

A target, a prospect. Moonflower knew what to do.

She slumped down in her chair, her shoulders up to her ears, rested her head in her hands. Let the air hitch in her chest, as if tears were a moment away. Gave a quivering exhalation. Moved the heels of her hands to her eyes and sniffed hard.

Moonflower kept her head down and listened. Nothing. She let out a soft, high whine.

"Hey," a man said.

Moonflower startled, jerking her head upright.

He stood a few feet away, to her left, a tray in his hands

loaded with a burger, fries, and a drink. A slight man, round-shouldered, his slouch making his body a question mark. Tan slacks and a navy puffer vest. About thirty-five, she thought. Maybe forty, but his features were boyish. Boyish men don't age well, Mom had told her that. They sag and droop while their brothers crease and crack.

"You okay?" he asked, his face open and friendly.

Moonflower nodded and looked away, folding in on herself, her body telling him to go away, leave her alone. He would take no heed. She counted on it.

"Mind if I sit down?"

She turned her body away, showed him her back.

"Well, this table's free, I guess I could just sit here."

She heard a chair scrape on tile, creak as his scant weight settled into it. The fussing of his tray and food.

"You hungry?"

Moonflower didn't answer.

"Boy, they give you a lot of fries. I mean, I'm not complaining, I like fries. I like 'em a lot, but wow, that's a lot of fries. I guess I could just throw them away, but that's such a waste."

Moonflower turned her head, watched as he tipped some fries into the lid of his burger box. He reached the half-empty carton to her.

"Do me a favor. No point throwing them in the trash."

She hesitated. Then she took the carton from his hand. His finger brushed hers, his skin soft and moist, like a child's. She turned away from him, took a fry from the carton and put it into her mouth. Chewed and swallowed. Salt and grease. Her stomach gurgled in protest.

"So, Christmas Eve come around again, huh?"

She took another fry, forced it down, the salt scratching at her throat like rat claws.

"I know it's none of my business, but I gotta wonder, how come you're not at home? Where's your family?"

Moonflower kept her back to him, dropped her head down.

"Did you run away?"

She remained still.

"Is that it? Did you run away from home?"

She allowed her head and shoulders to rise, just a little.

"Yesterday? Day before?"

Moonflower didn't turn her head. "Two days ago," she said.

"Hm," he said, as if this meant something. "What happened? An argument?"

She scratched at her scalp, her fingers digging into drifts of black hair. "My stepdad. He . . . we don't get along."

He knew what she meant. She sensed his quickening.

"You don't want to be alone at Christmas," he said.

A fact. Not a question.

She chewed on another salty, scratchy fry, hoping she could keep it down.

"You don't have to be," he said.

One more fry. One more chew. One more swallow.

"Listen, I'm an elder in my church. We run a shelter for kids like you. Give them a bed, a safe place, somewhere they can gather their thoughts and decide what to do."

Now, she turned her head to him, glancing over her shoulder. Saw his round, shining, honest face.

"I mean, yes, it's run by the church, but there's no preaching, no pressure, we're not trying to convert anyone.

We just want to give people a safe place to be for a few days. Normally there's this whole process, they need an order from the city, social services, an induction and whatnot, but it's Christmas Eve. I'm sure if I took you over there, they'd give you a bed for the night."

"Where is it?" Moonflower asked.

He pointed a finger at the distance. "Just out of town a little. Not far. Fifteen, twenty minutes, maybe."

She turned away. Made herself smaller.

"What do you say? A warm bed for the night. Something to eat. They do a special dinner for Christmas."

Her stomach lurched and snarled. He laughed.

"I guess you can't claim you're not hungry. Come on, what do you say?"

She turned back to him.

"What's your name?"

"Craig," he said, smiling. "For my grandfather. I never knew him. My mother tells me he was a great man. What do we call you?"

"Monica," she said. "But everyone calls me Moonflower."

His smile widened, showing the gaps between his teeth. "Moonflower? That's pretty. So how about the shelter? A safe place, a warm bed, good food. How about it?"

"Okay," she said.

"Good," he said, standing. "Good. Let's go."

Dear Moonflower,

I almost forgot to write you this year, but I'm glad I remembered because, guess what? This has been a good year. I mean, a fucking great year.

I'm a little drunk, so this might ramble a bit. Where to start?

Well, at the age of twenty-five, I'm finally going to college. Yes, it's only Madison Technical College. Yes, it's only part time. Yes, it's only an associate degree. But, but, finally I'm making progress. And once I graduate, if I want to, I can transfer to UW-Madison and study for a full BAA.

I have Suzanne to thank for this. Mrs. McDermid, the regional manager, but she insists I call her Suzanne. I got to know her before Dad passed. She lost her husband to ALS maybe ten years ago, so I guess she had some sympathy for me. She stops by for coffee once a week or so, chats a while, asks how I'm getting along, asks about you. I show her photos, tell her all the funny things you've said and done, and I think she's genuinely interested. I guess you could say she's taken me under her wing. Anyway, she told me about this program run by corporate, where they fund adult education for their employees. An employee—like me, for example—has to be recommended for the program by a regional manager—like Suzanne, for example—as showing promise for future advancement in the company. They pay the tuition costs, allow time off when required, and they even pay for childcare if you need it.

"You've been dealt some shitty hands," she told me. "You deserve a break."

She's not wrong.

Life has kicked me in the ass over and over. I got pregnant when I was sixteen and gave birth at seventeen, and I don't regret keeping you—God, I could never regret you— but it's been hard. For you, I gave up the life I'd planned, and just when I thought I might get back on track, Dad got sick. Now here's a chance to start building something for myself, and for you, and yes, goddammit, I deserve this.

And there's something else.

There might be a man in my life.

I say "might be" because we've only gone out a few times, and even then, "out" is stretching it a little, seeing as at least three of those times were just drinks in the bar at my hotel.

His name is Peter, and he's a sales rep for Fender, the guitar company. Except it's not just guitars, they do all sorts of music-related stuff. He's based out of Scottsdale, Arizona, they have offices there as well as California, but he travels a lot for work. When he's in Wisconsin, he uses Madison as a base. He likes it better here than Milwaukee because it's more central and doesn't have the traffic, and he can drive as far as Chicago or even the Twin Cities when he needs to. He might stay for a week at a time, three or four times a year.

That's how we met. I was covering on the front desk late one night because Val had an emergency at home, and this man arrived wanting to check in. I'd say he was around thirty, longish hair, smart-casual. Just enough faded denim to suggest he wasn't a walking necktie like most of the business travelers we get. He asked if I was new here, and I said I'd been working here for a few years, but normally back office, not out front. That explains it, he said, otherwise I'm pretty sure I'd remember you. My God, I felt my cheeks burn red like a schoolgirl's, even at a line as cheesy as that.

I wound up being out front for a few days, on and off, and we got to chatting as he came back from his day trips, and by the fourth day I was actively seeking to be there. On the fifth evening, he said he was checking out in the morning, and he wondered if he could buy me a drink to thank me for all my help. God, I went bright red again, and I giggled like I was being asked to the prom.

Why? I mean, I'm a grown-ass woman, a single mother in fact, so why am I turning to jelly when this man pays me a little attention? It's not as if he's the first to ever try it on. Ask any woman who works in a public-facing job, we're never short of creeps who think we'll drop our panties if they give us a wink and a smile.

So why this man?

I don't know. He's good looking, yes, oh God yes, handsome even, but there's a quiet confidence about him. A steadiness, a strength. Like a rock in a river.

So, I told him employees were forbidden from socializing with the guests, but I do sometimes stop by the bar for a beer after work, and if he happened to be there too, well, I can't help that, can I? In the end, I had four beers and a scotch, and I had to get a cab home. But it was worth it. You'll find this out when you're older, but sometimes you meet people and things just fall into place, like you've known them your whole life and somehow forgot until the moment they walked through the door.

I told him the truth. About you, and our circumstances, how my life had gone off course. I figured why let him think he was flirting with a woman without commitments and waste both our time? It didn't matter. We spent three hours together, talking and laughing, and he said he'd very much like to do it again, next time he's in town. He didn't try to get me up to his room, or steal a kiss or cop a feel. He was a gentleman. So, I said yes, I'd very much like to do it again, next time he's in town.

That was back around March, so it must have been early June when he returned. I arrived at work on a Tuesday morning and there was a note on my desk saying a Mr. Peter Veste had asked for me the evening before, that he'd be out on business all day, but that he'd like to speak with me when he returned.

I couldn't sit still all day. There's a two-way mirror behind reception, the management offices behind that, and God, I barely took my eyes from it. It got to the point where my boss, Mr. Billingham, asked if I was feeling all right. I was supposed to finish at six, but I found some things I needed to get caught up on, and Mr. Billingham left for the day, and then seven came and went, then seven-thirty, and I thought, God, what a fool I am, and I called Mom and said sorry I was late, and I might be later still, and could she get your supper and put you to bed, and—

He walked through the doors at 7:48 P.M. carrying two guitar cases and a backpack slung across his shoulder.

I shot up from my chair like it'd been wired to the mains and somebody had flipped the switch. I stood for a few seconds, just watching, wondering what to do. I mean, it was obvious what I should do: slither on out there all casual and nonchalantly sexy and say, *Hi, I got your message.* Instead, I remained rooted to the spot, staring like a deer in the headlights until the phone on my desk shrilled, and I answered it, and it was Val at the front desk telling me there was a guest wanting to speak with me, and was I available?

I said, Please ask him to wait, I'll be out momentarily.

That was the longest one minute and forty seconds of my life, just standing there, trying not to appear too desperate.

Anyway, I went out, and he asked if our agreement still stood. I told him it did, and we had a wonderful night. And the next night, and the night after that. I had the next day off, and he made some calls, moved some meetings, and we spent the day together.

And the night.

It had been so long. I mean, it's not like I've been entirely chaste all these years, but it's been so long since it's been good. I've had my moments, but they were rarely anything more than disappointing sticky fumbles. Not like this. This? This was something different. I'll spare you the details, but . . .

There's no way to end that sentence that doesn't make me blush, or won't make future you throw up in your mouth.

When I got home at about 5:30 A.M., Mom was waiting in the kitchen.

She asked, Who is he?

I told her.

She asked, Was it worth it?

Yes, I said.

She asked, Is there a future?

I paused, then, on the threshold between the hall and the kitchen, my shoes in my hands, my shame not far behind, and I considered it.

I think so, I said.

Mom smiled and nodded. Good enough, she said. And she went to bed.

I love her for that. I remember how raw it felt, standing there, her knowing where I'd been, what I'd done. How open the wound. And she didn't judge me for it. She understood I had gotten something I needed, because at one time, she had needed it too.

We judge each other too much; we impose too many rules. And there are Boy Rules, and Girl Rules, and God forbid one should ever cross the two. A dad could welcome home his son in the early hours and quietly admire his tomcatting around the place, but a mother should scorn her daughter for seizing a moment with someone? My mother, your grandmother, has no use for that bullshit, and neither do I.

Let's just spell this out: I got laid, and it was good.

That's all there is to it.

Except, it's not, because Peter came back in September, and we did it all again. And now he's coming to visit for the New Year. He'll be here in three days. He's a good man, and I know you'll like him.

Love, always,
Mom

19

She's not in danger.

Rebecca repeated that mantra, over and over. All these years, and she still didn't quite believe it. Not then, not now. But still, it was the truth.

She had seen the mark first. The small man, tan pants, blue puffer vest. She had pointed to him as subtly as she could. He made his approach, like she knew he would, and Moonflower played her part exactly as she should have. Everything was right.

Except it wasn't.

Rebecca saw the cops only a few seconds after the man sat down. Over at the pretzel place, buying coffee. A man and a woman, him thick around the middle, her broad-backed with her hair pulled tight into a bun. Neither of them looking at anything in particular. Certainly not looking at her or Moonflower. Why would they?

Even so, the sight of them placed a chill at Rebecca's center. She forced herself to quit staring at them, instead stealing glances over the top of her own coffee cup as she pretended to take a sip. The male officer turned his back to the counter and let his gaze crawl around the food court, sliding over the tables, the chairs, the scattering of customers. Until it reached her.

Did he pause?

It seemed to Rebecca that the travel of his attention slowed as it passed her. Only for a moment, so short a time it couldn't be measured. But she felt it. Like a fingertip on her forehead. No, she told herself. She was imagining things, exhaustion and fear getting the better of her.

The male cop inclined his head toward his female partner, said something. She didn't turn from the register where she paid for their drinks. But her left hand went to the radio handset clipped to her breast pocket. She leaned her head into it and spoke five syllables. Only five, no more.

They took their coffees and chose a table, the woman facing Rebecca, the man with his back to her. Maybe twenty, twenty-five feet away. The woman surveyed the room, just as her partner had done, a slow sweep from one side to the other. This time, there was no question: her gaze had paused on Rebecca.

The tight ball of fear in Rebecca's breast unraveled into panic. It was all she could do not to throw her cup down and run for Moonflower. Her higher mind told her to be still, to watch, to see what might happen. She realized then that she'd given the two cops all her attention and had no idea what her daughter was doing.

The man in the tan pants and blue puffer vest had taken a seat at the table next to Moonflower's. She held a carton of fries in one hand, nibbled at a fry in the other. Rebecca watched the man's lips move, guessing at what he said. Probably offering a safe place for the night, somewhere with food and a warm bed. All Moonflower had to do was go with him and all would be well.

Sure enough, he stood, leaving most of his food uneaten. He gestured toward the exit. Moonflower glanced that way, then looked back to him. Come on, he probably said, let's get you somewhere safe and warm. Moonflower hesitated, then stood. The man smiled. She smiled back, nervous, shy.

Good girl, Rebecca thought. You got him.

Moonflower's eyes flitted in her direction. Fear gripped Rebecca.

Stop, she wanted to cry. Call it off. They're watching.

But were they?

She allowed herself one glance at the cops. They were deep in conversation about something, their focus on each other and their coffee.

Rebecca looked back to Moonflower and gave a hint of a nod. Moonflower returned the gesture and followed the man away from the table, away from the food court, toward the exit and the bitter cold evening beyond. When they were almost out of sight, Rebecca stood and followed. Casual, unhurried. She did not look toward the cops again. Something told her that to do so would bring their scrutiny. She strolled toward the exit, her pace steady and even, quickening only as she neared the doors and saw the thick snowfall outside. The cars in the lot blanketed in white, the tire tracks fading in the lanes between the parking spots.

For a sickening moment, Rebecca couldn't see

Moonflower or the man who'd led her away into the bleak evening, but then she spotted them, heading for an aging Dodge SUV at the eastern end of the lot. Rebecca's van stood at the western end. A car paused and allowed her to cross, and she headed toward the van, looking back over her shoulder as she went, keeping her daughter in sight.

No sign of the cops following. She had worried over nothing.

Everything was going to be all right. She was sure of it.

"It's going to be okay."

She said it aloud to make it true.

20

"We got eyes on her."

The message came over the radio as the four vehicles made their way along Route 66, holding a steady speed through the light traffic. The city had begun to quiet, its good people heading home to be with their families. Donner traveled in the passenger seat of the lead car, an unmarked black SUV driven by Agent Rollins, Agent Chin in back. The other two agents followed in an inconspicuous sedan, the state troopers behind, and the Flagstaff PD cruiser bringing up the rear.

Donner lifted the handset and thumbed the button.

"What about the kid?"

"She's alone."

"You sure?"

"Yep."

"All right. Just hold back and keep her in sight for now."

"Wilco."

He returned the handset to its cradle. "How far to the mall?"

"Two, three minutes, max," Chin said. "The van's in the northern parking lot, at the front of the main building."

They approached a Taco Bell on the left, a Burger King, a Jack in the Box, their bright lights cutting through the thick snowfall, the interiors near empty.

Donner felt an instinct nag at him. He lifted the handset once more.

"Both marked vehicles," he said, "hang back. Pull into one of those lots and wait for my call."

A pause, then two calls of grumbling agreement.

"They won't like that," Chin said. "Calling them out on Christmas Eve, then telling them to wait on the sidelines."

"I don't give a shit what they like," Donner said. "She sees two marked cars pulling up, she panics, she runs."

"Fair enough," Chin said.

They passed an RV dealership on their right, closed for the holiday, all the vehicles coated in fresh snow. Ahead, beyond a mattress showroom, the Flagstaff Mall's sign, metallic lettering on stone. Rollins steered the SUV into the parking lot, a half empty expanse of asphalt bathed in artificial light.

The radio crackled.

"She's on the move, heading for the north exit."

"All right," Donner replied. "Keep your distance, don't spook her."

He spoke to Rollins, pointing to a tall vaulted wooden canopy over glowing doorways. "Is that it? The exit? Swing over that way."

Rollins did as instructed, navigating the lanes between

the rows of cars, the SUV's tires hissing on the slush of snow melted on the salted asphalt. A few turns, and they skirted the main building, the entrance up ahead.

"She's out," the radio said.

Donner leaned forward, peering through the fat tumbling snowflakes. Rollins slowed as they neared the entrance with its wooden canopy. There, a woman, quick in her step. She paused at the curb, her gaze scanning the parking lot until she saw something far behind them. She did not see the men who watched from the slowing SUV. Rollins brought the car to a stop. The woman took it as permission to cross, and she jogged across the road and away, heading for the far side of the lot.

Rollins went to move off, but Donner touched his arm and said, "Wait."

"We can't just sit here," Rollins said.

"She's not interested in us," Donner said. "But if we tail her to the van, then she might be. Pull in there."

"That's a disabled spot."

"What, you scared you'll get a ticket?"

Rollins tightened his jaw, but he obeyed, pulling into the space. He applied the parking brake but kept the engine running.

Donner watched the woman as she made her way toward the far end of the lot, sometimes walking, sometimes jogging. She seemed to dissolve and rematerialize as she passed in and out of the reach of the lights. Beyond, Donner made out the blocky shape of a van. He lost her in the dimness for a few seconds, then the van's headlights ignited.

"There she goes," he said.

The van pulled out of its space and headed toward the parking lot's exit. Too fast, its wheels spinning on the slush, the rear fishtailing.

"Go." Donner tapped Rollins's shoulder. "Go, go."

Rollins put the car in gear and set off, following the lanes until he slipped in thirty yards behind the van. Donner reached for the radio handset.

"We're on the move. Marked cars, stay a quarter mile back, I'll keep you updated on our position. Agent McCreary, fall in behind us, but keep your distance."

All three cars responded in the affirmative.

The van reached the exit and signaled right, turned, little traffic to impede it. Rollins followed, keeping his speed in check, keeping her in sight. Donner spoke into the radio again.

"Okay, headed northeast, I think, on . . . what is this?"

Chin reached over his shoulder and took the handset.

"Northeast on Eighty-Nine," he said. "Standby."

Rollins gave Donner a sideways glance. "Been out of the field for long?"

"Fuck you," Donner said. "Just follow her."

21

His name was Craig Watters. He had a little girl around Moonflower's age, but he hadn't seen her in six months. His wife had left and taken Julie and her little brother with her. Just up and left. He was real glad he had the church for support. Lord knows how he would've coped otherwise. They stood by him when it really counted, like a church should. Good people, all of them. Not like his wife. She'd abandoned him for no good reason, taken his kids away, left him all alone. He'd had to put their house on the market. No offers yet, but the realtor had said it was slow out there right now. Maybe in the spring it would pick up.

Moonflower pretended to listen as he drove, the stores and the drive-throughs fading away, the lights of the city falling into the distance behind them. She suppressed the urge to fidget, the muscles of her arms and thighs jittering and rippling. Spasms threatened, but she kept them at bay.

Not many cars on the road. Dark out here, the SUV's

headlights picking out the pine trees through the snow as they whipped past. The windshield wipers swept away sheets of white with each stroke. The car's heater blasted warm air around her. Not that she cared.

The traffic thinned as they headed farther out of town. They passed a few clusters of buildings, forlorn at the roadside, and soon all was dark. Moonflower peered out the passenger window. The trees flashing by, dim channels between them. Such lonely country. A place where a person could get lost and no one would ever miss them.

Craig turned right into a small housing development, a gathering of modest one story homes, all prefabs with wooden fences. Lights in the windows, glowing cheer. Moonflower could feel the people inside. Families with young kids, elderly couples sharing the warmth. Happy people, she felt. A sadness rang in her, one she'd felt many times before. How long since she'd spent a Christmas Eve in a warm home with lights and a tree? Gifts waiting for her, good smells from the kitchen.

"Is this where the shelter is?" she asked, knowing the answer.

"No, it's a bit farther out," Craig said. "Out in the sticks a little. They do outdoor activities there, nature walks, camping, that kind of thing. That's why it's out of town."

He took a right onto a narrower road that curved between the trees. Full dark now, no light but from the SUV, her vision filled with cascading snow. A world of white and black.

"Not much farther," he said, smiling.

His gaze went to the rear-view mirror, and his smile dropped. Moonflower looked back over her shoulder, out through the rear window. A pair of headlights maybe a hundred yards behind. She looked back to Craig, his attention flitting between the mirror and the road ahead. His pulse quickened, and his breathing. She could hear his heart rattling, smell the sweat on him, the fear and the need of what he planned for her.

"How far?" she asked.

He glanced away from the mirror to her. "Not very. We're nearly there."

Moonflower looked back again, saw the headlights following. Then they blinked out, as if they'd never been. She turned back to Craig, his eyes locked on the mirror.

"Shit!"

His foot slammed on the brake pedal and the SUV skidded on the snow. The car fishtailed side to side, rocking Moonflower in her seat, until it shuddered to a halt.

"Shit," Craig said.

He gripped the steering wheel hard, the muscles in his jaw working. Then he turned and stared out of the car's rear window, seeking, searching. After a few moments, he let out a lungful of air.

"Sorry for my language," he said. "I missed the turn."

He put the car in reverse and wrapped his arm around the back of the passenger seat as he backed up.

"Here we go," he said, and turned the SUV onto an unmarked trail. "It's just up here a little. You'll be safe, I promise."

The car juddered all around as it traversed the rough ground. Moonflower reached up and took hold of the grip.

"There's a shelter out here?"

"Yeah," Craig said. "Like I told you, they do all sorts of

outdoor activities. That's why it's all the way out here in the forest. We'll be there in a minute. Wait and see."

The trees thickened all around, the trail narrowing. The glare of the headlights on the falling snow obscured the way ahead. A film of sweat appeared on Craig's forehead as he leaned forward, peering into the near distance. He jerked the wheel this way, that way, as his course wandered. Eventually, he eased off the gas, applied the brake. They entered a small clearing, and ahead, coated in snow, there stood a low cabin.

As the car halted, its tires crunching snow, Craig said, "We're here."

He shut the engine off, pulled the key from the ignition, and opened the driver's door. Lowering himself from the seat, he said, "Come on."

He stood there, waiting, the door open. Smiling at her. "We're here. Out you come."

Moonflower stayed put. She felt his fear and excitement edge into frustration.

He closed the driver's door, trudged around the front of the car, through the snow, and came to the passenger door. He opened it and stood back.

"Let's go," he said.

Moonflower leaned forward and studied the cabin. No lights in the windows. No sign of life. It looked like no one had been here in years.

"What is this place?" she asked.

He reached in, took her hand. "It's a safe place for you to stay. Come on."

She allowed him to guide her out of the SUV. Her feet sank into a carpet of snow, an icy breeze whispering through the trees to wrap around her.

"Come on," Craig said, walking toward the cabin, releasing her hand.

He turned back to her, grinning, rubbing his hands together, shivering with cold. He had not dressed for this. None of this was planned. It was all opportunity. But that was all his kind needed. She had given it to him, like bait to a fish, and he had gobbled it up. Now to wind in the line.

"This isn't a shelter," she said. "It's just an old shack."

He stopped, offended. "It's a good cabin. It was my grandfather's. The roof's sound and the walls are solid. It's dry inside, and we can get a fire going, it'll be warm as you like, I promise."

"But it's not a shelter," Moonflower said. "It's just a cabin in the woods. Why did you bring me out here?"

She knew the answer, but she asked it anyway.

Craig shrugged and smiled, his eyes glinting in the darkness.

"Because I wanted to help. Because no one wants to be alone on Christmas. I don't. Do you?"

"No, but . . ."

He took a step closer to her. "But what?"

"You're a grownup man, and I'm just a kid. I shouldn't be out here with you."

Craig gasped, held up his hands.

"Oh, my goodness. Is that what you think? Do you think I would . . ."

Moonflower shuffled her feet in the snow, looked anywhere but at him.

"I don't know, I mean, you hear things. You seem nice, but . . ."

He took another step. Close enough to reach out and touch her, if he wanted to.

"Honestly, that's not who I am." He brought his palms together in beseechment, a mimicry of prayer. "I just wanted to give you a safe place for tonight. Somewhere warm. We can go inside, I can light a fire, there's blankets, there's food in the cupboards. I've got canned spaghetti, there's potato chips, I think there might be some candy bars. What do you say? Do you want to go inside and take a look? I'll stay out here while you go in and see what it's like. What do you—"

Moonflower heard the string slap the bow's limbs, heard the arrow whip through the cold evening air. The sound of it piercing the meat of Craig's neck.

He froze, his eyes wide, his mouth open. A choking sound from deep in his throat. He reached up, touched his fingertips to the arrow's shaft, then cried out at the pain. Disbelief on his face, as if something impossible had happened, something beyond the realms of all imagining. His lips worked, trying to form a word. Help, maybe. Then a cough from deep inside him, and bloody sputum fell from his mouth. He dropped to his knees, his hand still reaching toward the arrow, but his fingers not quite daring to touch.

Mom stepped into the clearing, the bow in her left hand, the quiver hooked to the belt at her waist. She reached for the sheath at her hip, drew the knife from the leather. Craig tried to turn his head to see her, but the movement pulled an agonized squeal from him. Mom slung the bow over her shoulder as she stepped up behind him. She pulled the arrow free of his neck and dropped it into the snow. Then she grabbed him by the hair, yanked his head back, and pressed the tip of the blade against his throat, close to his Adam's apple.

"You ready?" she asked.

Moonflower stepped close and nodded.

Mom drove the blade in deep, so deep the tip emerged at the other side of his throat. Craig's eyes bulged. Moonflower lowered herself to her knees, her eyes meeting his.

"I'm sorry," she said.

"Now?" Mom asked.

Moonflower nodded.

Mom whipped her hand out and forward, opening his throat.

The blood came, sweet and hot.

File #: 89-49911-17
Subject: Rebecca Carter
OO: Flagstaff
Desc: Letter, Handwritten
Date: 12-25-2005

Dear Moonflower,

I don't know if you'll get what I mean, but this year, more than any other year, I feel like a real person. I mean, a real person, with a real life, with real plans, with a real future. Does that make sense?

God, where to start? I got my associate degree from Madison Tech, and in October, I started working toward my BAA at UW-Madison. Just think, if I write a letter every two years, next time you hear from me, I'll have a proper degree from a proper college. All thanks to Suzanne McDermid. God bless her.

It hasn't been easy. Some days I barely get a moment to lift my head and look around. It's work, study, mom, study, work. Barely room for any kind of a life in between. Thank God for your grandma. I couldn't have done this without her. And she's so good with you, and you with her. Sometimes I look at the two of you together and I wonder if I should've let her raise you as her daughter. She suggested that once, when I was pregnant with you. She would have been young enough then. Raise you as her daughter, my sister. I was horrified at the time, but looking back, maybe it wasn't such a terrible idea.

She's a better mother than I am. That's not me being self-effacing, it's just a statement of fact. I wish I could be as good as her, as calm, as in control, but I can't. I do my best, and I pray to God that's enough.

So many nights I lie awake, telling my pillow I'm not good enough. Not good enough for my job, not good enough for Peter, and worst of all, not good enough for you. Those nights are so long, the dark lying heavy on me, the minutes crawling by while I pick myself apart, piece by hateful piece.

Why can't I just be happy?

I should be, shouldn't I? Everything's going right. I'm getting the education I should've had six years ago—no, eleven years ago! I like my job, I love my family, I have a good man in my life, and I have you and all your glorious love. So why can't I be happy? What's wrong with me?

Nothing. There is nothing wrong with me. I just have this feeling inside that I don't deserve it. Like at some point, the universe will tap me on the shoulder and say, nuh-uh, this good stuff isn't for you. And then it's going to blow everything apart. Burn it all to ash.

But maybe it won't. Maybe everything will be all right. Maybe, just maybe, I deserve this. I've worked hard at my job, I've studied hard at college, and swear to God, I couldn't love you any harder if my very soul depended on it. So maybe things are good because I deserve them to be good.

I have news. Well, not news, I guess, seeing as you won't read this until years later, if you ever read it at all.

There's a big music trade show in Anaheim in January. It happens every year. Peter wants you and me to go with him. Well, not to the show itself, but we can if we want to. Apparently, there are always lots of rock stars there (would you believe, Peter knows Eddie Van Halen?!). During the day, Peter will have his meetings while you and I do as we please, enjoying the sunshine, going swimming, whatever. Maybe even go to Disneyland! Like a real vacation.

Imagine it! Just imagine.

I know you've only met him a handful of times in the two years we've been dating, such is the nature of long-distance relationships, but I've seen how you two get along. How you make each other laugh. It fills my heart from the bottom to the top, I swear to God.

Imagine. Imagine a future. A home of our own, a family of our own.

A house, a yard, a dog or a cat. Maybe a little sister or brother.

Jesus Christ, how white-bread, how vanilla. How dull could I be?

But still. Imagine it.

Dare I?

Dare I imagine it?

I do.

I dare.

Love you,
Mom

22

Rebecca released her grip on his hair, let him fall into Moonflower's embrace. She turned away, no desire to see any more than she had to. Hearing it was enough. The desperate slurping and gulping, punctuated by gasps for air. All this time, and she hadn't grown used to it.

She walked a circle around the clearing, catching snowflakes on her tongue, so cold they burned. A childish desire took hold of her: she opened her mouth, extended her tongue, allowed a flake to fall upon it and dissolve. She remembered being a girl in Madison, how the winters seemed to last forever. How she dreamed of growing up and moving away to somewhere warm, where the sun shone all year round, where the biting wind didn't blow in from the lakes and drive the cold into your bones. She would never have that, she knew, and a selfish part of her resented it.

Life isn't fair. Her own mother had repeated that often. You do the best you can with whatever the world dumps in your lap. Plan all you want but know that the ground can drop from beneath your feet at any moment. So here she was, in a forest on Christmas Eve, catching snow on her tongue while her daughter fed.

Moonflower was all that mattered. Keeping her alive was the only meaning in Rebecca's life. She would do so until her last breath.

Behind her, the frenzied sounds of feeding had ceased. She turned and saw Moonflower kneeling beside his body, breathing hard, her bloodied hands in her lap. A look of shame and regret on her face. The same look she always had when she'd finished feeding, hating herself for losing control, even if it was only for a few minutes. It didn't matter how often Rebecca reminded her it wasn't her fault, that the men they preyed on didn't deserve any better.

"You done?"

Moonflower's head snapped up as if she'd forgotten Rebecca was there. She blinked, then nodded.

"Okay."

Rebecca crossed the clearing to her, the knife still in her right hand. She placed the bow on the ground and knelt beside the body, its odors reaching into her nose, mouth, and down into her stomach.

"Go clean up," she said.

Moonflower stood upright and stepped away. She gathered a handful of snow and used it to clean the blood from her fingers, then another to wipe around her mouth. There were fresh clothes in the van, and wipes to properly cleanse her, along with the plastic sheeting and the other items they would need over the coming hours.

But there was one task to perform first.

Rebecca leaned over him, saw the red maw beneath his chin. She probed with the tip of the blade, feeling, feeling, until it pressed against and between something hard. Putting her weight on the base of the handle, she pressed down, severing his spinal cord. It was unlikely Moonflower had infected him—that would require her blood to mingle with his while he still lived—but Rebecca would take no chances. As she withdrew the blade, her stomach lurched. She turned away, vomited coffee and bile into the red-stained snow. Always the same. It never got easier. Faster, cleaner, more efficient, but never easy. She spat, wiped her nose on her sleeve, blinked the tears from her eyes.

When she looked up, she saw Moonflower standing quite still, staring into the trees. Rebecca's eyes followed the direction of her gaze, seeing only falling snow and darkness.

"What?" she asked. "Baby, what is it?"

Moonflower raised her right hand, the skin still stained red, and pointed.

"Mom, someone's—"

Blinding light, bright as the sun, searing Rebecca's vision. Voices shouting, barking like wild dogs, "*Freeze! Drop the knife!*"

Rebecca raised her hand to shield her eyes from the light. She saw Moonflower rooted to the spot, snow falling all around her, the flakes dancing in the glare of the flashlights.

"*Drop the weapon, now!*"

"Baby," Rebecca called.

"*Drop it!*"

Moonflower turned her face to her.

"Drop the goddamn knife!"

"Run," Rebecca said. "Baby, run."

Moonflower didn't move except to shake her head, her eyes wide with fear.

Rebecca pulled cold air into her lungs and roared at her daughter.

"Run!"

2 3

Donner could see almost nothing.

The snowfall had reduced visibility to barely twenty feet as they had left the main road and headed deeper into the forest. They'd kept a prudent distance as they left the city, but not so far that they didn't see the van turn off the highway and into a small housing development. Chin had warned Rollins to be careful, ease back, as the van exited the development onto a smaller road. The woman would spot them easily out here with no other traffic, even with the snow.

Rollins had followed her onto the road, the SUV smoothing out the difference in the surface quality, but not by much. Up ahead, the van's tail lights seemed to blink in and out of existence.

"You're losing her," Donner said, "you're losing her."

"No, I'm not," Rollins said. "Jesus, don't lose your shit, all right? This isn't my first time, you know?"

"You lost her," Donner said.

"What? No, I . . ."

He leaned forward over the wheel, peering out through the snow.

"Goddammit."

"Keep going," Chin said from the back. "We'll catch up."

Donner rested his forearm on the dash as he stared ahead, searching for red lights among the falling white. The glare from the SUV's lights made the world look like it was made of falling stars, all around, blotting out all else. Then the van's rear loomed in front of them, stationary, as if it had materialized out of the cold winter air.

"Shit!" Rollins spat as he stood on the brake pedal.

Donner braced himself against the dash, ready for the impact. It didn't come. The SUV skidded and fishtailed, but it halted a few feet from the van's back doors, which stood open, the SUV's headlights revealing the clutter within. The driver's door stood ajar.

Donner eased the SUV's passenger door open then drew his weapon from the holster beneath his coat. He slid down from the seat, his feet settling into a bed of snow, and positioned his forearms in the gap between the door and the SUV's front pillar, aiming along the length of the van. He heard the SUV's driver's door open and Rollins climb out.

"No one there," Rollins said, his weapon drawn anyway.

Donner glanced over, saw Chin follow him out.

"I think you're right," Chin said, "but be careful all the same. Rollins, you take the driver's side, Donner, you take the passenger side. Let's go."

The three of them advanced toward the van, weapons drawn and ready. Donner lost view of the others as he skirted the passenger side, watching the wing mirror for any sign of movement within. He approached the door and reached for the handle. Donner took a breath, swallowed, and counted to three before grabbing it and hauling the door open. He leaned back, wary of an attack, visions of a madwoman slashing at him with a hunting knife. One glance inside, duck away, then another, before he was sure no one waited for him. Rollins stood on the other side, examining the empty driver's seat.

"Nothing," Chin called from the rear of the van.

"She left in a hurry," Rollins said. "But where to?"

Donner stepped away from the van and turned in a circle, examining the tree line. There, no more than five yards away, a trail running between the pines.

"Here," he said, heading that direction. He saw the fresh tire tracks on the ground. "There's someone else out here."

He began to follow the tracks, but Chin grabbed his sleeve.

"Hold up. The others aren't far behind. If we wait a minute, we can—"

"There's no time," Donner said. "God knows what she's doing out here, who she's come after. There could be another victim at the end of this trail. We have to take her now."

"No," Rollins said, snowflakes settling on his eyelashes. "This goes to shit, we all get it in the neck. You think I'm going to risk a disciplinary for you, you're dumber than I thought."

"Fuck you, Rollins," Donner said. "I could give two shits what you think. I'm in charge of this operation, and I say we go in."

Chin considered for a moment, then said, "If this goes bad, it's on you."

"I know. Let's move."

The three of them followed the trail deeper into the trees, their feet kicking snow. They held their silence as a clearing came dimly into view up ahead. Dark, no moon, but the city's light reflected from the low cloud cover allowed the form of the world to be seen through the snow. A dilapidated cabin and an SUV. Donner tapped Chin's shoulder and pointed to the space between them. Two people, one kneeling over the other. The sound of retching. Donner signaled silence to the others and advanced toward the clearing.

It was the woman, a knife in her hand.

"Now," Donner whispered.

Chin flicked on his flashlight and shouted, "Freeze! Drop the knife!"

The woman, one hand raised against the light, turned to the far side of the clearing, over by the cabin, and said something.

"Drop the weapon, now!" Rollins commanded, his own flashlight aimed at her.

The blade glistened red, but the knife remained in her grasp. She spoke again.

"Who's she talking to?" Donner asked, trying to see, but the flashlight beams obscured everything they didn't touch.

The others didn't hear him, both shouting as they crossed the clearing to her, demanding she drop the goddamn knife.

Now she took a breath and bellowed one word.

"Run!"

A movement by the cabin, so quick Donner might not have seen it at all. He sprinted in that direction, but the snow slowed his feet before he tripped on a felled branch and sprawled in the cold white. He clambered to his feet, glancing back over his shoulder. "Stay on her," he said, and took off running.

Donner reached the treeline, his eyes searching for movement ahead, and kept going. He thought he heard the sounds of branches slapped aside, but his own breath thundered in his ears, the cold searing his lungs as he ran. His feet tangled in roots and branches, caused him to stumble, but he kept upright. Snowflakes filled his mouth as he gulped cold air, his lungs aching. He paused, leaning against a tree, its bark coarse on his hand, peering through the gaps in the forest all around him.

Donner had no flashlight, but as his eyes adjusted, he realized it offered an advantage. The reflected light from the cloud cover allowed him to see deeper into the trees rather than pulling his vision to the flashlight's beam. He stood still and let his gaze travel all around, seeking movement. From behind, he heard more noise, the other agents and the cops arriving on the scene. He glanced back in that direction, saw the flashlight beams dance.

As he turned his head away, he caught the shape of a girl, hugging tight to a tree trunk. He focused on her, and he became certain she was looking back at him. Twenty yards away, maybe less. He kept his weapon lowered, his voice as calm as he could manage.

"Stay there," he said. "Nobody's going to hurt you."

He took two steps forward.

The girl looked back toward the clearing and the dancing lights.

He moved closer. "It's okay. Everything's okay."

A beam of light speared through the trees, flitting across her features, showing her pale skin and dark hair. And the smears of red across her face and clothing. In the clearing, the woman cried out in pain. The girl flinched at the sound. She returned her gaze to Donner. He saw hate and fear in her eyes.

"Please," he said, quickening his pace. "Stay still. You're safe, no one's . . . wait!"

She took off through the trees, and within moments, he'd lost her.

2 4

Moonflower ran.

Low hanging branches whipped at her face and chest. She didn't care. Her feet glided over the snowbound roots and pine needles, the wind cold against her skin. The man called after her, breathless, telling her to stop, stop, no one would hurt her.

But they would.

She knew that in her bones. Just like Mom had always told her. They would take her away and lock her up, starve her.

They would hurt her like they hurt Mom. Moonflower could hear her cries even now. She slowed, dared a glance back at the clearing. It glowed with light, the forest echoing with voices. Among them, Mom, in pain.

She could go back. She could try to save her. But there were too many of them. As quick as she was, she might not be quick enough. No, she would not go back. Not now. Better to wait. Better to run.

But she would keep her promise.

File #: 89-49911-18
Subject: Rebecca Carter
OO: Flagstaff
Desc: Letter, Handwritten
Date: 11-10-2007

I have nothing.

2 5

Rebecca sat alone in an anonymous office, floating in a sense of calm she hadn't felt in years. So, this is it, she thought. This is what the end of everything feels like. She had wondered many times about this moment. The inevitability of it. She had expected to feel many things: fear, anger, defeat. But not this cool wash of calm, as if suspended in still water. As if the one thing she'd fought so hard and so long to prevent was the one thing that could bring her peace.

She had not fought them when they came for her, when they screamed at her to drop the knife. When she'd been sure Moonflower had lost herself among the trees, she had let it drop to the snow-covered ground and raised her hands above her head. The rest was a smear of light and noise and pain. She remembered one of them pushing her face down into her own vomit and kneeling on her back as she cried out in pain, a cable tie binding her wrists. More flashlights, more voices. Someone, a woman, reciting a list of rights. The back of a car, traveling at speed. Being searched and stripped of her clothes and boots, given plain gray sweats and white tennis shoes in their place.

And now here, someone's office, hands cuffed to a chair. The same woman who'd read her rights, and stripped and searched her, watching from the corner. The insignia on her shoulder said she was Flagstaff PD. Her name tag read SGT. B. TODACHEENE. She hadn't said a word since they'd been in this room. Barely even moved.

Now Rebecca wanted to speak. A nagging, gnawing want scratched at her chest, causing a ripple in the calm. She swallowed and asked the question that had been creeping into her mouth for some time.

"May I please have a cigarette?"

Her voice seemed hollow and metallic, as if emanating from a speaker, not her own throat. The cop didn't answer.

"There's a pack in the coat I was wearing. And a lighter. Could I have one, please?"

Nothing. Not even a movement of her eyes.

"I guess not," Rebecca said.

Knowing the answer, spoken or not, eased the craving. She felt her body soften, sinking further into the chair. Fatigue replaced the desire. When had she last slept? She counted through the hours, but before she could reach back far enough, the door opened, and a man stepped through. The one who'd chased Moonflower into the forest. The one who'd lost her. He wore casual clothes, now dirty, torn in places. A gun in a holster strapped beneath his arm. He carried a notebook, a pen, and a bundle of pages.

"Sergeant, you can take a break. I'll call you if I need you."

The cop nodded, left her place in the corner, and exited the room. The man locked it behind her, slipped the key into his pants pocket. He sat down opposite Rebecca, slumping into the chair, looking as tired as she felt.

"Can I have a cigarette?" Rebecca asked. "I asked the officer, but she didn't answer me. There's a pack in my coat."

He didn't reply, didn't lift his gaze from the notebook, leafing through the pages. For the first time, Rebecca felt a chime of fear. This man knew her, knew what she'd done. He would burn her for it.

After a time, he glanced at his wristwatch, then at the clock on the wall behind her.

"Merry Christmas," he said.

She turned to look at the clock. It was past midnight. She thought of Moonflower out there in the freezing cold, alone and afraid. Her daughter would survive, there was no question of that. But what would she do? The chime of fear turned to a peal.

"I'm Special Agent Marc Donner, FBI, Cybercrime Division," he said. "And you are Rebecca Carter, forty-five years old, born in Madison, Wisconsin. Parents Jonathan and Denise Carter. Correct?"

"That's right. I should have a—"

"A lawyer, yeah. We can't get one this time of night, not on Christmas. This is not a formal interview, but I must remind you of your Miranda rights. Anything you say can be used against you, et cetera, et cetera. You want to talk to me or claim the Fifth? Between you and me and these four walls, the smart thing to do is say nothing at all."

"I don't care," Rebecca said.

"You sure?"

"I don't care. If I did, I wouldn't have told you my real name."

Donner grinned, nodded, and lifted the first printed page in front of him.

"Yeah, your real name, let's start with that, because Jesus, this is something. You're a goddamn miracle. Lazarus, raised from the dead."

Rebecca couldn't keep the dry and bitter laugh from her mouth.

"Yeah, I know," Donner said, echoing her laughter. "Crazy, isn't it? You were declared legally dead nine years ago. And yet here you are, big as life."

"That has nothing to do with me," Rebecca said.

"No? So, where've you been all these years?"

"Around," Rebecca said.

"Around," Donner said, smiling. "Getting into all sorts of trouble. In fact, I've been following your exploits for close to two years. You've left quite a trail behind you. Now, here's what I know for sure: You murdered Craig Watters earlier this evening. You cut his throat, and if the other bodies are anything to go by, you severed his spinal cord while you were at it. Correct?"

She held his gaze and said, "Correct."

"Why did you do that?"

"Because he was a pedophile. A pervert who preyed on children."

"I checked. He had no convictions for any sexual offense against anyone, child or adult. In fact, he had no criminal record whatsoever. Never so much as been arrested or even suspected of a crime. What makes you think he was a danger to children?"

"I didn't think," Rebecca said. "I knew."

"You knew? Knew how?"

She didn't answer. Instead, she asked again for a cigarette, told him about the pack in her coat.

"Your clothing's been bagged up for evidence, including anything that was in your pockets. I quit a year ago, so I guess you're out of luck."

"Maybe someone else here smokes."

He stared hard at her for a moment, then got to his feet and went to the door. He unlocked it and stepped out, locked it again from the other side. Taking a risk, Rebecca thought, leaving her alone like this. She was cuffed to the chair, sure, but it wasn't fixed to anything. What was to stop her waiting for him with the chair raised high, ready to smash it—

Before she could complete the chain of events in her imagination, the lock rattled once more, and he entered then locked the door again. Donner carried a pack of Lucky Strikes and a cheap lighter. He fished one from the pack and placed the filter between her lips, sparked the lighter. She drew in a chestful of smoke, felt the brilliant rush of nicotine through her brain. He placed the pack and the lighter on the desk in front of her. Right there, inches away, but entirely unreachable.

"You have Sergeant Todacheene to thank," Donner said as he returned to his seat. "It's no smoking in here, but given the shit you're in already, I don't think anyone's going to be overly concerned."

Rebecca lowered her head so she could reach the cigarette with her fingers. Donner sat quiet for a while, watching her draw and exhale until the cigarette was half burned away.

"Better?" he asked.

"Yeah," she said. "Thank you."

"How many more have you killed?"

He asked it casually, as if he was asking how many pairs of shoes she owned.

"I don't know," she said, honestly. "A lot."

"This year, say. How many?"

She thought about it for a moment.

"Eight or nine. I guess tonight makes ten."

"We only found three."

"I'm good at it."

Her answer caused something to flicker behind his eyes. Repulsion or admiration, she couldn't be sure.

"Good at it," he echoed. "That you are. Now, the three we found this year all had records, for anything from possession of child porn to assault, including Bryan Shields up there in the hills near Golden, Colorado. But Mr. Watters, he had nothing."

"Just because he'd never been caught doesn't mean he didn't do it."

"Doesn't work like that," Donner said, shaking his head. "What gives you the right to execute a man for something you think he might have done?"

"It's not what he might have done. It's what he was going to do."

"Enlighten me. What was he going to do?"

"He brought a little girl out to a cabin in the forest. A little girl he'd just picked up in a shopping mall. You tell me, what do you think he was going to do?"

"A little girl," he said. "You were using her as bait."

"I wouldn't put it like that."

"I can't think of it any other way. And now she's out there somewhere, alone, in freezing weather. We have a team out searching for her, all those cops that helped arrest you earlier, and whoever else they could get hold of this time on Christmas. I pray to God they find her. If they don't, in these conditions? She won't survive the night."

Rebecca felt a glimmer of a smile on her lips. "She'll be fine," she said.

"I hope so," Donner said. "Who is she?"

"Monica," Rebecca said. "At least, that's what she was christened. I've called her Moonflower since she was a baby. After the flowers my mother grew in our old greenhouse. They're pale white, like she was."

Donner turned two pages back in his notebook, traced the words with his fingertip.

"Monica?" he asked. "Monica Carter? Your daughter?"

"Yes," Rebecca said, "my daughter."

His gaze lifted from the page to meet hers, his eyes locked on her.

"According to my notes, your daughter died fifteen years ago."

"That's right," Rebecca said. "And then she came back."

2 6

Donner leaned back in his chair. He breathed in, tasting the cigarette smoke that drifted between them. It triggered memories: sneaking a drag during school recess, the nicotine's kick enhanced by the danger; good meals finished and digesting in his belly while his lungs filled with smoke; the first time he and Liz had made love, holding it to her lips, then his own, both of them drawing on the cigarette, its embers lighting the room red. He desired now to feel the filter between his lips, the firm paper-wrapped cylinder of tobacco between his fingers, the dirty scratch of tar in his lungs. The pack lay on the table between them, glowing red and white beneath the fluorescent lights. He ran his tongue behind his teeth, wetting his mouth, and returned his attention to the woman opposite.

Insane or a liar. One or the other.

He asked, "What do you mean, she came back?"

Rebecca Carter didn't blink. "I mean what I say."

"How did she come back?"

Her gaze left him, retreated to somewhere distant.

"I don't know how, exactly, just that she did. I prayed. My mom and I, we both prayed. We were never a religious family, but Mom and I got on our knees that night and begged God and Jesus to give her back. And yeah, the next night, there she was, tapping at my bedroom window. But God had nothing to do with it."

Donner watched her for a moment, imagining her holding her daughter as the life flowed out of her into the dirt. He couldn't bear to hold the image in his head, so he leafed through the sheets of paper in front of him, spread them out, reports, inquiries, conclusions. He'd read through more without printing them: handwritten notes, official statements, a coroner's report.

"Maybe I'm not understanding something here," he said. "Your daughter was murdered. Attacked in a park not far from your home, her throat torn open. Just like the man you killed tonight."

Rebecca's eyes flickered, memories splintering and reforming behind them as he spoke.

"It was me who found her," she said. "Does it say that in your notes? She was late home from her friend's place, it had gotten dark, and I knew she'd walk through the park. So, I went to look for her, and I found them, her and the man who attacked her. I say man, but it was hard to see in the dark. He might have been a kid for all I could tell. He was small, I remember that. I heard it first, her crying out, and this sound, this wet chewing sound, coming from some bushes. I went running over there, and I must have startled him because he ran away and left her. She died in my arms. I remember screaming at her to stay with me, but it was no good. She was gone. I used to hate him, whoever he was, for doing that to her. But then I realized, he was just hungry. He needed to feed, just like she does now. He gave her whatever it was he had, and that's no more his fault than it is hers."

"That doesn't make any sense," Donner said.

She smiled and said, "No, it doesn't, does it?"

Donner checked his notes again.

"Your daughter was pronounced dead at University Hospital, Madison, Wisconsin. I have the date and time here. There's no question. So, what am I not getting? People don't come back from the dead, no matter how much we want them to."

"I know," Rebecca said. "But Moonflower did."

Her expression didn't change. Her gaze didn't wander. None of a liar's tells. She believes it, he thought. Absolutely and completely. There was no point trying to challenge her delusions. He had no choice but to follow this road wherever it would lead.

Donner went back to his notes. The reports. The unending horror of it. Somehow, the child's murder wasn't the worst of it.

"Approximately thirty-six hours after your daughter was attacked in that park, before a full autopsy could be performed, her body went missing from the morgue. Two days after that, your own mother reported you missing."

Now she blinked, a shadow crossing her face.

"Leave my mother out of it," she said, her voice cracking.

"I can't," Donner said. "Tell me what happened in those two days, Rebecca. Trying to hide anything won't help you now. Just tell me the truth."

She stubbed the cigarette out in the ashtray that sat on the edge of the desk. Ducked her head down to press her thumb and index finger against her eyes. Then she reached for another, but the handcuffs snapped taught, cutting her short.

"If I take those off, you won't hurt me, right?"

"No," she said.

"I'm bigger than you," he said, "and stronger. If I have to put those back on you, especially if it requires the assistance of my colleagues outside, well . . . it won't be gentle. Do we understand each other?"

"Yes," she said.

Donner stood and walked around the desk, taking the key from his back pocket. He undid the cuffs, ready for any change in her demeanor, any sudden shift in her position. None came, so he tossed the cuffs onto the desk and lifted the pack of Luckies. He held it out to her, let her take one and place it between her lips. It wasn't until he brought the lighter toward his own mouth that he realized he'd taken one for himself. He paused for a moment, wondering if he should, before sparking the flame. His chest filled with heat, and he resisted the urge to expel it with a cough. The nicotine caused a nauseous bloom in his head. The second drag was better, the third delicious. He lit hers, waited as she inhaled and exhaled, both of them savoring their sin.

"I didn't steal her body," Rebecca said. "The police came to our house, asking questions. I mean, Jesus, they'd barely left it for those few days, but that morning, they came back, asking about her body. But they had no proof, no evidence. I don't think they even really had a suspicion. They knew I hadn't taken her."

"Then who did?" Donner asked, returning to his chair.

"No one," she said. "She got up and walked out all by herself. My little girl, she walked all the way back to our house and she knocked on my window. I hid her in the basement for a day or so, even my mother didn't know she was there, but she couldn't stay. And when the cops came around, I knew what I had to do."

"You had to run," Donner said.

"That's right."

"With the body of your murdered daughter."

Rebecca took a drag on the cigarette and shook her head.

"No," she said. "It was five in the morning when I walked out of the house to my shitty little Hyundai, and Moonflower walked right beside me, carrying her own bag. I called my mother from the road later that day. That was the last she heard of me."

Smoke hung heavy in the air above them, an acrid blue cloud.

"That didn't happen," Donner said. "I'm sorry, I know you want it to be the truth, you might even believe it's the truth, but it's not. And while you're telling me this nonsense, a little girl is out there lost in the freezing cold."

"She's not lost," Rebecca said. "She'll find her way back to me. She always does."

27

Moonflower had been walking for a long time. She didn't know how long exactly, but it had been hours, anyway. At first, she had run blindly through the trees, whipped by low branches, roots and foliage snatching at her feet, until the shouting voices and darting lights had fallen into silent darkness. Then she had slowed, stopped, her chest swelling with air, expelling it, deep hard breaths. She turned in a circle, once, twice, three times, snow falling all around. No landmarks in the forest, nothing to orient to. Not even a star in the cloud-bound sky.

She remembered once, when she was little, getting lost in a shopping mall. She'd been there with Mom and Grandma, looking for new shoes. They had been walking between stores, and Moonflower had spotted something in a window: a toy horse with a doll on its back. It wasn't a toy store, but for some reason, there were toys in the window. She had only paused for a moment to look and see, but when she raised her head, neither Mom nor Grandma were in sight. She remembered that feeling at her center, like a balloon whose string had been cut, letting it drift into a perilous sky. Untethered. She wouldn't have known that word back then, not when she was little, but she knew it now.

I am untethered, she thought.

The fear came then, washing over her like a cold river, threatening to sweep her away in its current if she didn't hold her footing. She became still and quiet like a mouse, eyes closed tight, feeling and hearing everything around her. The ground beneath her feet, the cold air on the skin of her face and hands, and in her lungs. The heaving and sighing of the branches above her head.

And the light. Moonflower could feel it reflected from the clouds, the lights of the city, the thousands of torches borne by all the people who lived and breathed there. She opened her eyes and looked up at the sky, the dim orange glow. Turning, she could see its source. She could feel it. All those lives, all those beating hearts, clustered together in their homes. They would have taken Mom there, to the city.

She felt a tugging at the string that was tied to her heart. It had not been cut, she was not untethered. It pulled her toward the light and the city and the humming life.

Hours ago. Miles away. But her feet did not hurt, she was not tired.

Once, in the depths of the forest, she saw and heard men and women with flashlights, the beams cutting through the trees, catching snowflakes. She knew they were looking for her, so she clung to the dark pools between the trees until they passed.

Now, here she was, skirting the boundary of a small airport. Quiet now, hardly anyone there, but still lit up like a beacon. She made her way along the wire fencing, letting the shadows melt into and out of her. She had been on an airplane once, when she was little. Mom's friend Peter had taken them to California, and she and Mom had gone to Disneyland. She had liked Peter, and she sometimes wondered what had happened to him.

The thread tugged, pulled her away from the airport boundary, toward a low building surrounded by a metal fence. An empty parking lot and a stretch of waste ground between here and there. Mom was in that building. She could feel it as hard and real as the bones beneath her skin.

Moonflower walked around the edge of the parking lot, beyond the reach of the lights, keeping to the dark places. She was good at that, finding the shadows, and letting them find her. Like slipping in and out of existence, there one moment, gone the next. The trees provided all the cover she needed.

Soon, she reached a road that turned around the building, leading to its own small parking lot and gates. Tire tracks, laid not very long ago, but already losing to the snowfall. She crossed the lot, quick and sly like a cat, and came to the fence. Up and over, easy, crouching down at the other side between the trees and low bushes. She studied the building for a moment, saw the bars on its windows, felt the low hum of people inside. And there, among them, pulling at the thread: Mom. Moonflower did not sense fear in her. At least, not as much as she might have expected. Instead, an exhausted calm, still but brittle. Mingling with the dozens of other scents, she caught bitter cigarette smoke. On the left side of the building, facing the road that led to the airport, light cast on the snow.

And a shadow.

Moonflower moved toward the building, pressed herself tight to the wall, and approached the corner. She stole a glance around the brickwork and saw a policewoman, propping open a fire exit with her shoulder. Her face glowed ember orange as she drew on her cigarette.

Don't hurt her too bad, Moonflower told herself. Not if you can help it.

Quiet as the falling snow, she moved.

File #: 89-49911-19A
Subject: Rebecca Carter
OO: Flagstaff
Desc: Newspaper Article, Madison Standard
Date: 11-10-2007

LOCAL COMMUNITY IN SHOCK AT MURDER OF TWELVE-YEAR-OLD GIRL

Madison police officers have described the murder of twelve-year-old Monica Carter as "brutal." The attack took place yesterday evening in the quiet, wooded Glen Oak Hills Park in the suburb of the same name. According to reports, the child's mother, Rebecca Carter, 29, was looking for her daughter in the park when she came across the attack in progress. The attacker fled when disturbed. Ms. Carter attempted first aid, as did paramedics, but Monica was pronounced dead on arrival at University Hospital. The cause of death was preliminarily listed as massive blood loss caused by trauma to the throat.

A Madison Police Department officer spoke on condition of anonymity: "I've never seen anything quite like it," the officer said. "The paramedics were already on scene when I got there, but there wasn't much they could do. The kid had already lost so much blood. The mother was hysterical, understandably, so me and my colleague were primarily concerned with trying to calm her down and get an idea of what had happened.

"I've attended a lot of sudden deaths, suicides, murders, accidents, whatever, but this was different. When a kid this age is attacked, there are certain things you expect to see, but not in this case."

The officer refused to elaborate further.

At a press conference this morning, Lieutenant Dean Brookmyre, Madison PD, stated that the suspect who fled from the scene was described as a young man, aged anywhere from mid-teens to early twenties. He is of slender build and medium height, blond hair, dressed in casual clothes. Lt. Brookmyre appealed for anyone who was in the area of Glen Oak Hills yesterday evening to get in touch. Police are particularly interested in anyone seen running through the area, or matching the description given.

Lt. Brookmyre said: "This was a brutal murder of a young girl in what should have been a safe public space. Our thoughts and prayers are with Monica's family at this most difficult time. Please be assured, this police department is putting everything we have into apprehending the killer of Monica Carter."

A full postmortem examination will be carried out within the next twenty-four hours. Anyone with information is asked to contact Madison Police Department. The investigation is ongoing.

2 8

The FBI man watched and listened with the earnest attention of a parent hearing a child blame their imaginary friend for a broken vase. Rebecca lost the urge to be honest she had felt only a few minutes before. She slumped down in her chair, pulling the last of the cigarette into her lungs.

"Doesn't matter if you believe me or not," she said. "I don't care. Anything else you want to know about me, about what happened, I'm sure it's all in your notes you got there. It was in all the papers at the time. I assume you have access to old newspapers and stuff."

"Yeah," he said, one corner of his mouth hinting at a smile. "At the library, same as you."

She smiled too as she stubbed the cigarette out on the armrest and dropped the butt to the floor even though the ashtray was in easy reach.

"I used to love the library. So did Moonflower. We still like to read. Not much else to do out on the road. We like mysteries. Moonflower used to love the Nancy Drew books, but now she likes grown-up mysteries. I used to worry she was too young for them, but then I realized that was ridiculous."

Donner made a serious face, which seemed to take some effort.

"So, how old is she?"

"The night she died, she was twelve." Rebecca counted the years in her head, and when she realized she was too tired, she counted them on her fingers instead. "That makes her twenty-seven, right? But really, she's still twelve. She's been twelve for fifteen years."

"Long time," Donner said.

She knew he was patronizing her, and she didn't care.

"It's funny," Rebecca said, "I remember thinking when she was about nine months old, how I'd miss her. That version of her. Do you have kids?"

He hesitated, something moving behind his still features, then said, "Two girls."

"They never tell you this in the books, all those how-to-raise-a-child guides: you miss them when they change. Like when Moonflower was nine months, or when she was two. I miss those versions of her. I grieve for them. Isn't that strange? How you can grieve for your own living children? The four-year-old, the six-year-old, all those different stages when they change, when they show you who they are, all those versions of themselves they leave behind. Those children are gone, and you miss them, even though they're still alive, still with you."

Something shifted in him. Rebecca couldn't tell quite

what, but her words had pained him somehow. He tried to hide it, but he couldn't.

"I guess I never thought of it like that," he said.

"I have," she said. "I think about it all the time. And how I grieve for all the changes that will never come. How she'll never be anything but what she is right now. I'll never meet those versions of her that should've been. No sweet sixteen, no prom, no first boyfriend, or girlfriend, whatever. No graduation, no college, no career, no wedding, no children. I'll never be a grandma. I lie awake at night and think about that. What I lost. What was taken from me."

Rebecca wanted another cigarette but resisted the urge to ask.

"What about the men you killed?" Donner asked. "What did you take from them?"

Sonofabitch, she thought. Letting her spool herself out like that, then grabbing at the thread.

"They were abusers. I never hurt anyone who didn't deserve it. And I only did it because I had to. There was no other way."

"No other way to what?"

"To keep her alive. That's all that matters. Nothing else. I will keep her alive because she's all I have in the world. And she's such a good girl."

In spite of it all, Rebecca felt a warm smile spread across her lips as she spoke.

"She's such a sweet soul, so kind, so loving. Whatever happens next, you remember that. She's my good girl, my Moonflower. And she's still human. She's not an animal, she's not a monster. She's a human being, just like you and me, just like your—"

A crashing noise from outside froze the words in her mouth. Furniture toppling, equipment falling to the floor, plastic smashing on tile. A man's voice rising, then falling into nothing.

Donner sat upright as he looked to the door behind her, his face slack, his mouth open.

"She's still human," Rebecca said. "Remember that."

Another man's voice, shouting, barking commands. Then gunfire, one shot, a pause, then two more in quick succession.

Donner stood, his chair tumbling back onto the floor.

The same man's voice stretched by a scream, a choked gurgle, something falling heavy against the wall outside the room.

Silence now, time pulled long and thin.

Rebecca said, "You should let me go now."

2 9

The adrenaline hit Donner's system hard, his every sense sparking with electricity. He stood still and listened but could hear nothing over his own heartbeat, his urgent breathing, the rushing in his ears.

He looked down at Rebecca Carter. She had said something, but he'd lost it in the fear.

"What?"

"Let me go," she said.

"What are you talking about? There's—"

The door handle rattled, then something slammed into the wood, a violent impact that reverberated through the room. Donner felt the force of it through the floor.

"Who's out there?" he asked, his voice wet in his throat.

"You know who," Rebecca said.

Donner reached for the holster, fumbled at the clasp. For a moment, he wondered if he'd ever drawn his weapon in the field. When doing raids, yes, but never like this. Never to actually defend himself.

Another slam against the door, hard enough to loosen the frame. Rebecca looked once over her shoulder, then back to him as he drew the pistol from the holster.

"Put that away," she said.

Donner kicked the felled chair out of the way and backed himself against the wall, the pistol raised. Safety off, he racked the slide to chamber a round, then aimed at the door.

"It won't help you," Rebecca said.

"Be quiet," he said.

She closed her mouth and became still, watching him.

He waited, trembling and crackling with energy that could find no release. Nothing happened.

Come on, he thought. Do it, goddammit. Just do it.

He could feel it on the other side of the door, the presence, whoever it was. Listening, sensing him, hearing the thunder in his chest.

Then nothing.

He inhaled, swallowed, exhaled, wondered if they had—

The door exploded inward, the lengths of the frame splintering and flying. His finger reflexively squeezed the trigger of his pistol, and he fired blind into the wide-open mouth of the doorway. Part of his mind registered Rebecca throwing herself to the side, tipping the chair and letting it carry her to the floor. The other saw the girl lunging at him, hands outstretched, her eyes wide, her teeth snapping.

Donner cried out, squeezed the trigger twice more, even though he knew she was unarmed. It didn't matter. She twisted her body as she came at him, the bullets slipping past and into the darkened hallway beyond.

Then she was on him, a wild and clawing thing, her

fingers grabbing at his hair, her nails tearing his scalp. He fell to the floor, the pistol flying from his grasp, the child following him down, and he felt her breath on his skin, saw the blood on her lips, the meat between her teeth. Somewhere far away, he heard a man scream and knew it could not possibly be his voice even though it sounded so very like his own.

Donner saw her mouth open wide, her bloodied teeth bared, as she lowered her face to his. His right hand stretched, reaching for the pistol while his left seized her throat, tried to push her away, but she was so strong. She took hold of his forearm, twisted and pulled, and he felt his shoulder stretch, followed by a lightning bolt of pain. Another scream from far away, tearing at his throat.

"Baby, no."

The child hesitated, then opened her mouth wide once more.

Human, the woman had said.

But she was so wrong.

"Baby, stop."

The girl astride his chest, her mouth an inch from his naked throat.

"Don't." The woman crawled to them on her elbows and knees. "Let him go. We have to get out of here."

The girl growled and turned to her mother.

"Moonflower, sweetheart, you need to stop. We have to go."

Rebecca came closer, brought her face close to the child's, inches away from Donner.

"You came here for me. That's all. Now let's go."

The girl turned back to Donner, her eyes filled with

animal hate and hunger. She grabbed a handful of his hair and slammed his head against the wall. Immense pain blossomed at the back of his skull, bloomed and swelled, silvery and cold. The world flickered in and out, his vision swirling with blots of inky black.

Then the world came back with a sickening jolt, and he was alone on the floor, and pain rang out like church bells. Donner rolled onto his side, dragging one useless arm behind him, and vomited until his stomach had nothing left to give. Then the darkness took him again.

3 0

Moonflower ran to the parking lot, dragging Mom by the hand.

Mom cried out, told her to slow down, but Moonflower couldn't. The blood ran too fast in her veins, made too much noise. The jangling, ringing clamor of it in her ears. Like every bell on earth chiming at once. Every red cell singing to the stars above.

She felt the cold air on her skin and stopped, her feet skidding on the snow. Mom fell to the ground beside her. Moonflower looked up at the sky, saw nothing but a dark blanket. She wanted the stars and the moon. She wanted to sing to them. But they remained hidden by cloud.

She sang anyway, her voice rising up from her chest to the heavens.

In the near distance, dogs joined her song. In the city, in the cold yards and warm houses, and in the streets, and farther away, in the forests. They all sang to her and to the moon. She wanted to go to them, the wild ones, find them among the trees and run and hunt with them. They would accept her as their own, because it was the truth. Had always been.

Moonflower let go of Mom's hand and walked farther into the lot. She looked east to the forested hills, listened to the songs the wild dogs sang to her. Coyotes, yes, not far away. But farther, deeper in the dark channels between the trees, there were other, larger animals. Thick gray fur and long yellowed teeth. The ancient dogs, hated and hateful, roaming where humans would not.

She opened her mouth, filled her chest with icy air, and sang out to them. She listened, hearing the echoes of her own voice from far away. Then they answered, the ancient ones, whooping and howling, and she desired to go to them, but two hands seized her shoulders and spun her around.

"Moonflower," Mom said. "Look at me."

Kneeling, she raised her hands to cup Moonflower's face and leaned in close.

"Baby, look at me."

Moonflower looked, but she did not speak. She listened instead to the songs of the dogs that lived far away in the hills and the trees.

"Oh God, you're bleeding."

Mom went to touch the cut above Moonflower's eye, where that man had swiped at her with his gun before she tore into his neck. Moonflower reflexively pulled her head away. Mom knew better than to touch.

"Listen to me," Mom said.

Moonflower looked to the hills.

Mom shook her, hard.

The singing faded, leaving only the rush of blood in her ears.

"Baby, are you here with me?"

Moonflower didn't know the answer to the question. Part of her was, yes, because she could hear and see her mother right there in front of her and feel her fingers gripping tight to her upper arms, so tight it hurt. But part of her was out there, miles and miles away, singing with the ancient dogs to the absent moon.

Mom shook her again, harder, so hard it hurt Moonflower's neck, and she couldn't hear the dogs anymore, only her mother's hard voice.

"Moonflower, I need you here with me now. I need you to be in control of yourself. Do you hear me?"

Moonflower blinked. She pointed to the darkness in the east.

"There are dogs," she said. "Out there."

"I know, baby," Mom said, "I heard them. But we have to go. I need you here with me now, all of you, and we need to go. Do you hear me?"

Moonflower blinked again. "Yeah," she said.

"Are you with me?"

"Yeah, I'm with you."

Mom took her in her arms, squeezed her tight.

And still, somewhere, the dogs sang.

File #: 89-49911-22
Subject: Rebecca Carter
OO: Flagstaff
Desc: Letter, Handwritten
Date: 12-25-2008

Dear Moonflower,

I suppose this is the last letter like this I'll ever write. I don't know why I'm even writing it. What's the point? What's the point of this and all the others? My intention had been to give them to you when you turned sixteen or eighteen or twenty-one or some arbitrary age that meant you were old enough to understand them.

Jesus, what's there to understand? Just a lot of bullshit scribbled down by a girl too damn stupid to know she was cursed. Sixteen, eighteen, twenty-one. I don't think you'll ever be those, even if you survive till you're a hundred. I'm sitting here in this shitty motel room, watching you try to sleep, and you haven't aged at all in the fourteen months since you came back. You and your body should be changing so fast it'd make your head spin, but you're not changing, not even one little bit. Somehow, that scares me more than anything.

You're always hungry. So, so hungry. You can only go a few days on the animals I manage to catch. You need blood like your own. Blood like mine. I've tried to feed you as best I can, but I can only give so much. I'm running out of places to put the needle. It's making me so tired and weak. And there's an infection now. I can see it creeping up my leg from the last puncture. I need to get antibiotics from somewhere. If I don't, I'll die. And then you'll die, and I can't allow that to happen. I must live so that you can live. I'll get the medicine from somewhere, somehow. I have to.

I think I'm rambling. I have a fever, and it's clouding my mind. I have to stop writing soon. Everything hurts. Even the sound of the pen on paper is like pins in my brain.

You're the only good thing I have left in the world. Two years ago, I had everything. I had a future. But I should've known it would be taken from me. Because everything I reach for, everything I grab hold of, it turns to dirt in my hands.

I miss my mom so much. I think about her always. I think about her taking me in her arms, telling me it's going to be all right. I know she worries about us, wonders where we are, if we're even alive. I've wanted so many times to find a payphone and call her, just to hear her voice. But I can't. They might find us and take you away from me.

That's the worst thing I can imagine: losing you. If I lose you, then there was no point to any of it. Every single day of my life, from the moment I was born, would be a waste of existence.

I'm going to stop writing now. This pen feels like a shovel in my hand, and all I'm doing is digging a hole for myself to lie down and die in.

I don't know where to go from here. I don't know what we're going to do. All I know is I have to keep you alive, no matter what. That's all there is.

I love you, always and forever.

Mom

31

They had been driving for an hour along narrow, winding mountain roads, and Rebecca had lost her bearings, no idea which point of the compass she faced. The adrenaline had subsided, leaving fear in its place, and she fought panic as she navigated the snowbound passes. She had taken the keys to the police cruiser from the unconscious officer who lay at the fire exit of the field office in Flagstaff. Something less conspicuous would have been better, but there was no time to hunt for keys to any of the other vehicles in the small parking lot. She couldn't guess how long it would take someone in the building to raise the alarm, but it wouldn't be long. There was no choice but to take the cop car, a Ford SUV, and go.

She slowed and eased the car to a halt. She shut off the engine and lights, then exited onto the snow-covered road. The weather had cleared, but she knew it wouldn't be for long. The sweats she wore offered little defense from the cold's bite.

Peering up at the sky, she could see the reflected light of the city in the near distance. She suspected it lay to the east or north of here, but there was no way to be certain. The car probably had a satnav system, but she was reluctant to switch on anything more than the engine and the lights, fearing it might send some signal that could pinpoint their position. Even an hour later, they hadn't put nearly enough distance between them and Flagstaff. She cursed quietly to herself.

She had asked Moonflower what happened outside the room.

"I hurt some people," Moonflower said.

Rebecca had barely glanced at the forms of the two men, one slumped against the wall outside the office that had served as an interrogation room, the other at the far end of the corridor, his head lying at an unnatural angle.

"I'm sorry," Moonflower had said. "I didn't mean to do it."

"I know, honey," Rebecca had said. "It's not your fault."

The alarm would have been raised by now, cops swarming the place. How long before they'd have road-blocks in place, patrols out looking for the stolen car? Only a matter of time before they had a helicopter in the air, its searchlight skimming the trees.

Rebecca thought about her van. Was it still sitting out in the wilds, waiting to be towed away? She supposed there were cops out there, tending to the scene. Were they searching the van now? Everything she owned was in there. Every last shred of her life.

She thought of the letters, folded pages bound together with a rubber band. Lost now. Moonflower would never read them. And her journals. Rebecca imagined cops and agents poring over her most private thoughts, and she bit on her knuckle to keep herself from crying out in the darkness.

"Mom?"

Moonflower's voice startled her. Rebecca turned to see her looking back from the passenger seat, her mouth still ringed with drying blood, her clothes sodden with it. The cut above her eye already healing.

"Where are we?" Moonflower asked.

"I'm not sure," Rebecca said.

"Where are we going?"

"I don't know," she said, climbing back into the car and closing the door. "All I know is we have to ditch this thing and get something else. And soon."

Moonflower fell silent and Rebecca knew her daughter had more questions that she couldn't answer. She started the engine and set off again, keeping her speed in check. After a few miles, she saw dim lights up ahead. She felt a spark of hope that threatened to die before it could kindle. Leaning over the steering wheel, she squinted, trying to pick out any details.

As they drew nearer, she saw small prefab homes sitting in wire-fenced yards, single- and double-wides, some with lights in the windows, others in darkness. Some kind of tiny, isolated town. The homes grew in number and density as she followed the twisting, undulating road. She noted the vehicles she passed, mostly SUVs, all of them old. It occurred to her that she could stop and check if any careless owners had left their keys in their cars. Unlikely, she thought, and she couldn't risk a resident investigating the strange woman poking around their home.

The spark of hope Rebecca had felt a few minutes before began to fade as the homes thinned out again and she realized she was leaving this place behind. Then she saw something that made her take a sharp breath: a yard surrounded by chain-link fencing, a cluster of cars and trucks inside. There was an office and a workshop, the police car's headlights picking out a hand-painted sign that said BILL'S AUTO REPAIRS.

She brought the car to a halt at a chained gate and studied the buildings and vehicles inside. A small prefab office with a flat roof and cracked windows adjoined a workshop with a roller door. Big enough for one car and no more. No alarm boxes that she could see.

Half a dozen vehicles sat in a row, all of them old, some of them on blocks. But not the GMC van. At least twenty years old, she guessed. Rusted and dirty.

Probably keys inside the office. She could break in and take them. Maybe some tarps around to hide the cop car. Might be a day or two before anyone would return here and find the GMC missing, the marked Ford SUV in its place.

But only if the van's engine ran.

"Please, God," Rebecca whispered.

3 2

Donner sat on the edge of the hospital bed, his packed bag next to him, looking out at the snow-capped mountains. The phone pressed against his ear with his right hand, his left arm in a sling. His shoulder hadn't quite been dislocated, but near enough to cause it to throb with his heartbeat.

"I'm sorry," he said for the third time in as many minutes.

"So you keep telling me," Liz said, "but that doesn't fix anything."

"I know."

"Do you? Do you really?"

"Liz, I—"

"We waited for you. We waited, and we waited. And you think you can just call me up and say you're sorry? Like that makes everyting okay?"

"No, I don't, but it's still true. You have to believe me, I had no choice."

"There's always a choice."

"No, there's not. I had one chance to catch a killer I've been chasing for two years."

"See, that's just it, isn't it? There wasn't one single agent in the whole of the FBI but you that could've done this. Don't you see, it's always you? You at the center of everything. Not me, not your kids, just you."

His anger rose, and he could not quell it.

"Goddammit, Liz, people died."

"Don't," she spat. "Don't you dare try to lay that kind of guilt on me. Tell me something, and tell me truthfully."

Donner bowed his head and said, "What?"

"If you hadn't pursued this, if you had come home to your family like you were supposed to, would those people have died?"

He thought of the CCTV footage he'd been shown that morning. That same brilliant glare obscuring the girl's image as he'd seen in the security video from the gas station two days before. One angle from outside where Sergeant Todacheene had been smoking at the fire exit. Her turning toward the glow, then the creature that looked like a girl hurling itself at her, smashing her head against the doorframe.

Then the corridor inside, Agent Rollins striding along, one hand going to the weapon holstered at his waist. Thrown aside like a broken toy, colliding headfirst with the wall, his neck taking the brunt of it. Finally, Agent Chin aiming his pistol, shouting something, opening fire. The glowing form of the girl simply moving aside, stepping out of each bullet's path, then she's on him, dragging him to the floor. He slams his pistol against her temple, rocking her head, before she tears into his neck.

Rage and sorrow chased each other through Donner's heart. He hated Liz in that moment because she was right, whether or not he could ever admit it to himself. If he'd gone home to be with her and their children, everything would've been different. He raised the phone up above his head, ready to throw it at the closed window. A knock on the door behind him stayed his hand.

Donner turned his head and saw Sergeant Todacheene in the doorway. She wore plain clothes, a plaid shirt and jeans, a bloodstained gauze pad taped to her temple.

"I gotta go," Donner said. "Can I talk to the girls later?"

"No," Liz said.

"What? Come on, I just want to—"

"This family doesn't begin and end at your fucking whim, Marc. You don't get to be a father just when you feel like it. God, you hurt them so bad, you have no idea. I have to protect them from that. I have to."

"Liz, please."

"Goodbye, Marc."

She hung up. Donner gripped the phone hard in his fist, felt the metal and glass flex. Had he been alone, he would've smashed it on the floor. He glanced back over his injured shoulder at Todacheene.

"Now's not a good time," he said.

"I don't care."

He exhaled, deflating, sinking into his own lap.

"They found my car," she said, entering the room and stepping around the bed. She sat on the windowsill, facing him. "Auto shop about ten miles from here. Little half-assed place that keeps old junk running way after it should've been scrapped. Swapped it for a van."

"What kind of van?"

"GMC," she said. "Old model, ninety-eight. Owner didn't know anything about it till he went to open up this morning, found a Flagstaff PD Interceptor sitting in his yard."

Donner tried to read her expression, but it was blank as a fresh sheet of paper.

"At least that's something," he said. "Has your department put out an alert? She'll have swapped the plates, but still."

Todacheene laughed and shook her head. "Are you serious? How many old GMC vans do you think are out there? It's thirty-six hours since she took off. Wherever she is now, it's a long way from here."

Donner realized he was grinding his molars, his jaw muscles hard and tight. He consciously relaxed them, massaged each side in turn with his right hand.

"What happened?" he asked.

"You know what happened," Todacheene said.

"I mean, to you. At the field office, what happened to you?"

She looked over her shoulder, out of the window, toward the mountains.

"Nice view," she said.

"What happened?" Donner asked.

She turned her stony gaze back to him. "I'll tell you the same as I told the other feds that came asking: I saw nothing. One minute, I'm standing there at the fire exit, having a smoke. Next minute, I'm waking up on the ground with a motherfucker of a headache, and all hell's breaking loose around me."

"That's not all, though, is it?" Donner said, not letting her stare him down. "What did you see?"

"Not a goddamn thing," Todacheene said. "And you'll tell them the same if you have any sense."

"You saw the girl," Donner said. "You saw her, didn't you? You saw what she did."

"I didn't see a damn thing," Todacheene said, standing upright. "That's what I've said all day today, and that's what I'll say tomorrow, and the day after, on and on until they stop asking. Whatever madness you brought here with you, I want no part of it."

She came close, standing over Donner.

"I knew Agent Rollins. Not real well, but we were on speaking terms. He didn't deserve what happened to him. To die like that. You brought that on us. When you get back to the Hoover Building in DC, and you're sitting at your nice comfortable desk, I'd like you to reflect on that."

She went to the door.

"I'd offer you a ride to the airport, but . . . I just don't want to. See you around."

Donner had no reply. He watched her leave, then looked to his hands lying flat in his lap, one of them holding his phone. It vibrated, the display showing a photo of McGrath, one he'd taken at some burger joint in DC, a milkshake mustache on her upper lip, her middle finger raised to the camera.

He rejected the call.

33

Moonflower slept long and deep those first few nights, like diving in a great black ocean. The hunger had been sated, her mind and body exhausted.

She dreamed of dogs.

Not the ones who skulked at the edges of ancient camps, hoping for scraps from the beasts who walked on two legs. Not the ones who grew fat at their masters' feet, kissing the hands of those who beat and cowed them.

No. She dreamed of the dogs who ran free among the trees, running and hunting, teeth stained red and yellow.

They needed nothing from the beasts who walked on two legs.

Neither did she.

When she woke, she remembered little of the dreams. All forgotten except running, running, running . . .

File #: 89-49911-25
Subject: Rebecca Carter
OO: Flagstaff
Desc: Letter, Handwritten
Date: 08-15-2010

To Whom It May Concern:

If you are reading this letter, it means either I'm dead, or I've been captured. In case I'm no longer alive, or I've been injured during my arrest and am unable to communicate, I want this letter to serve as my confession: I, Rebecca Carter, am guilty of murder. To date, I estimate that I have killed around fifteen men and one woman. I accept full responsibility for their deaths, and if I am alive to do so, I will take whatever consequences arise from them.

Let me be clear about one thing: my daughter, Monica, has never harmed anyone. All these killings have been committed by me and no one else.

If it makes any difference, all the people I've killed have absolutely deserved it. They were all predators. Most of them will have had criminal records, probably for minor offences, but those minor offences would eventually have led to major crimes. I know in my heart that my actions have spared many children from unspeakable suffering. That is how I sleep at night, and how I can live with myself.

If she is in your custody, please treat Monica with kindness. Whatever you may think, she is not a monster. She is a good girl with a kind soul. She should not be punished for my actions. If she has escaped, which I think is more likely, then please don't pursue her. No good will come of it.

I don't believe in God, but I ask forgiveness from the world for what I've done. I hope it will be clear why I did it, and that it was done out of love.

Please don't hurt my daughter.

Rebecca Carter

3 4

Rebecca opened the van's rear doors and brutal light flooded in. The trees did little to hide the sun. She lifted a handful of stones from the plastic bag beside her and climbed out, feeling her joints grind and groan, the knots of her lower back loosening. Chilly out, but not the bone-deep cold of a week ago.

"Happy New Year," she whispered to herself.

The dogs whined and growled. Four of them this morning. Two medium-sized mutts, a small Jack Russell, and a skinny coyote. The Jack Russell was new. It wore a collar. Somebody, somewhere, was probably franticly looking for it.

Rebecca threw the first stone, aiming for none of them in particular. They scattered away from its trajectory, the coyote most wary, but they remained at the edge of the clearing.

"Get out of here," she shouted. "Go on, git!"

She kept her eye on the largest mutt and threw another,

putting her weight behind it. The stone hit the dog's flank, and it yelped.

"Git!" she shouted again, and the dogs retreated into the trees, far enough that she lost sight of them. But she knew they were still there, still watching.

Once she'd found a shaded spot to use for a toilet, she returned to the van and climbed inside. She pulled the doors over, left them open a crack, enough to allow a shaft of light through. And some air. An odor lingered within, a low animal smell, and she hoped it was the van itself. The plywood flooring was rotten with damp, and mold laced the plastics and carpeting of the cabin.

But maybe it wasn't the van. Maybe it was something else.

Her daughter huddled at the back, against the bulkhead. This van had no access from the cabin to the rear, and it was darker back here, more claustrophobic. Moonflower had slept deeply the first two or three days, but less and less since then.

"Did you get any sleep?" Rebecca asked.

"A little," Moonflower said.

"Try and get some more."

"I'm hungry."

"You just fed a week ago."

"Yeah, but I'm hungry."

"We can't hunt that often. It's a miracle we've survived this long. If we take any more, it'll draw attention. We can't take that risk."

Moonflower leaned forward, her voice rising.

"But I'm hungry."

"I can't help that," Rebecca said, her patience thinning.

"I could go out myself."

"No, you can't."

"Why not? There are plenty of animals around. There's rabbits and deer and—"

"Maybe one of those dogs."

Rebecca saw the anger flare in her.

"Not the dogs," Moonflower said.

Rebecca slumped against the side wall of the van and closed her eyes.

"I'll go out later, see if I can find something."

Moonflower didn't answer. She huddled back into the corner, her fingers fidgeting, her nails clicking off each other in a stuttering rhythm.

Something had changed a week ago in Flagstaff. Her Moonflower, her good girl, had gone somewhere and not come back. Not fully. When she'd been out in the forest all by herself, it was the animal part of her that had drawn her to the FBI field office. It had given her the will to hurt those people and take her mother back from them. But now the animal remained, and it was always hungry, its mouth always open. Rebecca had seen this animal before, had caught its scent, but it had always receded when its hunger had been met. But not this time.

Moonflower had huddled in the back since they'd taken this van, sullen and quiet, speaking only to snap and snarl at her mother. They had been driving near constantly, stopping only to sleep and eat. With the wall between the cabin and the load bay, Rebecca hadn't seen much of her daughter. She would never admit it to a living soul—she could barely acknowledge it within herself—but a low-down part of her might have been glad of it.

In the six days since Christmas, they had crossed into Nevada, heading northwest, skirting Las Vegas, and on to Northern California. They had been driving in aimless circles for the last four days, keeping to the forests, while Rebecca tried to think of some way forward. Some direction they could travel that would lead to safety, any safe harbor, anywhere. But she could think of only one, and she didn't want to go that way.

The dogs had begun trailing them three days ago. One mutt at first, then another joining later the same day. If Rebecca had been following any plan, had any sense where she was going, she could have left them behind, but instead they kept tracking the van down among the trees. Yesterday, the coyote appeared, staying apart from the other two. Then this morning, the Jack Russell. Rebecca knew what drew them, what scent they followed miles through the forest. The thought made her shudder.

"What are we going to do?"

Moonflower's voice startled Rebecca, and she realized she had slipped into a shallow slumber.

"I don't know," she said.

"We can't keep driving in circles."

"If you have any better ideas, I'm listening."

She hadn't meant her reply to sound so mean but it came out that way nonetheless. Moonflower's head dropped and she folded in on herself.

"I'm sorry," Rebecca said. "I didn't mean it like that."

"There's one place we could go."

"No," Rebecca said, her heart hardening.

"You haven't heard what I was going to say."

"I know what you're going to say, and the answer's no."

"He might be able to help us, even if it's just somewhere to hide for a few days."

"We're going nowhere near that man."

"We might not have a choice."

"There's always a choice, and the Nurse will always be the worst one."

Moonflower fell silent for a few moments, the air thickening between them, before she said, "I'm right, and you know it."

Rebecca didn't answer because, God help her, she did know it.

35

Donner sat still and quiet opposite Holstein. The same chair he'd sat in less than two weeks ago. Alone this time, McGrath reassigned for now. His shoulder still ached when he moved, despite the sling. All he could do now was wait still and quiet while Holstein read page after page of notes and reports. Twenty minutes he'd been sitting here, and Holstein had barely acknowledged his presence.

Five more minutes ground by before Donner felt he could hold his silence no longer. He opened his mouth, inhaled, but Holstein raised a finger without looking up from the page he read.

"Shut the fuck up," he said.

Donner swallowed his words and resigned himself to this purgatory. It was his first day back in the Hoover Building. He'd spent a night in the hospital in Flagstaff, recovering from the concussion. Every waking moment, a procession of agents and cops, all of them asking questions.

He'd answered them as best he could, but his memory was hazy, and what he could remember made no sense.

Rollins had died, he knew that much. His neck snapped like a twig. Todacheene had been knocked unconscious at the fire exit, claimed she hadn't seen or heard a thing, though Donner didn't believe her. Chin had been assaulted inside the building. Bad enough that he might never walk unaided again. That, and a chunk torn out of his neck. Most likely, he'd be pensioned off. Between him and Donner, they couldn't describe much of what had happened. And those they told didn't seem to have any desire to hear it. Like Holstein, who, after thirty-four minutes, was now ready to speak.

Donner had already sat through two interviews with agents from the Inspection Division. There would likely be more before the investigation was concluded and passed on to the Office of Professional Responsibility for adjudication. They would hand down their judgment, suspension or dismissal, whatever it may be, and he would have the opportunity to appeal. He had already decided he would not.

At last, Holstein spoke.

"You're placed on administrative leave with immediate effect, of course."

Donner had expected nothing less, so he didn't argue, just nodded.

"You can count yourself lucky in that regard. Summary dismissal wouldn't have been unwarranted, given the circumstances. You'll surrender your ID and weapon to me. Understood?"

"Understood," Donner said.

Holstein sat back in his chair and studied him.

"Marc, what the fuck happened out there?"

"Everything's in my statement, and in the interviews. I told the Inspection Division agents everything. Everything I can remember, anyway."

"Yeah, except nothing you said makes any goddamn sense."

"It's the truth."

"If I submit this to the OPR, they'll crucify you. You do realize that, don't you?"

"What do you want me to do, lie?"

"I want you to think about your future at the Bureau, assuming there is one. Then I want you to think about what happened that night, get it in order, and get it to make sense."

"My statement, and the answers I gave under questioning, that is exactly what happened, to the best of my recollection."

Holstein flipped through the pages until he found the written statement.

"You're saying a child did this. You're telling me a little girl overpowered a trained cop and three FBI agents, killing one of them. Snapped his goddamn neck."

"I didn't see any of that happen," Donner said. "All I saw was her breaking down a locked door and coming at me. I fired three shots, all three missed, she injured my shoulder and knocked me unconscious."

"A child did that," Holstein said. "A twelve-year-old girl."

"Yes, sir. Except, she isn't a child. Her mother said she was human. That's the last thing I remember clearly:

Rebecca Carter telling me her daughter was still human. But she isn't."

Donner regretted the words as he spoke them.

"Then what in the name of God is she?"

"I don't know, exactly. But I intend to find out."

Holstein's face grayed. He leaned forward on his desk and pointed at Donner.

"Now, you listen to me, and you listen good. You do nothing but go sit home and come up with something plausible to tell the Inspection Division. I'll use whatever leverage I have to make sure they disregard the bullshit you've been peddling up till now and allow you to make a new statement and give one more interview. That's the best I can do for you. But you listen well: you have no more involvement in this case beyond being a witness, and an unreliable one at that. If I find you so much as sniffing around this thing, I will recommend your immediate dismissal to the OPR Assistant Director myself. You understand? A man is dead, for Christ's sake. Another may never recover from his injuries. Haven't you done enough damage?"

No, Donner thought. Not nearly enough.

He found McGrath at the desk they had shared up until a few days ago. She did not smile as he approached.

"Hey," he said.

She nodded in return. He pointed to his old chair, asking permission to sit. She stretched her leg beneath the desk, kicked the chair out for him. He pulled it the rest of the way out and sat down. They sat in silence for a time before he asked, "How were the holidays?"

"Good at first," she said. "Then it all went to shit. Cara ate Christmas dinner all alone with Matthew while I sat in the other room for two hours being questioned by my own colleagues about that clusterfuck you caused in Flagstaff."

"I'm sorry," he said.

A series of emotions traveled across her face, anger to sadness and back again, then finally a blank acceptance.

"Yeah, I guess I'm sorry too. Maybe if I'd gone with you, things might have worked out different."

Donner shook his head. "No, they wouldn't. You'd have gotten hurt too, or worse, and we'd both be in the shit instead of just me."

"What the fuck happened, Marc?"

"Have you read my statement?"

"Holstein let me see it. But what really happened?"

"Honestly, I don't know. I have no idea what went on outside that room. I mean, I saw the CCTV footage, for all that showed. Did you see it?"

"Yeah, nothing but shadows and light."

Donner had been shown the images. Burning light flooding the frame every time the camera caught sight of the girl. Like she was a walking Roman candle.

He gathered his memories, put them in order, and recounted them once again.

"Everything was calm and quiet. I was talking with Rebecca Carter. Even without a lawyer, she was telling me everything. I had her. I mean, I had everything I needed to put her away. Then there's this commotion from outside. Shouting, gunfire, something hitting the wall. Then it was quiet for a while, I don't know how long, then there's something slamming into the door. It was like a battering ram. It hit the door maybe two, three times, and it gave way, ripped the frame right out of the goddamn wall. I got one shot off, aiming at nothing, and then I saw her. The girl. She had blood on her, I remember that. How red it was. And then she was coming at me. I fired twice, even though I knew she was unarmed. Didn't make any difference. Somehow, I missed. From less than ten feet."

He paused, seeking the words, making shapes in the air with his hands. McGrath watched him, her face unreadable.

"She flew at me, and each time I pulled the trigger, she moved out of the bullet's way. Just kind of . . . turned her body around it. Like she knew where the bullet was going, and she just moved out of the way. Then she was on me, and I remember the pain as she pulled my shoulder near out of its socket, and that's it. That's all I remember."

"A kid didn't do all that. A child can't dodge a bullet, and a child didn't kill a grown man with her bare hands and put three other people in the hospital. No way."

"She isn't a child. She looks like one, but she's not."

"Then what is she?"

Donner raised his hands to say, I don't know. He changed the subject.

"So, what's everyone saying about me?"

McGrath looked away and back again. "You really want to know?"

He forced a smile. "No, but tell me anyway."

"They think you've lost it. Opinion varies: anything from a trauma-related breakdown to full-blown batshit crazy. They say you're finished, there's no way you don't get pushed out. You'll be lucky if you get to keep your pension.

Some of them are angry at you. Some of them knew the agent who died, and they blame you. You're fucked, in other words."

Donner sank back into the chair, feeling everything drain from him. McGrath had never been one to sugarcoat things, but still.

"And what do *you* think?" he asked.

She whispered, Jesus, and stared at the wall behind him.

"Come on," he said. "Just give it to me."

"What do I think? I think I'm so fucking pissed at you it's all I can do not to punch you in your stupid throat. And I'm pissed at myself for letting it get this far. For not going with you. Fuck!"

She lifted a pen from the desk and threw it at him. Had he not ducked, it would've hit him square in the forehead. Then she kicked at him under the desk, her foot connecting with his shin.

"Ow!"

"You count yourself lucky that's all you get. Now, do you want my advice?"

Donner rubbed his shin and said, "I guess so."

"You drop this. You don't try to find this girl or her mother. Let it go. And you eat whatever shit the Bureau hands you. You be humble and contrite, you tell them your injuries have hampered your recollection. You lie through your teeth if you have to. Just tell them what they want to hear and pray to God you still have a job at the end of it all."

Donner couldn't meet her gaze. "I don't think I can do that."

"Goddammit, Marc."

"I need to know what happened. I need to know what she is—"

"Marc, stop."

"—how she could walk into that place and do so much damage and—"

"Shut your damn mouth."

"—and why she and her mother killed all those men. I need to know. It's driving me crazy. Maybe I'm already gone. But I need to know why this happened."

She speared him with her stare.

"You done?"

"Yeah."

"Then listen to me. I will be here for you, as your friend. I owe you that much. But you will not take me down with you. I've worked too hard and too long to throw it all away. I love you like a brother, I'll do what I can for you, but I won't piss away my career."

Her eyes brimmed, her cheeks red.

"I understand," he said, standing.

She stood too and came around the desk to him.

"You heard from Liz?"

"No," he said. "She's not answering my calls. Neither are the girls."

"Shit," McGrath said. "I'm sorry."

"Yeah. I can't blame them. I should go."

She shocked him then by taking him in her arms, holding him tight. In all the years they had worked together, through all the triumphs and defeats, through the best and the worst of it, she had never once embraced him. Now she did, and it frightened him.

"You take care of yourself," she whispered in his ear.

"Yeah," he said. "You too."

As he walked away, he glanced back over his shoulder and saw McGrath wipe a tear from her eye. She would be furiously embarrassed to be seen crying, so he said nothing and kept walking. When he got back to his car, Donner also wept, because he knew he would never see her again.

3 6

When the sun had dipped low enough behind the trees, Moonflower ventured out of the van and into the clearing. The forest's scents were carried to her by the breeze, and she saw them as colors, swept along by currents, like a flowing rainbow river. The earthy tones of moss and bark and dirt, the brighter greens of pine and ferns, the fiery reds of mushrooms. And the things that walked and crawled and climbed and flew between the trees. She smelled them all and saw their shades and hues. Every single one of them.

The world had grown so much bigger since a week ago. At once darker and lighter, every sound crisper, clearer, deeper, her senses overlapping so that even the scent of pine needles played on her tongue. She could hear the light beating down. Even now, as the sun retreated, she could feel the violent noise of its fingers reaching through the canopy. The clothes on her skin, every thread of the fabric, every stitch in every seam.

For the first day or so, it had been overwhelming. The world had become too much, a hurricane of noise and light and smell and taste. But then she found she could focus, pick through the constant stream, and seek out what she wanted to experience. Now, on the edge of the clearing, she sifted through the scents until she found what she wanted: a sweet, biscuity smell, yeasty and ripe, deep yellow ocher and chocolate brown. And she listened through the roar of the trees, the muted pounding of sunlight, the thunder in her own ears, until she heard them.

Over there, through the trees.

Mom had told her to stay in the clearing, not to wander into the forest. But Moonflower didn't feel inclined to obey that command, so she walked northeast, following the yeasty ocher scent. Before long, she had lost sight of the clearing behind her, but she was not lost, could not be lost. And ahead, gathered at the foot of a great tree, they waited for her.

"Hey," she said as she approached, her voice soft.

She reached out her hand, and one by one, they came, nuzzling and sniffing at her fingers. The two crossbreeds, matted coats over hard ribs, and a smaller Jack Russell. Moonflower hunkered down and petted them in turn, scratching behind their ears. Each of them rolled on its back, supplicating, showing their vulnerable bellies. All except the coyote, which held back, its head and tail down.

"Come," she said, holding her hand out to it. "Don't be scared."

But she knew they all feared her, even the little one, who was bravest of them all. They surely loved her, or they would not have followed over all these miles, but they were also terrified in her presence. As they should be, she thought. Lying there, their bellies and throats exposed, ready to be seized and drained of their blood.

Moonflower's stomach growled, and the coyote flinched and backed away.

"I won't hurt you," she said, reaching.

The coyote whimpered as it drew near, trembling, fear resonating from its core like a plucked string. It lowered itself as it came close, its belly brushing the ground.

"Come on," she said.

And now she could touch it, burying her fingers in its warm pelt. Softer than she'd imagined, she felt each hair against her skin, the warmth at the base, the hard bones of the animal's skull and neck. And its pulse, thrumming. She felt its blood through its skin, she could smell it, hot and sweet.

Her stomach growled once more, but this time the coyote did not retreat. Instead, it rolled onto its back like the others, showing its belly.

"You'd let me eat you, wouldn't you?" she whispered, as if it were a delicious secret between them and the trees. "I won't," she said. "I would never."

She wouldn't have to, she thought. Not with so many wicked men in the world.

Mom waited for her at the edge of the clearing. Moonflower saw the look on her face and resisted the urge to turn and walk away. She readied herself for the scolding that would surely come.

But it didn't.

"You're right," Mom said. "I don't want to, but we

don't have any other choice. We'll set off first thing in the morning."

"How long will it take from here?" Moonflower asked.

"A day," Mom said. "Day and a half, maybe."

Moonflower splayed her fingers on her stomach. "I don't know if I can wait that long."

"I'll try to call him, make sure he has something for you as soon as we arrive."

"I can't wait," Moonflower said.

On cue, her stomach growled.

Mom's shoulders slumped, her head bowed.

"I'll see what I can do," she said.

Most Wanted
https://www.fbi.gov/wanted/topten/rebecca-carter/

Rebecca Carter
Unlawful flight to avoid prosecution; Felony murder of a federal agent.

Reward:
The FBI is offering a reward of up to $200,000 for information leading to the arrest of Rebecca Carter.

Remarks:
Carter is believed to be traveling with a girl aged 10-14, described as slender with long black hair, whom she claims to be her daughter.

Caution:
Rebecca Carter is wanted in connection with the alleged murder of a federal agent in Flagstaff, AZ, in the early hours of December 25th, 2022, while escaping from custody. She had been arrested the previous evening in connection with a series of killings across several states. Carter is considered extremely dangerous and should not be approached by members of the public. If sighted, local law enforcement agencies should be notified immediately.

37

Rebecca drove through the night until exhaustion got the better of her. She found an abandoned industrial park on the outskirts of Scottsdale, a cluster of warehouses and storage units, their roofs sagging, the windows long shattered. The dark channels between the buildings provided cover for the van, and she parked up in the shelter of what was once a loading bay.

She climbed down from the cabin, went to the sliding side door, and pulled it open. Moonflower huddled there, against the interior wall, wrapped in a sleeping bag. Except she no longer looked like the girl she had been a week ago. She had become somehow hollowed out, her eyes sunken in dark circles, her skin stretched tight over her cheekbones. And the smell, a dark animal odor that Rebecca had hoped was something else. She sat there, twitching and fidgeting as she stared back.

"I need to sleep," Rebecca said as she climbed in and slid the door closed behind her.

Darkness swallowed them, and though Rebecca craved light, she did not want to look at her daughter. She felt around for her own sleeping bag and struggled inside.

"Can I go outside?" Moonflower asked.

"What for?"

"Just to walk around, get some air."

Moonflower's voice sounded brittle, stretched thin.

"It's too dangerous," Rebecca said.

"There's no one around. What could—"

"I said no. Now let me sleep."

A few seconds of silence passed before Rebecca heard a low, feral growl rise into a shriek, then the van rocked as something slammed into its wall, followed by a small whimper of pain.

Rebecca scrambled around through the detritus on the floor until she found a flashlight. She flicked it on and saw Moonflower rocking back and forth, cradling her left hand in her lap. On the van's metal wall, a dent around the size of a girl's fist.

"Let me see," Rebecca said, untangling herself from the sleeping bag. She crawled over to Moonflower and reached for her hand. "Come on, let me look at it."

Moonflower lifted her hand from her lap and gave a gasp of pain. The hand appeared to fold over on itself, the little finger tucked beneath the third.

"Oh, baby, what did you do to yourself?"

Moonflower bowed her head and screwed her eyes shut, tears rolling from them.

"Mom, I don't know what's happening to me."

Careful of the injured hand, Rebecca took Moonflower in her arms and rocked her gently.

"Everything's going to be okay," she said. "I promise."

After a time, she felt Moonflower's body soften against hers. She eased herself away and reached for the broken hand. "Let me see."

She could feel heat in the hand, swelling around the break in the metacarpal of the little finger. It would soon begin to knit. No time to lose.

"I'm sorry, baby, this is going to hurt."

Moonflower let out a high whine, fresh tears spilling, and nodded. Rebecca took hold of the hand in both of hers. In one quick movement, she pushed the bone back into place, feeling the grind of the fracture. Moonflower screamed then went loose, her eyelids flickering. Then she snapped back to herself, leaned over, and retched. She brought up nothing but spit.

Rebecca held her again. "All done," she said. "It'll be healed by sunup. Come on. Lie down with me. Let's try to get some sleep."

She lowered herself to the van floor, bringing Moonflower with her, her chest to her daughter's back. She pulled the open sleeping bag back over them both and shut off the flashlight. They lay in the silent dark for time unknown, and Rebecca had drifted to the edge of sleep when Moonflower spoke.

"Mom?"

Rebecca startled. "Yeah," she said.

"Sometimes . . ."

"Sometimes what?"

"Sometimes I feel like I don't want to be alive anymore."

Rebecca felt something crack inside.

"Don't say that."

"Sometimes I wish I'd really died that night. That I'd stayed dead."

Rebecca closed her mouth, screwed her eyes shut. She said nothing because, sometimes, she wished that too.

She awoke with a start, and she cried out in the darkness, her arms empty.

"Moonflower?"

No answer. Rebecca scrabbled around, blind, seeking the hard cylinder of the flashlight. She found it and flicked the switch, aimed the beam into each corner of the van, the fright of her sudden waking growing into a deeper fear.

"Shit," she said as she reached for the side door handle.

Cool air washed in, softening the van's stale odors. She climbed out, her joints complaining at the effort, and looked around. To the east, the sky had begun to change from black to deep blue. How long had she slept? No more than an hour. She walked to the rear of the van and peered into the darkness between the buildings.

"Moonflower? Monica!"

Rebecca walked in that direction, listening, hearing nothing but rusted door hinges creaking in the wind. She turned in a circle, casting the flashlight's beam. It did little to push back the darkness all around. She became still, called her daughter's name once more, and listened hard.

There, off to her left, a voice. A cry of pain and fear.

Rebecca took off running, calling between breaths. As she passed an open doorway, she heard the voice again, high and cracked. She skidded to a halt and went to the door. She aimed the flashlight inside.

"Help me! Please, help—"

A woman's voice, cracked and hoarse. The light could not find her. There was a room toward the back, beyond the hulking forms of abandoned machinery, some kind of office with a window and a door of its own.

"Oh God, please help!"

Rebecca entered the building, part of her wanting to run to the voice, part of her wanting to flee the other way. She approached the office, picking her way through the decayed remains of boxes and crates, their contents spilling out onto the floor. The door to the office lay open, and she could hear rustling from within, grunting, panicked breathing. Then a thin, high whine, like a fearful dog.

"Please, please, no, don't . . ."

Rebecca reached the doorway and shone the flashlight inside. She froze there, locked in place by what she saw.

A middle-aged woman, filthy face and clothes, prostrate among the detritus on the floor. A fist holding a clump of her greasy hair, a pale face down close to her ear.

It was not, could not be Moonflower. This thing straddling the woman's back, this creature with its sunken features and bared teeth, whatever it was, it wore Moonflower's clothes, her skin, her hair. But it was not Rebecca's daughter. It couldn't be.

Could it?

"Moonflower," Rebecca said.

It did not look up. Instead it sniffed at the woman's throat. She heard the growl of its stomach, saw its bared teeth.

"Moonflower, stop," she said, raising her voice as she stepped inside the office.

Still, this creature that looked like her daughter did not acknowledge her presence. Rebecca kneeled down. The woman stared up at her, eyes as wide and round as dollar coins.

"Help me," she said.

"Baby, stop. Let her go."

Rebecca reached out, but it slapped her hand away and snarled.

"Moonflower, look at me."

She reached again, but it lashed out, the back of its hand striking Rebecca's wrist, taking her balance. Rebecca fell to her side, the flashlight tumbling from her grasp. The office became a kaleidoscope of twisting shadows and silhouettes. She scrabbled for the flashlight among the scattered paper and cardboard. When she found it, she swung it back, aiming for the creature's head. It connected with a sickly thud, and the creature reeled for a moment before howling and launching itself at Rebecca.

The force of it lifted Rebecca from the floor, slammed her back against the wall, and now there wasn't enough air in the world. A supernova of pain blossomed from the base of her skull. The creature sat astride her, so heavy, pinning her into the angle where the floor met the wall. It howled again, its voice cracking under the strain of its fury.

Behind it, the woman clambered to her feet, made for the door, stumbled, righted herself again and ran. The creature leapt after her, its weight leaving Rebecca's chest, allowing her to grab a chestful of air. The woman screamed from the doorway as it lighted on her back. She somehow managed to stagger a few steps before its weight brought her down.

Rebecca got to her knees, then her feet, and lurched to the door, out of the office, her momentum carrying her to the writhing arms and legs on the floor, the howling, screaming voices weaving together in a maddening spiral of noise. She fell on the creature's back, wrapped her arms around it, pulled it away.

"Stop, baby, please stop."

They tumbled away together, their bodies one as Rebecca tightened her hold, and the woman got to her feet once more. She glanced back over her shoulder before running for the exit, gasping and yelping as she went. The creature tried to go after her, but Rebecca held on hard, slowing it down. It dragged her to the door then howled at the night.

In the distance, dogs answered.

3 8

The phone's screeching ringtone jerked Donner awake, disoriented, bile in his throat, a thick ache behind his eyes. He peeled his face from the thin pillow and blinked as sunlight forced its way through the crack in the curtains and hammered nails into his skull. The movement aggravated the ache in his shoulder, still tender after its injury, and he groaned. He looked around and realized he had passed out still fully clothed, one shoe on, one shoe off. It took a few moments to remember where he was: a cheap motel on the northern edge of Flagstaff, not far from the gas station where, on Christmas Eve, Rebecca Carter had tried to steal a cell phone.

"Jesus fuck," he said, his throat coarse and dry.

He reached for the nightstand and felt around for his phone, pushing aside papers, tipping over a glass. It rolled to the edge and fell to the carpeted floor. It didn't shatter, but it lost a sizable arrowhead from its rim.

"Goddammit."

The glass settled by the phone which lay face down on the floor. He grabbed it, checked the display: McGrath.

"Yeah," he answered.

"You okay?" she asked. "You sound like hell."

Donner maneuvered himself upright, trying not to bring more pain to his shoulder, and held the phone away from his mouth as he cleared his throat.

"Yeah, I'm all right."

"You been drinking?"

"No," he said, too quickly. "No. I picked up a cold or something, that's all."

The two-thirds empty bottle of vodka on the table across the room glared at him, called him a liar. That and the beer cans.

"You promise?"

He covered his eyes with his free hand and said, "I promise."

It wouldn't be the first he'd broken. Wouldn't be the last.

"Okay," McGrath said, but the doubt was clear in her voice. "Anyway, I got something. Just came in. A sighting just outside of Scottsdale."

Donner got to his feet, limped a few steps before kicking off the remaining shoe, and went to the map he'd pinned to the wall. A red circle around Flagstaff, a line connecting that to a point northeast of Santa Barbara where a spate of animal killings had been reported. He traced another line with his fingertip from there back to Scottsdale.

"Tell me," he said.

"A vagrant flagged down an Arizona state trooper on the edge of the city. Said she'd been sleeping rough at an old industrial park. She told them she was attacked by a child, that it dragged her into a building and tried to rip her throat out. She said it would've succeeded except a woman showed up and pulled the child off of her."

"A little girl?" Donner asked, but he knew the answer.

"Yeah," McGrath said. "Least, she says she looked like a girl, but the state trooper's report says she was hysterical, wasn't making a whole lot of sense. She kept saying it was a demon. There isn't much detail in the report, but it says the vagrant is known to police, history of mental health issues, drug and alcohol abuse, the usual, so her statement isn't being treated as a hundred percent reliable. She wasn't able to give much in the way of a description, but it sounds like them."

"Yeah, it's them," Donner said.

"And there's something else. It's pretty wild."

"What?"

"Flagstaff PD along with the local Bureau did a detailed search around the area of the cabin where Craig Watters was killed, where Rebecca Carter was arrested. Guess what they found."

"Goddammit, stop teasing it out. Just tell me."

Her silence told him he'd gone too far.

"I'm sorry," he said. "I didn't mean to snap. It's just, everything's . . ."

"Too much," she said, finishing his sentence for him.

"Yeah," he said.

"Then maybe it's time to step back. You don't have to do this to yourself."

"I do. I have to find them. Show Holstein and all the rest I'm not crazy."

"All right," McGrath said. "But remember this: I'm only helping you on the understanding that if you track them down, you call it in. You don't try to take them yourself. You promise me that."

"Of course."

"I don't believe you."

"I promise. Now, what was this other thing?"

She paused before she spoke, her frustration ringing loud through the miles between them.

"They found a shallow grave behind the cabin," she said. "A woman and two children buried there. They've been identified as Watters' wife and kids. The wife was blunt force trauma, the kids were strangled. Neighbors of his said she'd left him six months ago, took the kids to her parents in Oregon, at least that's what he'd told them. They suspected he was abusive, and that's why she'd gone."

"My God," Donner said, feeling a chill creep beneath his clothes and his skin. "She was right."

"What do you mean?"

"Rebecca Carter. She told me he was an abuser. I didn't believe her, there was no evidence of it, no record or arrests. But she was right. They didn't find this one online. They just picked him up at random in a shopping mall. And even so, they got the right guy."

"It doesn't change anything," McGrath said.

"Maybe. Maybe not. I'll drive down that way tom—"

He realized he'd said too much and snapped his mouth shut.

"Drive? Where are you? I thought you were at home."

Donner searched for a lie but could find nothing.

"Talk to me, Marc. Where are you? What are you doing?"

"I'm in Flagstaff." He forced a smile, hoping it would be audible in his tone. "Scene of the crime, you know?"

"For God's sake, why?"

Tell her or not? His mind lacked the clarity to form a lie, so he swallowed and told the truth.

"You know Edward Chin was discharged from the hospital a few days ago, right?"

"No, Marc," McGrath said, exasperation in her voice. "Don't do it."

"I just want to talk to him, see what he remembers."

"Don't. It'll get back to Holstein. It's all they'll need to shit-can you, and maybe me along with you."

"A few questions won't hurt anyone," Donner said.

"I swear to God, Marc, if you do this . . ."

"What?"

"Don't make me say it."

He leaned on the table with his free hand. "Go on and say it. Lay it all out."

"If you do this, we're finished. Not just as partners, but as friends. Remember I said to you, one of these days, there'll be a line I can't cross? This is the line, Marc."

Donner listened to her breathe for a few moments, then said, "All right. I won't talk to him."

"You swear to me."

"I swear to God," he said.

McGrath went quiet for a moment, and Donner pictured her at her desk, kneading her brow with her fingertips like she always did when something bothered her.

Eventually she asked, "Anything from Liz?"

"No," he said. "Not yet."

"Shit, I'm sorry. Do you want me to try? We always got along pretty well."

"No. I'll figure it out."

"Okay. Go easy on yourself, all right?"

"Yeah, you too," he said, and hung up.

He stashed the phone in his pocket and looked at the map on the wall. A red marker lay on the table beneath it. He pulled off the cap and drew a line from the point northeast of Santa Barbara all the way to Scottsdale.

"You're hungry, aren't you?" he said to the wall. "You wanted to feed, but you couldn't. So, you're going to try again."

He placed his finger on the map, looked at the routes heading east, away from the Phoenix metro area. Where were they headed? Mexico, maybe? That's where he would go if he wanted to stay out of sight. But why hadn't they gone that way a week ago? Tucson lay to the southeast, mountains beyond that, and the Coronado Forest. The kind of wilderness they liked to operate in. Yes, he thought. That's where they were headed.

Donner turned back to the table. The bottle and the cans.

"Jesus, man, get yourself straight."

He had so much to do. There was no room for alcohol in his plans. He went to the bathroom and grabbed the small garbage can from under the sink. Back to the table where he gathered up the cans, crushed them in his hand, and dropped them in to clatter against the rest. He lifted the vodka bottle, the remains of the clear liquid sloshing inside. What time was it? Past two in the afternoon.

He had ordered Chinese takeout last night and ate it while he leafed through his notes, reading some, writing more. One beer wouldn't hurt, he'd thought. Maybe two, but no more. He'd gone a year without. No sense going back now.

And yet, it wasn't enough. That was the thing, wasn't it? There was no such thing as enough. Only what he could take before the weight of it pulled him down into unconsciousness. How many times had his girls come down in the morning, ready for school, to find him passed out on the couch? More than he could count.

He lifted the bottle from the table, unscrewed the cap, and took a slug. And another, and a third, until the burn in his throat got to be too much.

"Goddamn," he said as he replaced the cap.

Mindful of the broken glass, he sat down on the edge of the bed. He gathered up the papers that had been scattered across the blankets, putting them back into order. Printouts of old articles from regional news outlets, copies of police reports, crime scene photos that McGrath had supplied to him. He had followed a hunch and come up with a solid lead: clusters of animal mutilations. Cats taken from yards. Rabbits left by the roadside. Young deer found in clearings. All of them with their throats opened, drained of blood. Most of them with puncture wounds consistent with a target arrow, just like the men who turned up dead. No one had spotted the link, not until now. Donner had spent the last two days tracing a path across the western states: one day, a small-town newspaper reporting missing pets somewhere north of Portland, OR, then a few days later, a man with a record goes missing from a suburb south of Seattle, WA, for his body to be found months later in the forests north of the city.

He sorted through the pages of handwritten notes until he found what he'd spent so many hours on the night before: a sequential list of locations, along with approximate dates. Bringing the remains of the vodka with him, he went back to the map on the wall. He placed the bottle on the table there, lifted the red marker in his right hand, and worked his way down the page in his left. When he was done, he stood back and took in his work.

A jagged red line crisscrossed state lines, town to city to forest, as far east as Texas, as far north as Montana. Not every cluster of animal deaths led to the body of a man, but that only meant no body had been found. They were out there, somewhere, in shallow graves or hidden beneath branches. The remains probably long picked over by carrion-feeders, coyotes and crows and insects. The red line connected all the way to Flagstaff in northern Arizona. And now it ran back to Phoenix.

He removed the phone from his pocket and took a photograph of the map. He opened WhatsApp and added the photo, along with a note:

Look at this. There's a pattern, and I know where it's going.

Donner pressed send and returned the phone to his pocket. He sat at the table and opened his laptop. The desktop showed shortcuts to half a dozen social media apps. He opened Kik and went to the profile page. Here, his name was Ryan Hersch, aged fourteen, with a photograph Donner had pilfered from some kid's Facebook account. His location said Mission Hills, Santa Barbara, CA. He changed it to Oro Valley, Tucson, AZ.

Before he could go any farther, his phone chimed in his pocket. McGrath replying on WhatsApp: *All I see is a bunch of red lines on a map. It's not a pattern, Marc. Don't drive yourself crazy with this. Please.*

He wanted to reply, tell her she was wrong, she must be

blind not to see it. But right now, she was his only friend in the world, and he couldn't afford to drive her away. He tossed the phone onto the pile of papers and returned his attention to the laptop.

Ryan Hersch, aged fourteen, resident of Oro Valley, Tucson, AZ. New to the area, seeking to make friends, into MCU movies, *Star Wars*, Call of Duty, avid reader, plays piano and guitar, hopes to form a band one day. Donner made the profile public and began his search. Baited the hook.

They were out there somewhere, the woman and the girl, seeking their prey.

"Come get me," Donner said.

3 9

The shudder of the van's dying engine shook Moonflower awake. She cried out in the darkness, feeling the overwhelming urge to thrash her arms and legs, but they couldn't move. It took a few moments to realize they were bound, her wrists strapped together, and her ankles.

What had happened? Had she been bad?

She searched her memory, reaching back over the last days and hours. The last thing she could grab ahold of was lying down here, in the van, with Mom. Mom's arms around her. Shivering even though she wasn't cold. Her stomach tying itself in knots, gnawing hunger. And then, somehow, slipping into a swampy sleep. She had dreamed of running with the dogs, weaving through derelict buildings, hunting their prey together in the rubble. Then a great stretch of nothing, like she had been entombed in her own mind.

Moonflower became still and waited, listening. The driver's door of the van opening and closing, the suspension rocking, footsteps walking around to the side door. It slid open, and Mom stood there, silhouetted by artificial light, watching.

"Mom?"

The silhouette shifted, the head tilting as Mom studied her.

"Baby, is that you?"

Moonflower tried to sit upright, but the bonds would only allow her to roll to her side.

"Mom, what's happening? Where are we?"

Mom crawled inside, unclipping the knife from her belt. Moonflower recoiled, fearful of the blade. But Mom would not hurt her, she knew that.

"It's okay, honey, just let me . . ."

She took Moonflower's wrists and slipped the blade beneath the nylon twine that held them together. The serrated edge sawed at the rope until it came loose, then Mom moved to the twine around her ankles. When she was free, Moonflower retreated to the far side of the van's interior.

"Why did you tie me up?"

"I had to, sweetheart," Mom said, her voice soft and smooth. "If I hadn't, you would've hurt yourself. Me too."

"That's not true," Moonflower said. "Why would I hurt you?"

Mom crawled toward her over the mattresses and sleeping bags. "It wasn't you, baby. It was the other thing."

"There's no other thing," Moonflower said. "There's only me."

Mom took her hand. "Then where have you been?"

"Right here."

"You know, you nearly killed someone. A homeless

woman. She must have been sleeping in one of those build-ings. If I hadn't come along, if I hadn't stopped you . . ."

Fear rose in her, tears rising with it. Moonflower swal-lowed, didn't want to cry like a baby. Somehow, that seemed like the worst thing that could possibly happen, even though she had cried in her mother's arms countless times.

"That's not true," she said. "I'd remember it."

"It doesn't matter. We're here now."

Moonflower looked past her, through the open door. A walled yard, garbage piled high. Somewhere close, she heard great engines, roaring and whirring, the heave and sigh of hundreds of people packed into halls and corridors. An airport.

"Come on," Mom said.

Moonflower hesitated before following her out into the night. A plane roared low overhead, making her flinch. It descended out of sight. She looked around the yard, the scrap piled against the walls, the shell of a car mounted on bricks. And rats hiding, watching. She could feel them in the dark places.

"I've been here before," she said.

"Not for a few years," Mom said. "Come on."

She took Moonflower's wrist and led her up a short flight of steps with a railing at one side, to a steel door. A security camera mounted above it, a peephole at eye level, a buzzer fixed to the wall. Mom pressed it with her thumb, and an electronic rasp came from somewhere inside the building. When nothing happened, she pressed it again.

She was about to ring a third time when a crackling voice broke from a hidden speaker. "Who's that? What do you want?"

Mom looked up at the camera and said, "It's Rebecca. Rebecca Carter, and my daughter. I tried to call ahead, but you didn't answer."

"Jesus Christ."

The second word faded as if the owner of the voice had turned away from the microphone, followed by a click. Mom thumbed the buzzer again, and one more time, held it there, the noise scratching at Moonflower's ears.

"Get out of here," the voice said. "You were on the news. They know who you are. You can't be here. Now go, please."

"We need help."

"I don't care. I can't help you. Go, or I'll call the police."

"You won't call the cops," Mom said, smiling.

"I guess we'll see," the voice said, like a child's taunt.

"I'll tell them what you've been doing here. In fact, if we get caught, that's the first thing I'll do. I'll tell them everything I know about you."

"You know nothing about me."

"I guess we'll see."

Quiet then, and Mom turned to look at Moonflower, wicked glee in her eyes as bolts snapped and keys turned in locks. The door opened and Guthrie Chambers's round face appeared in the gap.

"For Christ's sake, come in," the Nurse said.

File #: 89-49911-28
Subject: Rebecca Carter
OO: Flagstaff
Desc: Journal Entry, Handwritten
Date: Unknown

I killed a man two nights ago. I didn't think I could do something like that, but I did. I didn't mean for it to happen, it wasn't planned. The plain fact is, if I hadn't killed him, I don't know what he would've done to us.

It was late, and the van had broken down. I wasn't sure where we were, just that it was somewhere south of Portland. It was raining hard, and it was cold. I was looking under the hood, trying to figure out what had gone wrong, but I know nothing about engines.

A pickup truck pulled up alongside the van and a man asked if I needed help. I told him no, but he asked if he could take a look at the engine. There was no reason I could think of to refuse, so I let him. He looked at it a while, the rain pounding down, and then he said he could see the problem, some part or other needed replacing, and there was an auto shop in the next town along that would have it, and he could maybe even fix it, but it wouldn't be till morning. He said he could tow us as far as his place, then go get the part as soon as the auto shop opened.

I said no, but he said he couldn't bear to leave us stranded out there in the middle of nowhere. He seemed kind and decent, and I was so cold and tired, and so hungry. I had given Moonflower something to eat earlier in the day, and it had left me feeling dizzy and weak, like my bones and muscles had gone soft. Maybe if I'd been thinking clearly, I would've resisted. But I wasn't, and I didn't. I couldn't.

I sat in the driver's seat of the van while he hitched up a towrope from the back of his truck. I had to steer and brake as he drove, pulling me behind. I've never done that before, and I was scared I would rear-end him. Twenty minutes later, we were at his place. It looked like an old farmhouse. Kind of rundown and threadbare, but clean. I don't know if it was a working farm or not. He didn't have the look of a farmer.

As we stood outside the house, a question occurred to me, so I asked it: Did he live alone? I felt uneasy even before he answered.

He said, yes. He'd lived there with his mother all his life, but she had passed just two months before. I told him I was sorry for his loss and thanked him for his kindness. I had turned back to the van, Moonflower waiting in the passenger seat for me, when he asked us to come inside, he had plenty of room. I told him no, we would sleep in the van, he had already showed us enough kindness.

"It's warm inside," he said, "and there's food. I made up a batch of stew this morning. There's plenty."

God, I was hungry. I hadn't realized just how hungry until he mentioned food. My stomach yearned at the idea of hot stew. I pictured it steaming in a bowl, felt it burning my lips and tongue.

"Okay," I said, "thank you."

I went to the passenger side to get Moonflower.

She asked me, "Who is that man?"

"Someone kind who wants to help us," I said.

I saw the fear on her face. "I don't trust him," she said.

I should've listened to her.

His house was indeed warm inside, and I ate two full bowls of stew along with I don't know how many slices of bread. Moonflower managed to eat just enough not to make him suspicious. She vomited it back up later in the bathroom, but I don't think he heard. He showed us to an upstairs room with a big old bed that Moonflower and I could share. Then he handed me a towel, said I could take a shower if I liked, and he'd have some hot chocolate waiting for me in the kitchen when I was done.

The shower was the first I'd had in weeks, and it was glorious. I stood under the stream of warm water and felt the knots in my neck and shoulders loosen, saw the grime in the creases of my skin wash away, and the grease rinse out of my hair. I thought again how kind this man was, helping strangers like us. I told myself he was just a decent human being, nothing more. Even so, I was glad the door had a lock.

When I was dried and clothed, I checked in on Moon-flower. She lay on the bed reading a paperback I'd picked up in a thrift store. I told her I'd be back soon and went downstairs, following the sweet and dark scent of choco-late. A mug waited for me on the kitchen table, steam rising from it. The man sat at the other side, sipping from his own mug.

He asked, "Better?"

"Yes," I said. "Much."

He smiled as I sat down, and I took my first proper look at him. I could see that he had tried to tidy himself up. He'd combed down his hair, shaved, changed his shirt. Part of me was bothered that he'd made this effort because he had to have a reason. But another part of me was flattered that he would take the time.

"You can do some laundry in the morning, if you like."

I became aware then that even though my body was clean, my jeans and shirt weren't. There was an odor of my own sweat about them, stale and bitter. I felt heat on my face and felt suddenly ashamed. I tried to hide it by sipping from the mug.

"I guess you've been having a hard time," he said.

I looked away and said, "Yes, real hard."

"Anything you want to tell me about?"

"No," I said. "It's nothing anyone can help me with."

"I guess I've had it hard too," he said. "Since my mother passed, it's been lonely out here. Real lonely."

"I'm sorry to hear that," I said.

I felt my nerves ring and my skin prickle. The light in the kitchen seemed so much brighter, the colors deeper. Every sound so much louder, his breathing, the nervous tapping of his fingertips on the table, the rain on the window.

He began to speak.

"Maybe . . ."

I knew in my gut not to encourage him to say anything more, I knew no good could come of it, but he found the words anyway.

"Maybe you've been lonely too," he said.

I kept my voice warm and steady and low as I replied.

"I have my daughter," I said.

"Yeah," he said, "but maybe you're lonely for something more."

"No," I said. "I'm not."

He traced the grain of the wooden tabletop with his finger, a delicate motion, as if he could feel the life of the tree it had once been.

"Your girl could have that bed all to herself," he said. "My bed's big enough for you and me both."

He glanced up at me, a smile flickering on his lips, but I could see the fear in him. I saw the force of effort it had taken for him to say it, and I pitied him.

"No, thank you," I said.

His hands started to tremble. He glanced up at me again, and I saw his eyes welled.

"I just thought, maybe . . ."

His voice quivered. Not with fear, but with rage. I could feel it radiate from him, seeking release.

"You've been very kind," I said, rising from the chair, "but I think we should go now."

"Please don't," he said, a desperate urgency to his voice.

"It'd be for the best," I said.

"I'm sorry I said that. I apologize."

"That's all right," I said. "I'll get my daughter, and we'll go."

"Don't," he said.

"I think I should."

He shot to his feet, and his chair toppled.

I took a step back from the table and said, "It's all right. We'll be out of here in a few minutes."

"Goddammit, I shouldn't have said that. I'm a fucking idiot. I'm sorry. Please don't—"

He slammed the table with his fist. Chocolate spilled from both of the mugs. I had backed halfway to the door, and I kept moving as I spoke.

"It's all right," I said, keeping my voice as light as I

could. "There's no harm done. I'll just be on my way and leave you in peace."

He grabbed his mug and threw it. It bounced off the table and smashed against the wall, steaming chocolate spraying across the room. It splashed on my face, and I cried out as I brought my hand up to where it burned.

"No!" he said, and came around the table, saying, "Sorry, sorry, I'm sorry, I didn't mean it."

I went for the door, telling him it was okay, but I felt his hand on my wrist, his hard skin scratching at mine.

"Please," he said, "I'm sorry, I didn't mean it."

I tried to pull away, but he dragged me back into the kitchen, all the time telling me he was sorry, he didn't mean it, begging me not to leave. I shouted at him to let me go and he tightened his grip, tried to get ahold of my other wrist. I shouted again, louder, and he went to put his hand over my mouth. I slapped it away, tried to jerk my captive wrist free, but now he snaked both his thick arms around me, and I realized then how broad he was, how tall, how strong. One hand covered my mouth, and he hissed into my ear.

"I'm lonely, that's all, I didn't mean anything by it. Just be still. Just stop—"

I lifted my right leg and placed my foot against the door frame. I focused every bit of strength I had into my thigh as I pushed both of us back, taking his balance. We stumbled into the table, and it scraped across the floor until it met the sink and cupboards beneath the window and stopped dead. He fell, taking me with him, and he lost his grip on me as he landed hard on the floor. I tried to scramble away, our legs tangling, and he got hold of my sleeve. I swung my left foot blindly and my heel connected with his groin. He grunted and released my sleeve long enough for me to grab the knife that had fallen to the floor beside the half-eaten loaf of bread.

I crawled away, the knife clasped in my right hand, and his hands swiped at my legs. I kicked hard, and I can't be sure where I struck him, but I felt bone beneath flesh and heard him cry out, then curse.

It was then that I saw Moonflower in the doorway, her eyes wide with fright, staring at me, then her gaze darting behind me. I rolled onto my side, saw him rising up, then falling, hands going for my throat.

There was no conscious decision to stab him. No thought of act or consequence. Only the instinct to raise my right hand to meet him, the blade disappearing into his chest. His face going slack with shock as he collapsed on top of me. The gurgling from deep inside of him. The warmth that spread from him to me, covering my hands and forearms, slick on my skin.

Moonflower moved then, quick, and pulled him away, rolling him onto his back. The knife remained in my hand and a red rose blossomed on his chest. His breath came in shallow gasps and he stared at the ceiling. I wonder now what he saw there as he lay dying, blood pulsing from the wound in his chest in time with his slowing heart.

I sat upright and backed away until I could go no farther, wedged into the corner between the cupboards and the back door. Moonflower kneeled over him, and I saw something in her face, like a wild desire, a desperate need.

I knew what she would do before she did it. The thought flickered in my mind to tell her to stop, but I knew there was no point. Nothing in the world could keep her from it.

Moonflower lowered her head to his chest, to the pulsing wound, and she fed.

All this time, I've been giving her what I could from my own veins. So much it almost killed me. And whatever animals we could catch. Rabbits, mostly. But none of it was ever enough, and by God, it never will be again. Not after this.

It occurs to me now that I never knew his name. I didn't ask it, and he didn't give it. Nor I to him. It doesn't matter now, I guess. What I do know is that everything has changed. Moonflower has fed and she will want to feed again. She will need it as surely as I need to breathe. I have to think about that, think about how we can satisfy her hunger.

Another thing occurs to me: I wonder if that man is still dead?

Moonflower died, then she came back, changed. What if that man did the same? Is it enough that she fed from him for this thing, whatever it is, to be passed on? Or does it take more? I've asked Moonflower what happened that night in Madison, when she was attacked. I've asked how this thing got into her and changed her, but she says she doesn't remember. The idea of that man being back there at that farm, hungry, seeking to feed, frightens me more than almost anything. If I had the courage, I would go back there to see if his body is where we left it. But I don't.

40

Rebecca followed Guthrie inside, her arm around Moonflower. She closed the steel door behind her and felt the dimness of the interior press on her. The decaying house stood on its own parcel of land close to Tucson International Airport. The compound was surrounded by ramshackle homes, auto shops, and freight companies.

"You owe me a padlock," Guthrie said.

"I didn't cut the lock," Rebecca said, "I cut the chain. You should invest in better security if you really want to keep people out."

"You're lucky I'm not working nights this week," Guthrie said, giving her a hard look over his shoulder. "What would you have done then?"

"I would've broken in anyway."

He grunted a curse and opened the door to what passed for a living room. The building had four rooms, plus a bathroom and a kitchen. Guthrie had taped newspaper to the insides of the windows and lived in a perpetual twilight. The few lamps around the place were fitted with the lowest wattage bulbs he could find, and the switches for the overhead lights had been removed from the walls, leaving tangles of exposed wires.

"Does the TV still work?" Rebecca asked.

"About the only thing round here that does," Guthrie said.

She spoke to Moonflower. "Baby, you want to watch something while Guthrie and I talk? Maybe you could find a movie."

Moonflower gave her a smile, the first to touch her face in days. Television was a rare treat for her. Rebecca struggled to remember the last time they'd seen one. Moonflower searched on an upturned crate that served as a coffee table for a remote control. She sifted through magazines, newspapers, and books, trying not to cause a landslide of paper.

"Here," Guthrie said, lifting the remote from the tattered couch.

Moonflower took it and examined the buttons before finding the power switch. Rebecca nodded toward the door, telling Guthrie to follow her. He did so and brought her to the kitchen at the rear of house, which connected to the rest of the rooms by a short corridor. They both sat at the folding plastic table by the sink.

"What do you want?"

"Sanctuary," Rebecca said.

"I don't do that anymore. Especially not for you."

"We need help. We need shelter. Just for a few days till I figure out what to do next."

"Go to Mexico," Guthrie said. "You could be in Juarez

by morning, or Tijuana if you leave right now. Think of all those fat white American men who'd just love to meet your daughter."

"Watch your mouth," she said.

Her expression must have reflected her anger because he flinched before ducking his head and raising his hands in apology.

"You know what I mean. Your methodology works down there. Easy pickings."

He was right, which only angered her more. She had been able to keep Moonflower alive all this time because the stupidest men were driven by their basest desires, and they were plentiful. All the more so in those places where the things they desired could be so easily bought with cash money. They had taken advantage before, and although Moonflower's hunger had been more than sated, it meant wading through the kind of filth that could never be washed away.

"We'll go that way soon," Rebecca said, "but not for a few days. We need things to settle down a little first."

"So, you bring your troubles to my door," Guthrie said. "I don't need them, thank you very much, I got plenty of my own."

"You've helped us before, and people like us. What's changed?"

"You're headline news. You're wanted in a murder case. The killing of a federal agent, no less. You know what kind of shit I could be in for harboring a fugitive?"

"I have no choice."

"But I do."

"You don't understand."

"I understand plenty. I help people like you because I want to, not because I have to. And in your particular case, in these particular circumstances, I don't want to."

Rebecca felt her anger seeking an outlet, rage becoming tears, and she would not cry in front of this man. Would not, could not.

"I think she's starting to turn," she said.

Guthrie exhaled as he sat back in his chair. He became distant for a moment, memories unwinding behind his eyes, then came back to himself.

"What's happened?" he asked. "What's changed?"

"You heard about Flagstaff, right? That's what's been in the news."

"I'm short on detail, but yeah, I know about it."

"I was under arrest, handcuffed to a chair, being questioned. She came and got me. She hurt some people in the process."

"Killed one of them, in fact."

Rebecca tried not to react to his barb but felt the shame flicker on her face nonetheless.

"Something changed that night. *She* changed. She became something else, at least for a while."

"Something animal."

Rebecca turned her gaze away. "She's not an animal."

"No, but *it* is. The thing inside of her. I know. I saw it in my mother too, before she turned. How long has it been?"

"Fifteen years."

"Long time," Guthrie said. "Not many last that long. Maybe it's time to let her go."

The shock of his words took a moment to penetrate, but when they did, they sparked a fury in her. She raised her right hand to strike him, but her better mind stilled it. He shrank back in the chair, fear in his eyes.

"Don't say that," she hissed, her open hand suspended in the air between them. "Don't you dare."

"You can't stop it," he said, his voice low and calm. "You can only hold it back. And you can't do that forever."

She lowered her hand to the table. "I can try, goddammit."

"All right," he said, his shoulders dropping in resignation. "If you want to keep it under control, to keep your daughter in control of *it*, you need to feed it. Remember, this thing, this hunger, this disease, whatever you want to call it, it is greedy, it is a glutton. If it isn't fed, it will come to the surface, it will take control of her. And once it does, she'll be lost to you. That's why so few survive a month beyond the initial infection. Its greed destroys them."

"Do you have anything?"

His lips pursed as he ran his tongue over his teeth. "I got something," he said.

Guthrie stood and went to the chest freezer in the corner. An old unit that hummed and rattled, the kind that might hold popsicles or frozen pizza in a small 7-Eleven. He slid one side of the top over and reached inside, pulled out a catering tub of ice cream, a packet of tater tots, and a large bag of ice, setting them on the closed half. He dipped his hands inside once more and pulled out two clear plastic pouches containing a deep red substance.

"Frozen is no good," Rebecca said. "The ice tears the cells apart when it thaws. And if there's glycerol, she can't take it."

"You telling me my business?" Guthrie asked, giving

her a sharp look. "Polyvinyl alcohol. They did research a few years ago, seeing how arctic cod could survive in freezing temperatures, and they found a few drops of polyvinyl alcohol could enable frozen blood to be thawed with minimal lysis of the red cells. Glycerol works, but its removal is too time consuming to be practical for most medical uses. So, they tried polyvinyl, the same stuff that's in PVA glue, and it worked after a fashion. Maybe not well enough for transfusions, but for our purposes? It works just fine. I only have a few of these left, donated blood at its thirty-five day use-by that would've been destroyed if I didn't have my ways and means. Fill the sink with water, please."

Rebecca stood and went to the steel sink. She was surprised to find it shining clean.

"Cold water," Guthrie instructed.

She plugged the sink and turned the faucet. The water thundered into the sink as he fetched another three bags from the freezer. He brought them two at a time to the sink and dropped them in the water. Four in total.

"Give them a few hours to thaw," he said as he returned the ice cream, tater tots, and ice to the freezer. "Should be ready by morning."

"Thank you," Rebecca said.

"I'm not acting entirely out of kindness. You got any money?"

"Pocket change, that's all."

"Shit," he said, drawing out the sibilant.

"Once she's well again, I'll get some, I promise. I'll send it to you."

"I won't hold my breath," he said. "You can stay for the

night, then I want you gone. No arguments, no just-one-more-days. Gone."

"All right," Rebecca said.

She turned off the faucet and looked at the packets of blood clustered beneath the water. Four pints that might bring her daughter back from the edge, or they might not. Guthrie was right: fifteen years was a long time. But she would not let her daughter go. She would die first.

41

Donner rang the doorbell and waited. He gave it a full minute before ringing again. Cupping his hands around his eyes, he peered through the frosted glass, trying to make sense of the light and shadow beyond, and saw a movement as someone approached. The door opened a crack and a boy looked out, no more than ten or eleven years old.

"Hey," Donner said. "I was hoping to speak with Edward Chin. I know he was discharged from the hospital. Is he home?"

The boy stepped away from the door, allowing it to open another inch in the winter breeze.

"Mom!"

Donner opened the door farther and stepped through. A woman's voice called out in reply, Cantonese or Mandarin, Donner didn't know. An elderly woman appeared in a doorway down the hall. The boy's grandmother, he assumed. She wore an apron and worried a dishtowel between her hands. She stared hard at Donner for a second before shouting a string of angry words at him that he didn't understand.

He stepped farther into the hallway, pushing the door closed behind him. "I'm sorry, ma'am, I don't know what you're saying. I need to speak with Edward Chin. Is he home?"

She continued to rant at him until another woman appeared from the kitchen, this one younger. The boy's mother, Agent Chin's wife. She said something to the grandmother in her own language, an instruction, and the grandmother took the boy by the arm and led him away. She scowled at Donner as they both entered the kitchen, holding his gaze until she was out of sight.

"Who are you?" the younger woman asked. "What are you doing in my house?"

"Ma'am, Mrs. Chin, I'm Special Agent Marc Donner. I was there the night your husband was injured. May I please speak with him?"

"Donner," she echoed, her arms folding across her body. "Yes, I know who you are, and no, you may not see my husband. He's not well, and quite frankly, I think you've done enough harm. I'd like you to leave now."

"Ma'am, I know this is an intrusion, but I've flown all the way from DC. I heard he'd made a good recovery and he was at home. I've tried to contact him, but he didn't reply. I wouldn't show up here if it wasn't so important to me. I swear to you, I won't take much of his time. I really need to speak with him. Please."

"I'm sorry, Agent Donner, but you've wasted a journey. Now, for the second time, I'm asking you to go. There won't be a—"

"Who is that? What's happening?"

The call came from upstairs, a man's papery voice.

"Honey, it's no one, just a salesman. I've told him to—"

"Agent Chin, Edward, it's Marc Donner." Donner went to the foot of the stairs. Mrs. Chin tried to block him, but he stepped around her. He expected to find her husband looking back down at him but saw no one. "I really need to talk with you."

"What about? I've given my statement. I have nothing more to say."

"I want to talk about what happened that night. What *really* happened."

Silence for long seconds, broken by Mrs. Chin whispering, you sonofabitch, as she forced herself between him and the stairs.

"All right," Chin called from upstairs. "Come up."

His wife glared at Donner. Donner said nothing as he passed her and climbed the stairs. He reached the landing and saw an open door leading to a darkened room. From out here, he caught a low odor that reminded him of caged animals. He approached the doorway and knocked on the frame.

"Just come in, for Christ's sake."

Donner stepped inside. It took a moment in the dimness to see Chin sitting on the edge of the bed.

"Close the door," he said.

Donner did as he was told.

"So, talk."

Donner came closer and said, "How are you doing? I heard you'd recovered better than expected."

"Better than expected," Chin echoed, his tone mocking.

"The doctors said it was a fucking miracle. They said I had hardly any chance of walking unassisted again, and here I am."

He stood upright from the bed, a dressing gown and pajamas hanging loose on his skeletal body. Chin had not been a large man when Donner had last seen him only a few weeks ago, but neither had he been this stick figure of a person.

"I need to talk to you about what happened that night."

"So you said. It's all in my statement."

"Your statement says you don't remember anything. But I think maybe you do."

Chin stared at the window, obscured by the closed drapes. "Why are you here? What do you really want from me?"

"I want you to tell them the truth. About the girl. About what she did that night."

Chin dropped back down onto the bed, his thin legs seeming to betray him. "I tried to tell them," he said. His fingertips went to his neck, brushing the faint remains of a scar. "They wouldn't believe me. Said I was misremembering, that my head injury had made me confused. So, I changed my story."

"You lied to them," Donner said.

"Do you have a family?"

"Not anymore. They left me."

"I guess you've met mine," Chin said, his gaze moving to the door and his home beyond this room. "I love my wife. I love my son. I need to provide for them. If I tell my bosses that a little girl nearly broke me in two and tore a chunk out of my neck, my career will be over. So yes,

Agent Donner, I lied through my goddamn teeth and I'll do it again and again for as long as I have to."

A deep growl sounded from Chin's stomach, and he doubled over, wrapping his arms around himself, his face twisted in pain. Donner took a step closer.

"Oh God, I'm so fucking hungry," Chin said. "Always, always hungry."

"Do you need me to get—"

"I eat and I eat," Chin said, "and I can't keep it down. I've seen my doctor and he says I'm fine. But look at me. I'm fucking starving to death."

Chin bowed his head, and his shoulders quivered. He brought a hand to his mouth, choked back a sob.

Donner came closer and kneeled down, his eyes level with Chin's. "Did she do this to you?" he asked.

Chin lifted his head, sniffed hard, wiped tears away.

"I can't have the curtains open during the daytime," he said. "The light hurts my head, like nails hammered into my eyes. It makes my skin burn. I've been sitting here in the dark ever since I got out of the hospital. And I'm so goddamn hungry. What's happening to me?"

"I don't know," Donner said, reaching out, taking Chin's arm. "But maybe if you tell the truth, if you tell them what really happened, maybe they can help you."

Chin looked down at the exposed skin of Donner's wrist. Donner felt a tingling sensation there, became aware of the pulse beneath his skin. He took his hand from Chin's arm.

"I've been having these dreams," Chin said. "I hardly ever sleep, but when I do, I have these dreams. I do things. Terrible things. To Sandra and Jason. I hurt them. I bite them. I tear them apart. I rip them to fucking pieces with my hands and my teeth and I eat them. I'm scared to close my eyes in case I see it again, their throats torn out, their chests ripped open. I see their hearts, inside of them, beating, and I rip them out and I eat them. And when I'm awake, and I see them, and I think about how their hearts taste. How good it feels to open their throats and taste their blood on my lips."

Donner got to his feet, took a step back.

"I'm going crazy," Chin said as he rose, pushing himself off the bed with his stick-like arms, tears streaming down his hollowed cheeks. "I'm losing my fucking mind."

Donner knew then that he'd made a mistake. He shouldn't have come here. McGrath had warned him not to, but he did it anyway.

"I should go," he said. "I'm sorry I disturbed you."

Chin took a step toward him and sniffed. Like a dog sniffs an outstretched hand.

"I'm hungry," he said.

Donner took another step back. And another.

"So fucking hungry."

"I should—"

Chin moved so fast, Donner had no time to react. The force of it pushed the air out of his lungs as his back hit the wall hard, Chin's hands grasping the lapels of his coat, pinning him there. Donner grabbed his wrists, tried to prize them away, but Chin was too strong. Chin sniffed at the air between them, and his tongue appeared from between his lips, wetting them. He brought his mouth close, so close Donner felt his hot breath on his throat. Donner's right hand went for his holster before he remembered he no longer carried a weapon, that it had been taken from him.

"Don't," he said. "Please don't."

Chin's mouth opened wide. Donner saw his lips pull back over his gums.

"Don't."

The door opened, light spilling in, a shaft of it slashing across them both. Chin released him and stepped back, shielding his eyes as he retreated to the bed. Donner's knees weakened, and he would have spilled to the floor had it not been for the wall.

"What's happening in here?" Mrs. Chin demanded. "What's going on?"

Donner forced himself to take one more look at Chin, sitting on the floor by the bed, his hands clinging to the blankets. His face contorted by the agony of his hunger. Donner pushed himself away from the wall, staggered toward the door, ignoring Mrs. Chin's insistence that he explain himself. She shouted after him as he descended the stairs.

"I called the field office. They said you're suspended."

He blotted out the sound of her voice as he reached the front door. The boy and the grandmother stood in the kitchen doorway, watching him, fear in their eyes.

"You shouldn't be here," Mrs. Chin called after him. "You have no business talking to my husband about anything."

Out of the door, running down the driveway, her voice ringing out behind him.

"I'll report this, you see if I don't."

She was still shouting as he reached the rental car, her

voice finally muted as he climbed inside and started the engine. As he pulled away, he caught a glimpse of her in the rearview mirror, standing on the sidewalk, bending at the waist as she roared her fury at him.

Donner drove aimlessly, turning one corner after another, winding his way through the suburbs on the edge of Flagstaff, until he reached the forests beyond the city. He pulled over and shut off the engine. Fear pulsed through him, waves of it, great hammer blows to his chest, robbing him of air.

"Jesus," he said. "Jesus Christ."

He lost track of time as he waited for the tremors to pass. When his heart had slowed and his breathing had come under control, he drove back into the city and found a liquor store.

4 2

It was dark out when Moonflower woke. She had feasted that morning, drinking from the plastic bags. The blood had been cold, but sweet nonetheless, and her stomach had fallen quiet. When she'd eaten, Mom had brought her to a room with a pair of metal frame beds, thin mattresses on latticed springs. The kind of bed you'd see in an army barracks. It wasn't until she saw the pillows and the blankets that she realized how weary she'd grown. She crawled into the nearest one and fell into a deep, dark pit of merciful, dreamless sleep.

Moonflower didn't know what time it was. She'd never had a good sense of time. For her, it was either day or night, the hours and minutes didn't matter a great deal. Mom still snored softly in the other bed, and Moonflower rose as quietly as she could so as not to disturb her. Mom needed her sleep. Moonflower could go days without, and often did, but Mom was different.

She let herself out of the room, stepped into the corridor,

and followed it to the living room. There, against the wall opposite the television, stood a table with a laptop computer on it. She went to it and pressed a key. The screen came to life, along with a box that asked for a password. Pity. She would have liked to go on the internet. She hadn't done it regularly since before she changed, and she knew there were all sorts of things out there. Ways you could talk to people all over the world. It said so in the magazines Mom bought. She left the computer, went to the corridor, and looked into the kitchen. Nothing of interest there. She went back to the living room and its couch.

The TV sat quiet and dark in the corner. Moonflower rarely got to see a television. Only when they had more money than usual, and Mom would treat them to a night in a cheap motel where she could shower or have a bath while Moonflower watched cartoons or old comedy shows.

She found the remote control and switched it on. Sitting down on the couch, she clicked through the channels. It didn't take long to find a rerun of that show Mom had liked so much. The one with the six pretty young people living in New York. Mom insisted that she hadn't named her after one of the characters—Monica—but Moonflower didn't believe her. The TV Monica had black hair, just like hers. Maybe a coincidence, but she doubted it. The episode had just started, and the characters were all hanging around the apartment, waiting to get ready to go out somewhere. Moonflower remembered this one; she liked when one of the boys put on all the other's clothes.

During the first commercial break, she heard the rattle and clunk of locks being opened. The noise sparked a small fear in her and she stared at the living room doorway and the door beyond that opened onto the yard. She heard breathless huffing as the door opened, whispered curses. Guthrie appeared there, surprise on his face at seeing Moonflower looking back. He wore his nurse's uniform, a jacket over his greens, and carried two plastic shopping bags.

"Dogs," he said. "Goddamn dogs in my yard."

He cursed again and pushed the door closed, leaning his back against it. Moonflower heard a chorus of barks from outside. It crossed her mind to ask him to let them in, but she knew he wouldn't. He dropped his bags to the floor and fastened the locks.

That done, he leaned into the room and nodded at the TV. "*Friends*, huh?"

The commercials had ended, and the show restarted. Moonflower scrabbled all around the couch for the remote she'd held only minutes before.

"It's okay," he said. "You don't have to turn it off. Watch it if you want."

Guthrie picked up the bags and went to the kitchen. Moonflower heard the rustling of plastic, then the clunk of a small door followed by electronic beeps, and finally a whirr. By the time he returned to the room, another commercial break had started. He carried a plastic bowl along with a fork, and a can of Budweiser. She smelled meat and rice, peppers and onions. It soured her stomach, and she tried to hold her hand over her nose without appearing to do so. He sat down beside her as the commercial break ended.

"Oh, yeah," Guthrie said as he stirred his food. "This is a good one."

They watched the show in silence, punctuated by Guthrie's chuckles. Moonflower fought the urge to get up and leave. She had no desire to appear rude, but she was not accustomed to being in anyone's company but her mother's. He did not speak until he had swallowed the last of his meal.

"You and your mom, you can't stay here much longer. Tomorrow at the latest."

Moonflower didn't reply. She kept her gaze on the television.

"I want to help," he continued, "but you two have too much heat on you. If the cops or the feds find you here, I'm in a world of hurt. If I'm locked up, then I can't help anybody."

Moonflower searched for something to say, if only to be courteous. When she finally found a question to ask, she realized she truly wanted to know the answer.

"Why do you help us?"

He took a sip of beer. "Hasn't your mom told you?"

Moonflower shook her head.

"My mother was like you," he said. "We lived in Tolleson, west of Phoenix. It was just me left at home. I was working at Lincoln Medical, in the emergency department. We had a lot of gun violence, lot of kids coming in with gunshot wounds. All these young guys getting shot up for no good reason. I did my best for them, saved a lot of lives. Anyway, I was living at home, I couldn't afford a place of my own. Mom worked nights at the local Sam's Club."

Guthrie's voice thickened as his eyes grew distant with memory.

"She was walking home one night, and someone

attacked her, right at the end of our block. One of our neighbors, Mr. Collings, he heard the commotion and went out with his pistol, took a shot at the attacker. He swore blind he didn't miss, he put that sonofabitch down, but whoever it was, they got up and ran off. Mr. Collings tried to get Mom to call the cops, maybe go to the hospital, but she said she was okay, she wasn't badly hurt, said I could look after her, me being a nurse and all. He walked her the rest of the way home and told me what had happened.

"She had a bite mark on her neck, just bad enough to draw a little blood. There was more of the attacker's blood on her than her own. I think that's how it spreads. It's not enough to get bitten, otherwise there'd be more like you. I think some of their blood has to get into yours to infect it, whether it's through a cut or into your mouth, whatever.

"Anyway, I wanted her to go to the emergency room, get it checked out, but she wouldn't listen to me. A few days go by, and the bite mark heals, along with all the other cuts and bruises she picked up. But she's sick. She doesn't like sunlight, says it gives her a headache, so she's living with the drapes closed. She's always hungry but she can't eat anything more than a few mouthfuls without puking it back up. Took a while to figure out what was wrong with her. It wasn't till I came home after a night shift and found her sitting on the kitchen floor, gnawing on our neighbor's cat's throat. Damn thing was still alive, thrashing around, scratching at her."

He mimed grappling with the cat, his hands outstretched in front of him.

"I pulled it away from her, asked her what the hell she

was doing, and she's sitting there on the floor, crying her heart out, telling me she's hungry, she's so hungry. And you know what I did? I kept hold of that cat, got a bowl from the cupboard and a knife from the drawer, and I cut its throat open. I drained every last drop I could out of it just so my Mom could eat something. Then I cleaned up and put her to bed.

"So, we knew then what it was, even if we couldn't really believe it. I did my best for her, found whatever animals I could, I even bought rabbits from the pet store. But it wasn't enough. Animal blood, it'll ease things for a little while, but it's not what you need. You need blood like your own. Thing is, my mom, she couldn't bring herself to hurt a person. She just wouldn't do it. So, I watched her starve to death. Took three months. She died in so much pain, like her own body was eating her alive. And she changed. Whatever was inside of her had taken control, and I had to lock her in our basement, chained to the wall. Lucky we had no neighbors close enough to hear her screaming. I told anyone who asked that she'd moved to be with her sister in Albuquerque."

His eyes glistened and welled as he spoke, and Moon-flower wondered how often he'd played it all through in his mind. How red and raw the memory.

"It took a long time for her to die. In the end, I just closed the door to the basement, and I didn't open it again till she'd been quiet for a week. I can't imagine what it was like for her. I hope she wasn't aware. I hope whatever it was inside her did the suffering for her. She didn't deserve it. She hadn't done nothing wrong. She was just in the wrong place at the wrong time. My mom died in agony rather than hurt another person. That's who she was. Anyway, that's why I help people like you. Because it's not your fault."

Guthrie drained the last of the beer and crushed the can in his right fist before tossing it onto the crate-turned-table.

"Are there many like me?" Moonflower asked.

"About a dozen that I know of right now," he said. "And there'll be twice as many I haven't come across, maybe more. I watch the news, search local newspaper websites, keep an eye on what's out there. I know the patterns to look for. Animal mutilations, people going missing. Sometimes I can make contact, sometimes I can't. Most of them don't last long. Lot of suicides. Or they get greedy, they lose control, they pick the wrong target, or they starve, or they do something stupid and get themselves killed. But a few last longer, and they're out there, just trying to survive and cause as little harm as they can. For the most part."

"For the most part?" she echoed.

"Some of them aren't good people," he said. "Most of them are like you. Never wanted to hurt nobody, they were just unlucky. But some of them aren't like you. Some of them, not many, but some, enjoy what they do. They're the ones you gotta stay away from. Them and their helpers."

"Am I one of the good ones?" Moonflower asked.

He regarded her for a moment, then gave her a shallow smile, and said, "Yeah, you are."

"What about Mom?" she asked.

The smile lingered on his lips a moment too long.

"I got some things I need to do," he said, standing and gathering the detritus of his meal.

He left her there alone with the six pretty young people on the television.

File #: 89-49911-32
Subject: Rebecca Carter
OO: Flagstaff
Desc: Journal Entry, Handwritten
Date: Unknown

I know how to do it now. I tried it and it worked. I can use the laptop computer I took from that man in Carson City. There's no limit to the email addresses I can have. I just need to delete them when I'm done. I've tried it with Myspace, and there's one called Facebook that's getting bigger every day. Then there are all the message boards and chatrooms. I just post a photograph of a girl, make up some things about her, her age, her location, her interests. Usually, I don't even have to start the conversation.

It's so easy to tell the real boys who reply from the pretend ones. Those men, they think they're so smart, so cunning, hiding behind pictures of fourteen-year-olds. But I can spot them. The leading questions they ask about parents and friends, are you lonely, do you wish you could talk to someone who'd actually listen. The real boys don't do that. They can be as disgusting as the grown men, worse even, but they don't know how to manipulate the way the adults do.

We don't have to do it the old way anymore. Sitting in some park or food court, Moonflower on her own, me sitting close enough to watch, waiting for some creep to notice her. She can spot them better than I can. She can smell it on them. We could wait for days for one to come along, one with the guts to make an approach in a public place. Even then, if we got one to take the bait, he might sense the trap and run before we can disable him.

There's no need to do that anymore. We tried it and it worked.

His name was Walter Chesney, forty-two years old. Online, he was Barry Tucker, fifteen years old. In real life, he had a wife and three kids, and lived on the outskirts of Reno. Online, he lived with his rich parents in their home on the shore of Lake Tahoe.

He found one of our Myspace pages, the one that belonged to Christina Cattaneo, aged thirteen, who looked a little bit like my daughter. She'd posted about her parents, nothing specific, but just enough to show she wasn't happy. Barry Tucker posted a response, struck up a conversation with Christina, which soon moved to instant messenger.

I knew almost straight away what he was. Boys can be clumsy and gross, they can be inappropriate, but this was different. His questions were too specific, the questions of a man in need of something. I played along, gave him just enough line to keep him on the hook. That went on for more than a week until we agreed to meet at South Lake Tahoe Ice Arena, 7:00 P.M., Sunday.

We got there a half hour early, entering a few minutes apart. Moonflower bought a Pepsi, I got a coffee. We sat on opposite sides of the little café. We barely glanced at each other for thirty minutes, and the longer we waited, the more nervous I became. What if I'd made a mistake? What if some poor, dumb innocent kid showed up?

It was five past the hour when a man approached Moonflower's table, and I felt a wash of relief. He spoke to her briefly, then sat down. I watched as he leaned in close to her, whispering. I had a good idea of what was being said. Probably something along the lines of, I'm Barry's dad, he's waiting for you somewhere else, I'll give you a ride there. The conversation lasted a few minutes before he stood. Moonflower hesitated, glanced at me, then got to her feet and followed him toward the exit. I did the same.

Outside, in the falling dusk, I saw him open the passenger door of a red Camry for her, then close her inside. I had one moment of fearful doubt, seeing her all alone in that car. Then I remembered how strong she is, how brave, and the fear dissolved like mist on glass. I kept the Camry in sight as I went to the van, then followed them out of the parking lot. It's fall now, not quite cold enough for snow, but too cold for swimming in the lake, so there aren't many tourists around. The roads were quiet, and I had to keep my distance as he drove out of South Lake, west toward Lake Valley. I don't know the area well, but I could guess what his plan was.

Sure enough, he turned off the main road and onto one of the dirt tracks that cut through the trees toward the lakeshore. I pulled up at the point he'd turned off and watched as his Camry went deeper into the dimness. I shut off my lights and followed, just close enough to keep his rear lights in sight. There wasn't much farther he could go, so I stopped, shut off my engine, and climbed out.

I made my way through the trees, staying off the dirt track, but keeping it in view. I'd gone no more than a hundred yards before I saw his Camry, its red paintwork glowing bright in what little remaining light could force its way through the trees. I circled around behind it, came to the passenger side, and approached as quietly as I could.

He hunkered down by the open door, talking to

Moonflower in the passenger seat. As I got closer, I heard him speak, his voice warm and friendly.

"He'll be here in just a minute," the man said, "I promise. There's a little private beach just there, through the trees, and he'll be here in no time. Why don't you come and wait for him with me? I promise you, he'll be along in—"

He didn't know I was there until he felt the sharp edge of the hunting knife at his throat. I heard his teeth snap together as he closed his mouth.

"Stand up," I told him. "Don't turn around. Take two steps back."

I gripped the back of his collar with my free hand, kept the blade at his throat as we moved in unison away from the car. He was a tall man. Slender, but athletic. The kind of man who cycles on the weekend, goes on mountain hikes, plays tennis with his friends.

I don't know if it was some kind of precognition, but the thought had just entered my mind that with his height, he could fight me and win, so I was ready when he turned and tried to backhand me. I ducked out of the way and rammed the butt of the knife's handle into the base of his skull, just behind his right ear.

He cried out and fell to his knees. I placed my foot on his back and pushed him the rest of the way down. Sitting astride him, I grabbed a handful of his salt-and-pepper hair, pulled his head back, and let him feel the tip of the blade beneath his jawline.

I put my mouth to his ear and said, "You try that again and I'll cut your fucking eyes out."

I looked up and saw Moonflower, still in the car, staring

back. I thought she might have been frightened, but instead she seemed entirely calm, passive even.

I spoke into his ear again. "What were you planning to do with her?"

"Nothing," he said, "I swear to God. My son wanted to meet with her, he's on his way, I swear on my—"

I dragged the tip of the blade from his jaw up to his cheekbone, leaving a trail of deep red behind. I pressed the blade in, feeling the tip grind against hard bone. He screamed, a desperate high wail that echoed through the trees. I moved the tip to the corner of his eye.

"Don't lie to me again," I said, "or I'll blind you. What were you planning to do with her?"

"I don't know," he said, crying, "I don't know. I didn't plan ahead."

"You'd have hurt her, wouldn't you?"

"I don't know, I—"

I shoved the tip of the blade up his right nostril. He screamed again.

"You would've hurt her, wouldn't you?"

"Yes," he said, tearful now, snot mixing with the trickle of blood from his nose. "Yes, I would've hurt her."

"You would've killed her and left her body out here, wouldn't you?"

"Yes," he said.

I forced his face down into the dirt and kneeled on the back of his neck. I reached behind and pulled the wallet from the rear pocket of his jeans. As he cried and whimpered, the sound muffled by the dirt, I opened it and went through the contents. Almost two hundred dollars in cash, a Bank of America debit card, a Mastercard, and an

American Express. A photograph of him with an attractive woman, along with a boy and two girls. His driver's license told me his real name.

"Walter Chesney," I said. "I'm going to keep this. You're going to give me the PINs for all of these cards, and if you try to cancel them within the next forty-eight hours, I will contact your wife and I will tell her what you tried to do here today."

I put the wallet into my own jeans pocket.

"Now, I'm going to let you up. If you do anything to piss me off, I'll cut you up so bad you won't be a threat to any woman or child for as long as you live. Understand?"

"Yes," he said through a mouthful of dirt.

I eased myself slowly off his back and stood, dragging him up by his collar. Blood pattered on the ground as it spilled from the open wound on his face. Moonflower looked down at it and I saw the hunger on her. She looked up at me, and I shook my head, no. Not this man, not today, not here. There was more planning to do. This was just a trial run.

I told him to put his hands behind his head and walked him to the back of the car. I made him face away and get to his knees while I opened the trunk to see if he had anything else worth taking.

Something cold spread inside of me when I saw what was in there, like I'd swallowed ice water. The trunk was lined with black plastic sheeting, taped up on all sides to form a seal. In the center, a box of surgical gloves, a knife, a small semiautomatic pistol, and a bundle of cable ties. He looked over his shoulder, his hands still behind his head, and saw what I saw. I know what went through his mind then: he wondered if he could reach the gun before I could stop him. His strength and height and speed versus my blade. But I felt a rage so hot explode in me that nothing in the whole wide world could have stopped me.

He spun as I lunged, his hand up, and my blade went through the palm of his hand and pinned it to his chest, blocked by his sternum. He cried out as I tried to pull the blade back. It wouldn't come free, so I balled my left hand into a fist and punched him hard on the nose, feeling it crunch beneath my knuckles. I ignored the pain that flared in my hand and yanked the blade from his chest and hand. He gurgled as he fell, landing on his side, blinking, unseeing.

The anger in me burned all the brighter, so I kicked him in the gut with all the strength my body could muster, and he gave a wheezing moan. I did it again and again, his stomach, his chest, his throat, and then his jaw, feeling it give under the force of my boot. I would have gone on, I would have kicked him to death, if it weren't for Moonflower's voice behind me.

"Mom, stop."

I did as she said, adrenaline roaring through my body, my lungs hauling at the air. Walter Chesney lay at my feet, half conscious, moaning as blood flowed from his ruined face. I screamed my rage at him, doubling over with the power of it.

Then I used my boot to roll him over onto his back. He blinked at the sky, and I wonder now what he saw there. It doesn't matter. Whether heaven exists or not, he will never see it. I knelt down beside him and beckoned Moonflower over. I saw her eyes brighten, almost glowing with her hunger.

I opened his throat, the sharp blade severing meat and gristle, and let her feed.

While she gorged herself, I gathered whatever was of use from his car. We left his body there, but first I used the knife to sever his spinal cord at the neck. I learned that early on. The only way to be absolutely sure they stay dead. Their hearts can't start to beat again, their lungs can't draw air, if the brain can't command it. And the brain can't live without blood and oxygen. The circuit, broken. Simple, really.

We returned to the van, both of us spattered in his blood. I drove through the night and into the morning until exhaustion said I could go no farther. It was stupid, leaving him there like that. I hadn't intended to do it. It was supposed to be a dry run, that was all. But he showed me who he was, and the rage took over. As I drove, I wondered how many he had taken before. I thought about the girls in the photograph, his daughters, and wondered if they had suffered under his care. I told myself I had spared them and others his cruelty.

He showed me who was. He showed me who I am.

I killed a predator named Walter Chesney and I'm glad I did it.

4 3

It was still dark out when Rebecca woke. After a moment of disorientation, she remembered where she was. The home of Guthrie Chambers. The Nurse. She couldn't recall how many times they'd taken shelter here before, perhaps half a dozen, but every time had been a test. Guthrie had taken a dislike to her from the start. She knew he only allowed them sanctuary for Moonflower's sake.

Rebecca looked to the other bed, saw it empty. She heard the hollow voice of the television in the next room and knew where her daughter was. Her back and shoulders complained as she sat upright; the endless days of driving had tied her muscles in knots. She got to her feet and ran through her routine of stretching exercises, feeling the muscles loosen. That done, she walked through the corridor to the living room. Moonflower was too wrapped up in a rerun of *Frasier* to notice her. Rebecca found Guthrie in the kitchen, sitting at the plastic table, typing on his laptop.

"You got anything to eat?" she asked.

He gave her a baleful look. "Most folks come here, they have the manners to bring their own food, and usually a little money along with it. I'll feed your daughter, but I don't have to feed you."

She went to the cupboard over the sink and opened it.

"Hey, don't . . . goddammit."

An open bag of chips and a box of Ritz crackers. She lifted them down, filled a glass from the faucet, and brought them all to the table.

"I don't know why I opened my door to you," Guthrie said, shaking his head.

"Because you're a decent man."

She brought a handful of chips to her mouth. Stale, but she ate them anyway. She washed the salt from her tongue with a glug of water.

"Why do you hate me?"

He returned his attention to the laptop's screen and said, "I don't hate you. I just don't like you much."

"Why?"

He closed the laptop and sat back, his gaze fixed on her.

"Because you're hard." He looked away, into the distance, then back at her. "No, that's not it. You've got something missing in you. People like your daughter, they can't survive without someone to look out for them, someone to keep them from hurting themselves. And most of them do it out of love."

"What, I don't?"

"I know you love your little girl, and you'd do anything for her, including killing a person. All of you folks do. Difference is, I think deep down, way down where you can keep it hidden even from yourself, I think you enjoy it."

"Fuck you," Rebecca said.

Guthrie gave a dry laugh. "Yeah, right, fuck me."

"It's not true. I do it because I have to, to keep my daughter alive. That's all that matters to me. Besides, they deserve it."

"All of them? Every single last one of them?"

"All of them," she said without hesitation. No need to think about it; she'd already lost countless hours of sleep with each choice to kill.

"And you're sure of that?"

"Yes, I am. But I take no pleasure in it."

"You're telling me, when some guy takes the bait, when you catch him on your hook, you don't get just a little bit of a thrill from that?"

"No."

"What about when he shows up at the rendezvous?"

"Stop it."

"And when you cut his throat, what about then? Nothing?"

"Nothing."

"I don't believe you."

"I don't care what you believe."

"Fair enough. When are you leaving? Real soon, I hope."

"Another two, three days."

"Shit. Come on, why? Your daughter ate her fill, you got a bed for a night. You can use my shower if you need it. What more do you want from me?"

"I just need a little time to line something up."

"Oh, I see. You want to reel in another fish. Got it. And you won't take any pleasure from this one either, will you?"

"No, I won't. Can I use your laptop?"

He stared at her a full five seconds before standing and pushing the closed computer toward her. "Just make sure you use the VPN. I don't need your shit getting traced back to me. I'm going to bed."

Rebecca watched him leave, then opened the laptop, quite certain she didn't feel the small sparkling thrill of beginning the hunt. She used the NordVPN app to connect through a server in the Netherlands before opening the browser. Then, out of habit, she googled her own name in case she'd been mentioned in any news stories. She was presented with the same list of links she'd seen on her phone over recent days, all reports on what had happened in Flagstaff. But here was something new, right at the top.

"Shit," Rebecca said.

The link was to the FBI's Most Wanted page. She clicked on it, trusting the VPN to stop them from tracing her back to this laptop. There, near the top of the page, the mugshot they'd taken in Flagstaff. Hair unkempt, dark rings beneath her eyes. Below, in smaller thumbnails, older photos, family snaps, smiles glowing from them. Rebecca ached at the sight of who she used to be.

It took an effort to drag her eyes away from the images and read the text. When she did, she felt the ache inside turn to something colder, something darker.

Two hundred thousand dollars.

"My God," she said.

44

Donner was retching into the cheap motel room's toilet when his phone rang. The day before, he had bought a bottle of scotch and a six-pack of Fat Tire and driven around the city before he returned to this place. He paid for one more night in advance, locked the door, started drinking, and didn't stop until he passed out in a chair in the corner.

At some point in the early hours of the morning, while it was still dark, he opened his eyes, lifted his head from the back of the chair, and saw Special Agent Edward Chin standing over him, dressing gown and pajamas hanging loose on his wasted body.

I'm hungry, Chin said.

Donner couldn't move, his arms and legs locked into position, while Chin climbed over him, snapping teeth seeking flesh. He wanted to scream, but his voice remained trapped in his throat no matter how hard he tried to force it out. Chin took hold of his hair, pulled his head back, exposing his throat. Sniffing, tongue wetting his lips, Chin brought his mouth down close to the skin, so close Donner could feel his lips and the teeth behind them. Then the hard pain as the teeth took hold, coming together, and now Donner needed to scream but he couldn't, and the teeth sank deeper and deeper and—

Donner fell back into the world, carried on a sickly wave of nausea, spilling from the chair to sprawl on the cheap carpet. He swung his arms and kicked at the air, before crawling away across the room. When he reached the corner, he turned his head to see nothing. Nothing at all, except the chair, the bed, the table with empty bottles. The map on the wall with its crisscrossing red lines. Then his bile rose, and he scrambled to the bathroom, not quite making it.

The following hours had passed in much the same fashion, straddling the swampy boundary between sleep and waking, lurching from ugly dream to lurid reality, occasionally crawling to the bathroom to void his stomach.

The muscles of his abdomen cramped with the effort of it, and he groaned as the phone chimed from the table in the bedroom. He hauled himself to his feet and staggered over there, arms outstretched for balance. His heart leapt when he saw Liz's name on the display. He coughed, spat onto the carpet, wiped his mouth clean, and answered.

"Hey," he said. "I've been trying to—"

"Marc, don't talk, just listen."

He blinked as the room came in and out of focus. "Okay," he said.

"Those messages you left last night," she said.

"Messages? I don't—"

"Just listen. Please."

He swallowed and said, "Okay."

"I know you were drunk, but those things you said. I can't get past that. You can't say things like—"

"Wait, what? What did—?"

"Shut up and listen."

Her voice was hard enough to distort in the earpiece. He closed his mouth.

"You can't say those things to me. Not ever. I want you to stop calling. If you don't, I'll get a lawyer involved, get a restraining order or whatever it is I have to do to make you stop. And if I have to do that, you will not see your children again. Never. Do you understand?"

Donner walked to the bed and slumped down onto it, one hand covering his eyes, the other holding the phone to his ear.

"I understand," he said.

"Okay. Goodbye, Marc."

She hung up, and Donner threw the phone across the room.

"Goddammit," he said. "God-fucking-dammit."

He hammered his fists against his forehead and whispered, what did you do, what did you do?

Before he could search through the murk of his dulled memory, the phone rang again. He stared at it, the display glowing bright through cracked glass at the other side of the room. Whoever the call was from, he knew things were going to get worse. Donner cursed and got to his feet, swaying for a moment before he found an uneasy balance. He retrieved the phone, saw McGrath's photo, milkshake on her lip, her finger raised.

She would know about yesterday. She would know he went to Chin's home even though she'd begged him not to. He considered ignoring the call, but he knew she would not stop until she got ahold of him. Donner lifted the phone and thumbed the green icon. He said nothing, listened to her breathing at the other end.

Eventually she said, "You piece of shit."

"I'm sorry," he said, meaning it. "I had to talk to him."

"I told you not to," she said. "I begged you, Marc, and you fucking did it anyway."

"I'm sorry," he said again.

"What the fuck did you say to him?"

"Nothing. I was only there for a few minutes. I just asked him some questions, but he . . . he was unwell."

Donner pictured Chin's hollow face, his bared teeth.

"Unwell," she echoed. "I just hope to God it was worth it, Marc."

He felt a cold finger on his spine.

"What? What happened?"

She took a breath and said, "Not long before midnight last night, Special Agent Edward Chin placed the muzzle of his privately owned Smith & Wesson revolver in his mouth and put a .38 bullet through his brain-pan."

Donner leaned against the wall.

"Oh, Jesus," he said. "Oh, fuck."

"You sonofabitch," McGrath said, her voice trembling, "they're going to destroy you. They're going to rip you to pieces, and you know what? You'll deserve it."

"Oh God, I never meant for—"

"I don't give a shit what you meant to happen or what you didn't. You're finished, Marc, you're done, and it's your own damn fault. Don't call me again, don't ask me for any favors, don't come anywhere near me, do you understand? You're on your own, Marc. Goodbye."

She hung up, and the phone slipped from his fingers. His back slid down the wall until he curled on the floor, his face in his hands.

He would have wept, but there was nothing left inside of him.

4 5

Moonflower watched television through the night, flicking from one channel to the next. Old comedies, nature documentaries, detective shows. At one point she stumbled upon a black and white movie about a bachelor in New York, a butcher by trade, who lived with his Italian mother while seeking a woman to love. Mom came into the room not long after it started, and she joined Moonflower on the worn couch. Moonflower rested her head on her shoulder, and Mom put an arm around her. She said the lead actor's name was Ernest something. The movie was sad and funny and sweet, and they watched it together right to the end.

After it was over, Moonflower asked, "When are we going to Mexico?"

"Not for a little while," Mom said. "It's too risky to try to cross the border now. There are people looking for us, and they've offered a big reward."

"Will Guthrie let us stay here?"

"I'm not giving him a choice."

Mom stood and went to the corridor. Moonflower switched off the television and followed her to the kitchen, finding her at the table, the glow of the laptop's screen reflected on her face.

"Are we looking again?" Moonflower asked.

"I'm just seeing what's out there. What about this one?"

Mom showed her an online profile. A boy just turned fifteen. Good looking, dark hair, only a few pimples.

"Are you sure it's fake?"

"Yeah," Mom said. "We've been messaging for a few days now. He has all the tells. Says he's in Sierra Vista, about eighty miles southeast of here, not far from the border. Says his dad's in the military, stationed at the base there. Maybe we could arrange a meet somewhere between here and there."

As if on cue, Moonflower felt the first stirrings of hunger in her stomach. It gave a low growl, and Mom turned her head.

"You couldn't be hungry again already," she said. "It's only been a day."

Moonflower put her hand to her belly and said, "I can't help it."

She felt the sickly weight of guilt, followed by a flash of anger at her mother for putting it there. It faded as quickly as it had flared.

"I'll talk to Guthrie, see if he'll give you some more. Maybe get some rest in the meantime."

The world beyond the paper-lined window had begun to lighten, turning from dark blue to milky gray, and Moonflower's head felt heavy with fatigue. Yesterday had been the first real sleep she'd had in days.

"Okay," she said, and leaned in to hug her mother.

Mom returned the embrace and kissed her cheek. Moonflower went to the bedroom they'd shared the night before and crawled into the bed, pulling the thin blankets up to her chin. She closed her eyes and wished for sleep to come.

When it did, she dreamt of dogs running through the trees, carrying her on their backs, howling and singing, the taste of warm, fresh blood on all their tongues.

File #: 89-49911-46
Subject: Rebecca Carter
OO: Flagstaff
Desc: Journal Entry, Handwritten
Date: Unknown

Something strange happened last night. I don't know if it's good or bad. I'm sitting in a man's home as I write this, and I don't know how to feel about it. I am not going to write his name, or the location, because I expect one day for these pages to fall into the hands of the authorities, and I have no wish to lead them to this man. The reason I have kept a journal all these years, and catalogued all these deaths, is that I want the authorities to know why I targeted those particular people. Their deaths were not undeserved.

This man, the one I'm writing about today, hasn't harmed anyone that I'm aware of. I'll call him the Nurse because that's his profession, and that's all the personal detail I'll give.

Moonflower and I were at a McDonald's. She was at the outside seating, I was inside, watching. We were waiting for our target to arrive. His online profile said he was Joshua, fourteen. I didn't know what to expect in reality, but by that point, he was fifteen minutes late. I was about to get up and signal to Moonflower that we should leave when a heavyset man dropped into the seat opposite me.

"Hey," he said.

I didn't reply. Moonflower watched from outside, worry on her face. I shook my head at her, told her it was no problem.

"Do I know you?" I asked.

"No," he said, "but I think I might know you."

I stood, ready to head for the exit.

"Go if you want," he said. "I won't follow you. But if you give me a minute of your time, maybe I can help you."

I hovered there, uncertain.

"Who are you? What makes you think I need your help?"

"You arranged to meet a kid named Joshua here, right?"

"I don't know what—"

"Except you knew there was no Joshua, just like I knew there was no Amelia."

"I need to go," I said, heading once more for the exit.

He called after me. "She's hungry, isn't she?"

I stopped and looked back at him, but I kept my mouth shut.

"I can help with that, for a start," he said.

"For a start?"

"You really think she's the only one?" he asked.

I hesitated, then I returned to the table and sat. Moon-flower stood outside the window, staring in. I motioned to her to sit down, and she did so.

"Talk," I said.

"There are others. Not many, but they're out there. I've been watching you for a year now. Moving place to place, leaving a trail behind you. Animal mutilations, first of all. Then a week or two later, a man shows up dead, his throat cut. Usually with some kind of record, grooming, child pornography, that kind of thing. A clear and simple pattern, time after time. You really ought to be more careful. Look how easy I found you. Only reason the cops or the feds haven't caught up with you, is they don't understand what she is."

He pointed out the window at Moonflower.

I tried to give him a hard stare. "And what exactly is that?"

He didn't answer my question.

"You've been lucky so far, but it's only a matter of time. The way you find your targets? That's real smart. But what you do with them after? That ain't so clever. Just dumping them where they can be found, right next to where you took them. I'm honestly surprised you made it this far."

"I don't know what you're talking about."

He smiled and said, "Course not."

"Last chance," I said. "Tell me what you want, or I get up and leave."

"To help," he said. "That's all."

"How?"

"I'm a nurse on a trauma ward. I have access to donated blood. Once it passes its expiry, it has to be disposed of. Usually incinerated. A few pints might find their way into my refrigerator. No one has to get hurt. You and your . . . your daughter, I assume? You don't have to cut open anyone's throat. No harm, no risk."

I looked out the window, saw Moonflower staring back at me, her face hollow with hunger. He followed my gaze.

"She needs it, doesn't she?"

"Leave her alone," I said.

"You can think of it as hunger, most do, but it's not that. Not really. That thing inside of her, if it isn't fed, then it'll eat her instead. It'll devour her from the inside out. It'll keep eating her until there's nothing left of your daughter."

"Shut your goddamn mouth."

The Nurse reached into his pocket and produced a stubby pencil and a small notepad. He scribbled on the top page.

"Doesn't have to be this way. I can't cure her, I can't drive that thing out of her. But I can get her fed for now, and I can show you how to manage her. How to keep her alive. That's what you want, isn't it? To keep her alive?"

"Yes," I said.

More than anything, I didn't say.

He tore off the top page of the notepad and slid it across the table to me. An address.

"You come see me at eight in the morning. I'll be off my shift by then. I'll have what she needs."

The Nurse stood and left the table, walked to the exit. He didn't so much as glance at Moonflower as he passed. Neither did I as I walked back to my van. She joined me there a few minutes later, climbing into the passenger seat as I started the engine.

"Who was that man?" she asked. "Wasn't he the one we wanted?"

"No, honey," I said. "Just some random weirdo who sat down and started talking to me."

"What do we do now?"

"We start again," I said. "Find a new prospect."

Moonflower's stomach growled, then, and I remembered what he said. The thing inside her, devouring her with its hunger. I pulled the piece of paper from the pocket of my hoodie and read the address. A two-hour drive.

I wondered again what he wanted from us. Everybody wants something.

4 6

It was past noon before Guthrie entered the kitchen, rubbing his eyes and yawning. He wore a dressing gown over an undershirt and boxers, slippers on his feet. Rebecca waited for him at the table. She had been awake since the early hours, and her own eyes felt dry and heavy.

As he passed her on the way to the sink, he said, "You still here?"

"Moonflower needs more."

He fetched a glass from the cupboard and filled it from the faucet. "Already?" he asked.

He tried to hide the concern in his voice, but Rebecca felt it. She considered lying to him, but realized there was no point. Even so, it grated on her to tell him the truth.

"The time between feeds is getting shorter," she said. "She's getting hungrier. It was only four pints yesterday. So, yes, already."

Guthrie emptied half the glass in one swallow, cursed,

and set it down on the draining board. He went to the freezer, opened it, and rummaged through the contents.

"I don't have much left, maybe two, three pints. Like I told you, the thing inside her is greedy. You can't hold it off forever."

He pulled three plastic pouches from the freezer and dropped them in the sink before turning the cold faucet. Water thundered against metal.

"That's all I got. She can have them when they're thawed, then I want you gone."

"We need to stay a few more days."

"You don't seem to get it," he said, turning from the sink. "I'm not asking you to go, I'm telling you."

"It's too dangerous for us to go anywhere."

"And it's too dangerous for you to stay."

She took a breath and said, "I'm not giving you a choice. We're staying."

"I see," he said, folding his thick arms across his barrel chest. "You cleared the browser history on my laptop, but I keep a key logger running on it. I saw what you were searching for, what you were looking at. Two hundred grand. Why don't I just hand you over to the feds? Hell of a payday for one phone call, and I'll be rid of you for good."

Rebecca's rage climbed up inside her chest. She forced it back down. Anger would do her no good now.

"Because I'd kill you if you tried," she said.

He smiled a razor-thin smile. "Ah, there it is. Your true nature."

"Yeah, I guess so," she said, standing. "I'm going to get some—"

He turned and opened the cupboard beneath the sink,

grabbed something long and black, and aimed it at her chest. An AR-15 rifle.

"I want you out of here right now," he said. "You can take that blood for the road, but you and your girl are going."

Rebecca placed her hands on the plastic table and said, "We can't do that."

He chuckled and said, "I'm not giving you a choice."

"Go on, then," she said, her gaze fixed on his. "Shoot."

The smile faded a little. "Don't push me."

"You don't have it in you," she said. "You don't have the nerve."

He laughed then and shook his head. "You honestly think it's never come to this before? I've been doing this for nearly twenty years. In all that time, do you really think I've never had to pull a trigger?"

Rebecca felt the smile fall from her mouth. She had no answer, but she didn't move.

Guthrie sighted down the rifle at the center of her chest.

"Do it," she said. "See what happens."

He flicked off the safety with a metallic click. Rebecca's heart fluttered in her chest, but she remained still. Sweat beaded on his brow.

"I'm going to count to ten," he said, his voice quivering low in his throat. "If you aren't gathering your shit by the time I get there, I will—"

"Don't point that at my mom," Moonflower said from the kitchen doorway.

Guthrie's eyelids flickered. He wetted his lips.

"We're just talking, sweetheart," Guthrie said. "Ain't nothing for you to worry about."

Moonflower stepped around Rebecca, stood in front of her.

"I said, don't point that at my mom."

Guthrie forced a smile but couldn't hold it. "Honey, I need you to go on out of here and get your things. Can you do that for me?"

"No," Moonflower said.

"Nobody needs to get hurt. I just want you out of here. That's all."

"Put it down," Moonflower said, taking one step toward him.

It crossed Rebecca's mind to put a hand on her shoulder and bring her close, but she decided against it. Guthrie moved his aim to Moonflower for a moment, and going by the shift in his expression, he knew he'd made a mistake.

"You heard her," Rebecca said. "Put the rifle down."

"I can't do that," Guthrie said, his voice trembling now.

"She won't ask again," Rebecca said.

"Come on, now," Guthrie said, an uncertain smile returning to his lips. "Let's just deescalate a little here, okay? You need to stay a little longer? Okay, let's talk about that."

"No more talking," Rebecca said. "You pointed that gun at me. I can't trust you anymore."

"Fine. Then get the hell out. I don't want to shoot you, either of you, but I—"

Moonflower moved so fast, Rebecca was barely conscious of it before her daughter slammed into his body, forcing his arms upward, lifting him off his feet. The rifle's muzzle flashed, and Rebecca felt the air around her flex and move with the pressure. Something tore past her ear and impacted the wall by the door. Without thinking she dropped to the floor and rolled away.

The rifle discharged twice more, one bullet blowing a hole through the table, the other hitting the ceiling, shattering a suspended tile into pieces. Through the ringing in her ears, she heard Guthrie grunt with effort as Moonflower wrestled him to the ground. Then a splintering, cracking sound, followed by his desperate scream of pain. The rifle clattered to the linoleum-covered floor, and Rebecca crawled toward it. As she came close, she saw the burst of white through red on Guthrie's forearm, the bone glinting wetly in the artificial light.

She grabbed the rifle's hot, smoking barrel and pulled it toward herself. Raising the butt to her shoulder, she took aim as he writhed beneath her daughter.

"Baby, get off him," Rebecca said.

Moonflower became still, her gaze fixed on the bloody torn flesh of his arm.

"I'm hungry," she said.

"I know, baby, and I have something for you."

"Is it cold or hot?"

"It'll be cold, same as before, but it'll give you what you need."

"I could just take what I need, right now."

"No," Rebecca said. "This isn't the way."

Guthrie had become still, his skin turned gray. In shock, Rebecca thought. Moonflower looked back over her shoulder.

"He would've killed you," she said.

"Maybe. Doesn't matter. Let him be."

"Why?" Moonflower asked.

"Because he doesn't deserve it."

Moonflower's voice hardened. "Why do you get to decide who deserves it and who doesn't?"

"Because I'm your mother."

"What if *I* think he deserves it? If he shot you, what would he have done with me?"

"Baby, that's enough. Get off of him."

"What would he have done with me?"

"Monica, listen to your mother."

Moonflower stared hard at her for an age, then leaned down and screamed into his graying face. She climbed up onto her feet. Rebecca extended her left hand, beckoned her daughter to come to her side. Moonflower ignored her and remained by Guthrie, glaring down at him.

Guthrie's mind seemed to return from wherever it had been, and he looked from Rebecca to Moonflower and back again. He went to move and cried out at the pain it caused in his broken arm. When the wave of agony had passed, he spoke to Rebecca.

"If you stay here, I'll find a way to turn you in. So, you have a choice: either shoot me or leave."

Rebecca's finger tightened on the trigger. Just a little more pressure and it'd be done.

"One or the other," Guthrie said. "Make your choice."

She pictured the rifle bucking in her hands, the flare of the discharge, the bullet piercing the space between his eyes.

Deep down, you enjoy it, he'd said.

But he was wrong. She was sure of it.

"Goddammit," she said, lowering the rifle. "Moon-flower, get your things."

47

Donner had set off from Flagstaff at eleven in the morning, heading for Tucson. He'd prebooked a motel on the northern side of the city and planned out his route. Even if he stopped to eat, he'd be there by early evening.

He had tried to call McGrath twice the day before, and once this morning. No answer. He didn't blame her any more than he blamed Liz for freezing him out. Truth was, he had fucked up. He had taken a can of gasoline to his own life and burned it all down.

But that wasn't entirely true, was it?

He hadn't destroyed it all by himself, had he? All this devastation began with a beast dressed as a child, and it would end with her. He was close now. He could feel it in his bones. If everything worked out as he had planned, he would have saved himself by this time tomorrow. Either that or he'd be dead. One of the two, and really, he was beyond caring which.

She had taken the bait. The profile he'd created a week ago. A stolen photograph, a fictional teenage boy with a fictional life, chatting online with an equally fictional girl. He was certain it was her. She had all the same tells. Hers was exactly the kind of online existence he had created many times over to lure in the kind of men she targeted. Except, he would put them in jail rather than rip out their throats, no matter how much he might have wanted to. It was almost too easy.

He arrived at the motel in Tucson at twenty minutes after five, checked in, and went to the miserable little room he'd booked. When the clerk had swiped his Visa, he had held his breath, unsure if he was already at his limit.

In the room, he checked his phone for messages. One from the pretend-girl's profile:

I'll be at Santa Rita Skate Park later. Wanna meet up?

He replied: *Sure, what time?*

Fifteen minutes passed before his phone chimed with a response: *How about 7:30?*

He thumbed out his agreement: *Great, c u there.*

Donner added a string of emojis and hit send.

Nothing to do now but wait. He lay down on the bed and thought about the unopened bottle of scotch in his bag. It would remain closed until it was done, no matter how thirsty he was. He set an alarm on his phone to stir him to move in an hour and ten minutes. Sleep would not come, so he lay still and imagined the pleasing burn of whisky in his throat.

He arrived at the skate park twenty minutes early. It would have been earlier, but he'd taken a wrong turn along the way and had to retrace his route. He parked the rental car in the small strip of a lot adjacent to the park and scanned the area. The park was illuminated by artificial light, showing the parched grass in a yellowy green. A bunch of teenagers in the skate park, some of them using the three concrete bowls, most of them just hanging out. Some younger kids were using the basketball court, and a group of men messed around in the largest of the three softball fields, taking turns to pitch or hit.

No sign of a lone girl, or her mother.

After ten minutes had passed, Donner got out of the car. He wore sweats and a hoodie, hoping to appear like he was out for a run. A scattering of trees surrounded the area. He moved between them, just a man out for an evening jog. It took another five minutes to make a circle around the park, pausing now and then to take in the scenery. Nobody paid him any attention.

Donner rounded the skate park once, jogging at an even pace, studying the kids gathered there. All of them with boards, most of them with safety gear. No girl waiting to meet a stranger. He widened his search, keeping watch for Rebecca Carter. Nothing.

He stopped in the fenced channel between the skate park and the largest softball field. The men who'd been playing there had ended their game and were making their way around the field's boundary fence, presumably heading to the parking lot. Donner turned in a circle, looking, searching. He checked his watch. Seven thirty-five. Maybe he'd been wrong. Maybe the girl was genuine.

No, couldn't be, he told himself.

Maybe they'd spotted him coming and fled. Yes, that was more likely.

"Goddammit," he whispered to himself.

"Hey," a man's voice called.

Donner turned toward it. One of the men who'd been in the softball field, shaved head, broad shoulders, a bat in his right hand. Two others followed. There had been five of them altogether. Where were the other two? One of the men produced a cell phone from his pocket and began filming.

"You looking for someone?" the first man asked as he came near.

Donner's nerve endings jangled, his skin prickling. "Just out for a run," he said, taking a step back.

"Yeah? I thought maybe you'd come here to meet someone."

Donner knew then what was happening, that he'd made a mistake.

"No," he said. "Like I said, just out—"

"Hey, is your name Cory?"

"No, you got me mixed up with someone else."

He turned to go but saw the other two men approaching from the other end of the fenced channel.

"I think maybe you sometimes call yourself Cory," the man said, close now. "When you're online, I mean. And I think maybe you were here to meet a girl named Melissa. Am I right?"

The man with the bat was within swinging distance now.

"I don't know what you're talking about," Donner said. Then he lowered his tone, looked the man hard in the eye. "My name is Marc Donner. Special Agent Marc Donner. I'm with the FBI, based out of DC. Now I suggest you and your friends back the fuck up."

Some of the men exchanged glances. He'd rattled them. But not the leader.

"All right, FBI man, show me some ID."

"I can't do that."

"Why not?"

"Because I don't carry it when I'm jogging. Listen, whatever you think is happening here, you got it wrong."

The man smiled and brandished the bat. "You know, I don't think I do. What's happening here is a citizen's arrest. Chris, call the cops. Jerry, take a hold of him."

While one of the men thumbed at the screen of a cell phone, another tried to take hold of Donner's wrist. Donner swiped at his arm with his free hand, loosening the grip enough to pull himself free.

"You're making a mistake," he said.

One of the men behind the leader produced a pistol, a Glock maybe, but Donner didn't have time to get a good look because now the leader was swinging the bat in a wide arc at his head. Donner ducked, balled his fist, and drove it into the man's solar plexus. He gave a strained Oof! and crumpled, the bat slipping from his grasp. The man with the pistol raised it, took aim, panic in his eyes.

A dozen possibilities ran through Donner's mind: fight them, reason with them, run, and more. Only one made any immediate sense. He sprinted for the skate park's wire fence, unsure if he could make it over. He jumped, grabbed hold of the upper bar, and hauled himself up, hooking one leg over the top. The men called out in confusion, but he ignored them, focused only on getting over the fence and away.

Donner landed hard on the concrete on the other side,

jarring his elbows and knees, sending shockwaves of pain through his limbs. He cried out, but didn't pause to assess his injuries, instead scrambling to his feet. Gasps and shouts came from the kids clustered around the bowls. He shoved one of them out of his way as he made for the open gate at the other side. In his peripheral vision, he saw the men split and run along the outside of the skate park. He could make it to the exit before them, he was sure of it, if he could block out the pain and run.

Through the gate, there, the rental car less than thirty yards away. Run, he told himself, run.

The men came from either side of the park, trying to flank him, but they couldn't get to him before he got to the car. No way. He put his head down and churned his arms and legs, a jolt of pain from his knees each time his feet hit the ground.

Donner was only feet from the car when a lightning bolt of pain shot through his left ankle. He felt it twist beneath him, robbing his balance, and he sprawled on the coarse grass and dirt, skinning his palms. Behind him, the pounding of feet, the panting of men on the chase. He screamed as he got to his feet and put weight on his left leg. Hobbling forward, he pulled the key from his pocket and unlocked the car. They were almost on him as he opened the driver's door and fell inside.

He pulled his injured leg in after him and slammed the door closed, hitting the lock button as they reached the car. They hammered the windows with their fists. The leader arrived last, still winded from the blow to his stomach, and slammed the bat against the driver's window, then the windshield. As Donner turned the key in the ignition, a crack appeared in the windshield glass, spidering out from the point of impact.

He put the car in reverse and accelerated backward, mounting the grassy shoulder before hitting the road on the other side. The leader threw the bat after him and it struck the car's flank as Donner jerked the steering wheel to the right. He straightened, put the car in drive, and floored the gas pedal. His wheels spun on the asphalt for a moment, shrieking, before the car sped away. Somewhere behind him he heard angry shouts, faint above the roar of the engine. Donner screamed damnation as he drove, his voice cracking with anger and pain.

4 8

They had been driving for two days, no particular direction, sticking to the small roads. Moonflower had spent most of that time in the rear of the van, in the dark, her stomach rolling with hunger and nausea, her legs and arms twitching. Mom had slept barely more than a few hours, her mood like the blunt edge of a knife. Moonflower knew how she felt; she too sensed her anger like a shark beneath the surface of the water, always ready to strike. They had hardly seen each other over the two days, but when they did, they sniped at each other.

Now the van was still and silent, and Moonflower waited for the side door to slide open. Eventually it did, and Mom climbed inside. She said nothing as she closed the door and gathered the sleeping bag around herself.

"What time is it?" Moonflower asked.

"Three," Mom said.

"In the morning?"

"Yeah."

"Where are we?"

"North of El Paso. Baby, I need to sleep."

Her voice was heavy with fatigue and stretched patience. Moonflower knew she should be quiet and let her mother sleep, but the need to speak was greater.

"I'm hungry," she said.

Mom gave a weary exhalation. "You had those four pints yesterday."

"It was the day before yesterday," Moonflower said. "You should've let me have him."

"We've been over this, baby, it wasn't—"

Moonflower felt the voice rise up from her core, a voice that didn't feel like her own when it reached her throat, scratching and tearing as it climbed into her mouth. "Goddamn you, bitch, I'm hungry."

It left a taste on her tongue, bitter and metallic, and pain in her throat and chest, as if she'd breathed in something caustic. They both remained silent for a time before Mom sat upright.

"You can't talk to me like that."

Moonflower wanted to say it wasn't her, it was something else, something that hid beneath her skin, a thing that feared the light. Instead, she said, "I'm sorry."

"Okay," Mom said. She crawled across the van's floor to her. "Baby, you need to keep it under control. Just another day or two. Can you do that for me?"

"I'll try," Moonflower said. "But I'm so hungry."

Tears came, hot as blood, rolling down her hollow cheeks. Mom took her in her arms and rocked her.

"I know, baby, and it's not your fault. You remember that, okay? It's not your fault."

Moonflower knew that. She had never chosen this, no more than Mom had, no more than any of the men whose lives she had drained from their veins.

"I have something," Mom said. "Someone in El Paso. A fake profile. I've been talking to him for a couple days. I've been waiting for him to ask to meet, but I'll ask him in the morning. We'll get you fed so you can be well. A day, two days at most."

"You promise?"

Mom kissed the hard ridge of her cheekbone and said, "I promise."

File #: 89-49911-50
Subject: Rebecca Carter
OO: Flagstaff
Desc: Journal Entry, Handwritten
Date: Unknown

These are the rules. Is that the right word? Maybe, I don't know, but it'll do until I think of a better one. We spent two days with the Nurse, and he told me his story. I don't know if I believe him, but I guess I have no choice. He's met others like Moonflower. Cared for them, sometimes. These are the things he says I need to know in order to keep her alive. Most of these are his rules, but some are mine:

She is human. He didn't say it, but it's my first rule. She is human. She is my daughter, and she is still a human being. Nothing will change that.

She is not immortal. She can die just like any person. She may heal faster than is natural, but what is fatal to anyone else is also fatal to her. Because she is human.

She is not some magical being. She can't shapeshift into an animal, with or without wings. She can't turn into a cloud of sparkling dust or levitate or any of that bullshit. Because she is human.

Sunlight will not make her explode into a ball of flames. It hurts her eyes, gives her an unbearable headache, and even a cloudy day will cause her a wicked case of sunburn. But she will not spontaneously combust. Because she is human.

She has a reflection. She can't bear the sight of it, but she has one. It's near impossible to take a photograph of her. I don't understand why, but her skin reflects light differently. Any photograph of her turns out a shapeless glare. But she has a reflection. Because she is human.

She must feed. Not every day, not even every week, but regularly. Animal blood will get her by for a while, but not indefinitely. Eventually she will need blood like her own or she will starve, whatever's inside her hollowing her out until there's nothing left. She can tolerate a small amount of regular food, but no more than a mouthful or two or she'll throw it up again. She needs water like all living things. Because she is human.

She is human. This is the first and last rule, because it is the truth. She is Monica Carter, my daughter, my Moonflower, and she is first, last, and always a human being.

49

Rebecca hadn't had a cigarette in more than twenty-four hours and the need scratched at the inside of her lungs and her throat. She thought, I wonder if this is what it feels like? Her hunger? This bone-deep want. She shook her head to dislodge the notion. Foolish, she told herself. There was no imagining what her daughter's craving felt like.

She took a Marlboro from the pack, held it tight between her lips, and sparked up. The nicotine hit like a velvet hammer, almost took her off her feet. She stood in the shadow of the RV park's small convenience store, a baseball cap pulled down low, her shades on. She wore them in the store while she bought the cigarettes with the last of her money. It might have made her stand out except this place was already filled with freaks and weirdos. Short of walking into the store buck naked, there wasn't much she could do to make herself appear exceptional.

The RV park was part of a sprawl of lots northwest of El

Paso, most of them occupied by trailer homes. The board outside the complex had boasted of a clubhouse, a play area, and a pool. The only thing of any use to Rebecca was this shitty little store and the cigarettes it sold. She dragged the last of the Marlboro down to the filter, crushed it under her heel, and lit another. Smoother this time, less of a rush, but good nonetheless. Stupid goddamn habit.

She could see the van from here, its metalwork dull in the morning sunlight. Early enough for the air to still carry the night's chill. The sun would warm things up soon enough. The peaks of the Franklin Mountains loomed to the east. Good place to lose a body. No snow, not enough tree cover, but it would do.

Moonflower slept in the rear of the van. At least, Rebecca hoped she did. Neither of them had managed much since leaving Tucson. Rebecca had been avoiding spending time closed in there with her daughter. The caged animal smell had become stronger, and Moonflower's moods more erratic. If they were hers at all, and not the foul humors of the thing that drove her hunger. Rebecca couldn't tell anymore.

A traitorous, evil thought had been lingering at the edge of her mind these last few days: What if Guthrie had been right? What if it truly was time to let Moonflower go? Fifteen years was a long time for her kind. The animal in her, that gluttonous thing, had risen closer and closer to the surface. But Moonflower could be saved, couldn't she? Brought back from wherever she'd been lost. Of course she could. Rebecca had to believe that. And exactly how much of her baby girl was there left to save?

"Shut up," Rebecca hissed.

"Excuse me?"

She looked up from the orange embers of her cigarette and saw an elderly man staring back at her, an overflowing shopping bag in his hand, his brow creased, his lips thin.

"Sorry," Rebecca said, "I was talking to myself."

She felt heat spread on her neck and cheeks, a sickly twist of humiliation in her stomach. The man's face softened, and he took a step closer.

"Is everything all right, miss? Do you need any help?"

A hundred replies flitted through her mind, all the things she needed, none of which she could ever ask for.

"I'm fine, thank you."

"You sure?" he asked, taking another step toward her. "You seem upset."

Please go, she thought. I can't take your pity.

"Honestly, I'm fine. Thank you."

Another step closer.

"If you need anything, my wife and I are—"

"Please, sir, just . . . just fuck off, okay?"

He regarded her for a moment, only the briefest flash of contempt on his face, immediately replaced by a sorrowful acceptance.

"All right, I'll leave you be. We're in that Winnebago Roam over there, if you need anything."

He turned and walked away, his labored breath misting in the cool morning air, and Rebecca felt a sour sting of regret.

"Sir?" she called after him.

He stopped and looked back over his shoulder.

"I'm sorry for what I said."

He smiled, nodded, and went on his way.

Rebecca hunkered down, her back against the store's side wall, holding her head in her hands. How had she become this hollowed out shell of a person? She had once been a girl of sixteen, of seventeen, wide-eyed with wonder at the life that lay ahead of her. So clean in mind and spirit. She remembered how jaded and cynical her school friends had tried to be, as if happy and hopeful were the most uncool things a person could aspire to be. Even when she became pregnant, the sense of the world ending, the sky falling, only lasted a week or so, and most of that had been fear of telling her parents. Once they knew, and they made it clear they would love and support her no matter what, her hope returned. It had stayed for the remaining months of her pregnancy, and for the twelve years, four months, and nineteen days that followed.

Now? She could barely see a day ahead of herself. Like driving in thick fog, the headlights obscuring more than they revealed. She tried not to dwell on the gulf between surviving and living, but the knowledge of it lingered always at the edge of her mind, and she hated it with all her heart. It was that hatred that drove her forward, but it was no less bitter for it.

Rebecca finished the second cigarette, ground it out on the concrete, and considered lighting a third. A small indulgence, and she allowed herself so few of those. No, she would not. Save it for later, when her work was done.

The pretend-boy claimed he lived near the University of Texas at El Paso, both his parents lecturers there. God, he was bored living near the border. His parents didn't understand him, wanted to force him to be academics like them, when all he wanted to do was travel, see the world, and play his guitar.

All of it bullshit. Rebecca could spot the lies a mile off. So, she fed him some of hers, how she wanted to experience so much, but her devout Catholic parents were stifling her, and couldn't they see that she wasn't like them?

They'd been conversing for four days. Normally, Rebecca would have liked to string things out a few days more. Let her prey's excitement grow, let his thirst build, get him to the point where he was easy to steer. But there was no time. Moonflower was too hungry to wait any longer. Rebecca would try to convince him to meet that evening. If he refused, they might have to do it the old way, like back at that mall in Flagstaff. The thought made her shudder as she stood and walked toward the van. Either way, this time tomorrow, it would be done.

Tomorrow.

Such an alien idea. That there could be a tomorrow. It stopped her, her heels grinding on the asphalt. She tried to picture a tomorrow, a day after this one, but her mind could not conceive of it. Closing her eyes, she imagined it, waking up. Both of them still alive, Moonflower's hunger sated, the beast inside her quiet for now. The image would not form, not even the broadest strokes of it.

Rebecca opened her eyes and turned in a circle. The stretch of RVs and trailers to the south, the mountain peaks to the east, urban sprawl to the north, nothing but wilderness to the west.

Is this where it ends? In this godforsaken place?

No, she told herself.

This is where it begins.

5 0

Donner sat at the table beneath the motel room's window, chipped Formica, more stain rings than he could count. He kept the drapes closed, his perpetual hangover rendering daylight unbearable. The drunk had swallowed him whole sometime around three in the morning, and he'd woken at eleven, vomiting up what remained in his stomach. He had eaten two cold Poptarts and had so far managed to keep them down.

I am unwell, he thought.

His next thought was: No shit, Sherlock.

Donner laughed aloud, then caught himself, placed a hand over his mouth. He scrolled back through the direct messages on his phone, lines of text blurring until he stopped them with his thumb.

OMFG, I'm so done with this gd house.
I no, fkg a holes all around me.
R u free 2nite?

OMG yes!
Do u no Limestone Ranch?
???
Housing dvlpmnt, N El Paso.
1 sec, lemme ggle. Yep, got it.
Park there, by all the new houses.
Ok.
Meet me there? At old playground.
Gimme sec, brb.
OK.

Five minutes passed.

Yep, what time?
6?
Ok.
Listen, do u hv any money?

Several minutes passed before he replied.

Maybe. Why???
I might need sum.
U running away?
Maybe. Not 2nite, but soon.
Will c what I can do.
Ok, thank u. C u at 6?
Yep, c u there.

Donner checked the time: three in the afternoon. He'd planned the routes. Thirty minutes to get there. Two and a half hours to get focused. He stood from the chair, the cushion wheezing its relief, and limped to the bed. The pain and swelling in his ankle had eased somewhat, but it remained tender. He'd taken more Aleve than he should, but it seemed to help.

The revolver he'd bought the day before sat on the nightstand. A knock-off Smith & Wesson .38, anyone who knew guns could spot it was a fake. But it had been cheap, and no questions asked. Eight round capacity, and the cylinder spun well, the hammer action was smooth. It would perform well enough for his needs.

He had sat here last night, on the edge of this bed, for an hour and a half. Pushing the cylinder free from the body, spinning it with his thumb, flicking it back into place. Testing the heft of it in his hand. Placing the muzzle beneath his jaw. Imagining the click of the hammer, the explosion beneath his chin, the bullet's path through bone and tissue, the gases blossoming in his skull, obliterating him and everything he had ever been. He wondered what had gone through Edward Chin's mind when he did exactly the same thing. Did he think of his wife? His son? Did he wonder about after, whether it would be a long stretch of nothing, or some kind of heaven, or a pit of fire? No answers to be found, and no courage to pull the trigger, Donner had gotten drunk and passed out.

Donner stood and went back to the table. A cheap notepad sat there, along with a pen. He'd bought them at some dollar store a mile or two before the motel. The first pages of the notepad were scarred with meaningless doodles, slashing lines, scrawled phrases that he could not read in his relative sobriety. He tore those pages out, tossed them at the garbage can, and missed.

Donner lifted the pen and brought the nib to the blank page. He started writing, grinding the words out, each one like pulling a splinter from his skin. Tears came, blurring the ink. He wiped them from the page, making it worse. Didn't matter. Probably no one would read it anyway.

When he was done, he read through what he'd written. He had so much to say yet so little to show for it. One and a half miserable pages of self-pity, barely a word of consequence. A whole life gone by, and it came to little more than a few scribbles on some dollar store notepaper. He tore the pages from the book, ripped them into squares, and tossed them into the trash can by the desk. Then he went to the bed, lay down, and stared at the ceiling, his fingers interlocked across his chest. He counted the minutes.

Nothing to do now but wait.

5 1

Mom dropped Moonflower at the edge of the housing development not long before five-thirty, the sun now hidden behind the low rooftops, the sky painted with deep orange and red strokes, fading to dark blue. A cluster of homes, newly built, most not quite finished. Limestone Drive, Sandstone Lane, Stonehill View. Moonflower walked through the development, observing the empty shells of houses, imagining the happy families that would occupy them one day. She could almost feel the life pulse in anticipation from inside. Unfinished yards, some of them with cement mixers, mounds of paving stones wrapped in plastic, ready to be laid. A year from now, maybe two, this place would seem like it had always been here, had never been barren scrubland where jackrabbits and cottontails foraged while raptors hovered above.

No one peered at her through the windows. No drapes or blinds twitched at her passing. If they had, she would have looked like another skinny kid, a little paler than most, walking home from wherever they'd been. The promise of happy family life all around caused her mind to wander through the possibilities that had been lost to her. If she hadn't been attacked all those years ago, if she hadn't died and come back, would Mom have married Peter? Would they have had a home like one of these? Maybe she'd have had a little sister or brother, maybe even two. A life of sunrises and sunsets, school, college, friends, boyfriends, holidays. Maybe she'd be married, have kids of her own, a house, a good job. An artist, possibly, she'd always been good at drawing and painting, and she missed having a pencil and a sketchbook. But she could have none of those things; she would remain locked in this body, exactly as it was, for as long as she existed. Places like this always made Moonflower grieve for what never was.

Within a few minutes, she reached the edge of the old park, long abandoned. A long stretch of stubbled grass, yellowed and dry, with a cluster of covered jungle gyms and a pair of swings at one end, the chains rusted. A pair of crumbling maintenance buildings thirty, forty feet from those. Perhaps, when the housing development was complete, they would raze this playground and rebuild it, new and shining. Moonflower imagined all the children who would play here, their ringing laughter.

A stretch of leveled ground lay to the other side of the park, sites marked out with metal stakes and ropes, showing where more houses would be built at some future time. Barely any trees. She could see in all directions.

Moonflower went to the swings which stood in their own sand circle, apart from the climbing frames. One seat had detached from its chains, and it dangled loose like a hanged man. She sat in the other, and the chains creaked and whined as she pushed back with her legs, held her feet straight out in front of her on the forward swing, tucked them beneath her on the way back, building momentum. All the time she kept her attention on the boundaries of the park, looking for a lonely man who wouldn't hurt a fly, honest to God he wouldn't.

Forward and back, forward and back, the creak of the chains establishing a loping rhythm.

Nothing to do now but wait.

File #: 89-49911-67
Subject: Rebecca Carter
OO: El Paso
Desc: Letter, Handwritten by Special Agent Marc
Donner (Note: Letter torn and reassembled, retrieved
from waste basket)
Date: 01-13-2023 (assumed)

Dear Liz,

I don't know if you'll ever read this. If you do, it's very possible I'm dead, and I'm sorry. It shouldn't have come to this, and it's my fault that it did.

As McGrath keeps telling me, I could just walk away. Pretend none of this happened the way it did. That would be easier. Just keep my mouth shut, say what they want me to say, make it all go away. Then I could get on with my life. I could maybe even keep my job. But I would never sleep easy again as long as I live, knowing that thing's out there.

Everyone thinks I'm crazy. Holstein, my supervisor, thinks so. So does McGrath, even if she wouldn't say it to my face. And I guess you think it too. I suppose you can't all be mistaken. I feel it in myself, like everything is teetering on the edge of something, about to fall, and nothing can stop it. So, yes, I might have lost my mind, but that doesn't mean I'm wrong.

I don't know what this thing is that I'm hunting. It looks like a child, not much younger than Emma, but it is not a child. Despite what its mother says, it is not human. No human, child or fully grown, could do what that thing has done. And I've seen what it did to Edward Chin, what it turned him into. I'm sorry he took his life. I would've done the same in his situation. But the fact is, he may have pulled the trigger, but that thing killed him as surely as it killed Rollins and all those men whose bodies were left out in the forests.

I have to do this. I have no choice. Someone has to stop this thing. No one believes me. Why should they? So, I'm left here to do this all alone. I can't blame McGrath. She's right to stay out of it. I have to face this whether I want to or not. That's all there is.

Liz, Emma, Jess—I'm sorry for everything. I'm sorry for being too buried in my own selfishness to see our family was coming apart. I'm sorry I missed so much of my girls' lives because I was too wrapped up in my work or just too damn drunk to notice the years pass. Most of all, I'm sorry I left. I don't know what I thought I would gain, but I know what I lost: everything. There's no getting it back now, whether I come through this or not, I know that.

Please believe this one thing: I love you. I have always loved you, my girls, and I always will, no matter what happens next.

I'm sorry,
Marc

5 2

Rebecca drove in circles around the area, looking for anything out of the ordinary. Anyone paying her too much attention, a parked car with occupants trying hard not to look at her, a maintenance worker on a telegraph pole not focusing on his or her labor. Nothing stood out to her, but she was conscious that a dilapidated van touring the area might draw attention, so she made her way back to the park.

There was Moonflower, swinging back and forth, just an ordinary little girl at play. Except she shouldn't be there, not in a deserted place like this. Rebecca pulled up at the northwest corner of the park and craned her neck to survey the surroundings. Nowhere close she could park and not be visible. She would have to move the van into the housing development, and come back on foot, find a decent vantage point. Checking the time on the phone she'd swiped from a gas station several days ago, she saw she only had twenty minutes. No time to waste.

Rebecca put the van in drive and made her way into the development. She eased the van onto an unfinished driveway and parked in the shadow of a windowless house. Putting the cap on her head, the shades over her eyes, she walked back to the park. Less than a minute. She'd have to factor that in when the target showed himself, getting back to the van, and picking up his and Moonflower's trail. But she wasn't worried about that. Moonflower would slow him down, whoever he might be. Whenever they got to where they were going, Rebecca would incapacitate him with the rifle she'd taken from the Nurse. She'd have preferred her Sage bow, it was near silent, but she had lost that along with everything else back in Flagstaff.

As Rebecca reached the western edge of the park, she slowed and looked all around. Moonflower remained on the swing, back and forth, and Rebecca heard the coarse whine of the chains. No cars parked on the road that ran alongside the park, nothing but open ground all around. An alarm sounded inside her, faint but insistent. It was too exposed here, Moonflower too out of place. She reminded herself they were out of options. It was this or the old way, trying to pick up some sad man in a shopping mall food court. She wouldn't put Moonflower through that again.

Rebecca scanned the area again. Hardly any trees, no real cover to speak of. Only the pair of small maintenance buildings closer to the playground could serve as a vantage point. She walked in that direction, head down, just a woman out for an evening stroll, minding her own business. Shadow pooled between the two small structures, one of them a shed, the other little more than a locked-up box, both of them falling apart. She lost herself between them.

Getting darker now, a steady breeze sweeping over the open ground. She pulled off the shades and cap and shoved them into the pocket of her hoodie and watched her daughter play. Rebecca felt a pang of longing for such normality. A little girl on a swing, using her legs for momentum. She remembered that feeling, the rush of the fall, the moment of weightlessness at the arc's zenith, then falling again.

A small, lone dog emerged from the housing development on the far side of the park. Matted fur, ribs showing. It approached, hesitated, came closer. It lowered itself so its belly scraped along the dried grass and dirt, halting a few feet from the swings.

Moonflower used her feet to slow her momentum, kicking up billows of dust, then stopped, the swing swiveling for a moment before it became still. She bent over and reached out her hand. The dog drew closer, and when it was within reach, it rolled onto its back and showed her the pale pink skin of its belly.

Rebecca allowed herself a smile, indulged in the fantasy that Moonflower was a normal little girl in a normal playground petting a normal dog. Maybe it could be her dog, and after, they would walk it home together and Rebecca would admonish her baby girl for feeding it scraps from the table.

The dream broke apart in her mind. She felt something cold touch the core of her, and that small alarm she had been ignoring for the last few minutes swelled like a poisoned wound. Something was wrong. She couldn't place what it was, but the stillness of this place had become too still, the quiet *too* quiet.

Rebecca opened her mouth, inhaled, ready to call to her daughter, tell her to come here, they were leaving. But a voice from behind trapped the breath in her chest.

"Rebecca Carter."

She spun, almost overbalanced, reached out a hand to steady herself against the rusted metalwork of the shed. A man stood there, an N95 mask over his nose and mouth, and a pair of safety goggles over his eyes. Her mind scrambled to place him for a few moments, then she recognized the voice that spoke her name: Special Agent Marc Donner, FBI, his hollowed eyes seeming to have aged a decade in the few weeks since she'd left him cowering on the floor of the Flagstaff field office.

Rebecca had no more than a second to register the small metal cylinder in his raised right hand before his finger pressed on the top and a liquid came spraying out, into her eyes, her nose and mouth, onto her skin. Cold for a moment, then heat, building and multiplying until it scorched the light from her eyes. She tried to inhale so she could scream, but her lungs pulled in the fiery liquid, torching her from the inside.

She screamed anyway, a guttural cry of pain and fear that stretched all the way from her stomach to the heavens above.

53

Good, Donner thought. He wanted it loud. Louder the better. Bring the creature running.

Rebecca's hands flailed blindly, reaching, searching, her eyes red and blind, snot spilling from her nose, sputum from her mouth. She coughed and howled and gagged. Donner had been maced before, he knew what it felt like, so he gave her another blast as she collapsed to the ground. Then he looked across the park to the playground.

The child, the monster, stood by the swings, staring back at him, a cowering dog at her feet.

"Come on," Donner whispered. "Come at me. Do it. Do it."

She remained still, but he could feel the rage from here.

"Come on!" he shouted, pulling the mask from his mouth, the goggles from his eyes. The mace that hadn't been swept away by the breeze burned his nostrils and throat, brought water to his eyes. He blinked and wiped it away.

The creature charged then, all fours, galloping like the animal it was. Fast, so fast he thought for a moment he wouldn't be ready for her. He pulled the stun gun from his pocket and readied it, his thumb on the button.

She came at him, closer, closer, wait, not yet.

Jesus Christ, don't fuck it up.

Closer, closer.

Now.

He raised the stun gun as she leapt for him, her teeth bared, a devil's shriek sounding from her throat. She rammed into his chest, pushing the air from his lungs as he was thrown to the ground, her hands grabbing at his throat. He lifted his right hand, his thumb already on the button, sparks arcing between the prongs. As her mouth dipped toward his throat, he drove the prongs into the hollow beneath her jaw. Her body stiffened like a wooden plank, her eyes wide, her teeth clenched tight. She rolled away, gasping, her arms and legs convulsing.

Rebecca's ragged voice raged behind him.

"You motherfucker, what are you doing? What are you doing? Moonflower? Baby? Can you hear me? Kill him, you hear me? Kill him!"

Donner pocketed the stun gun and pulled the taser pistol from the holster on his waistband. The creature had begun to recover and push itself upright. He pulled the trigger. Twin darts shot forth, trailing black and red cords behind them, and buried themselves in her chest. Her body went limp and hit the ground hard, throwing up dust. The girl began to writhe, whimpering. Donner pulled the trigger again, sent another flood of electricity through the cables and into the prongs that pierced her skin. Her body stretched and stiffened, and a choked gurgling sounded from deep in her throat. Donner held the trigger as long as he dared, longer than any human could withstand it, but reminded himself this thing was not human. Whatever humanity it had ever possessed had been left on a mortuary slab a thousand miles and fifteen years from here. He released the trigger, and the creature went slack and loose, its eyelids flickering, spittle hanging from its lips.

Donner pulled the backpack from his shoulders and fetched the cable ties from inside. He rolled the creature over, kneeled on its back, and bound its wrists and ankles.

"Motherfucker, motherfucker, I'll kill you if you hurt her, you motherfucker."

Rebecca swiped at empty air with clawed fingers. He ignored her strangled curses and reached into the backpack once more, took out the spit hood. The woman crawled toward him, unseeing, reaching and feeling with one hand as she cursed and spat. Donner pushed her away, hard, and her back slammed into the shed wall. He placed the mask over the creature's head and mouth, pulled the ties as tight as they would go. The mesh hood had been designed for a full-grown adult, and the hard plastic lower portion hung loose over her mouth, but it would suffice for now.

Rebecca continued her furious curses and threats, her voice thin and cracked, her hands outstretched, searching the air for him and her daughter. Donner stood upright, listing as his weight triggered pain in his ankle. He grabbed the creature's collar below its throat, and lifted it.

"Shut up and listen."

"You bastard, I'll kill you, I'll—"

He kicked Rebecca square in the thigh.

"Shut up and listen if you want to see this thing alive again."

She leaned back against the wall, blinking, blinking, tears streaming from her red eyes. Her mouth wide, air wheezing in and out of her.

"There's a bag in front of you. There's a thirty-ounce bottle of saline solution inside. Get it now."

Rebecca hesitated, then scrabbled around the dirt in front of her till she found the bag. She pulled the bottle from inside, already fumbling at the cap.

"Open it and pour it into your eyes."

She did so, saltwater splashing all around her.

"Don't waste any. You'll need all of it."

She blinked up at the sky, pouring more carefully now, coughing and spitting away any that flowed into her mouth.

"Now, listen to me. You'll find your daughter at ABC Auto Center. It's an old salvage yard about two miles east of here. There's a workshop there. Get moving before someone comes by and calls the cops. We'll be waiting."

He limped away, carrying the creature by its collar, impossibly light, its heels dragging on the ground. With his free hand, he pulled the revolver from its holster beneath his arm. He headed south, toward what had once been some kind of recreation center, long abandoned. His car was parked on the other side. Beyond that, the remains of a basketball court, and a cluster of rundown homes. Someone might have heard the woman's frantic screaming, and he would be ready. If anyone emerged from their home to challenge him, ask him what he was doing with this child, he would tell them he was FBI and to mind their business. And if anyone tried to stop him, he would shoot them. He would not hesitate.

As Donner rounded the building, and the rental car with its cracked windshield came into sight, he knew he should have felt something. Guilt, anger, anything, but he had no room for emotion now. There was so much to do and so little time to do it in.

5 4

Moonflower lingered on the edge of consciousness. She was aware of movement, of being weightless and suspended above the ground. She lost herself for a while, then came back, rolling like dice in a cup. The mechanical hum of an engine, a man's strained breathing. Something hard and painful bound her wrists together, and her ankles, and some kind of material covered her nose and mouth. Her arms and legs would not obey her commands to strain at the bonds, to break them, her muscles hanging from her bones, heavy and useless. She drifted in and out of the world, staying a little longer each visit. By the time the car halted, she was able to keep her mind in the present.

The engine died, and moments later, cool evening air washed over her as the door at her feet opened. She turned her head, trying to see who reached in for her, but she could not. The mesh hood that covered her head robbed her of what little vision remained. He smelled of stale sweat and fresh fear as he dragged her out of the car and carried her toward a ruin of a building, limping, his step uneven. She tried to kick and writhe, but her limbs didn't have the power to do more than twitch at her command.

"Who . . . who are you?"

The hard plastic over her mouth muted the words, but he heard her well enough.

"You know who I am."

As he carried her into the building and hit a switch on the wall, she craned her neck, tried to see him. The single fluorescent light above stuttered into life, but still she could not make out his features.

"Please, I don't know what's happening."

"Quiet, now," he said as he limped toward the center of the floor.

He dropped her on the stained concrete. She rolled to her side and looked up at him. Now she could see through the mesh. It took a few moments to understand, but then she knew. She had left this man on the floor of that field office in Flagstaff, cowering, certain he was about to die. But Mom had told her to let him live, and she had obeyed.

"You know me?" he asked.

Moonflower nodded.

"Listen to me," he said, wincing as he hunkered down beside her. "I don't want to hurt you, and I won't if I don't have to. I just want everyone to know the truth. To show them I'm not crazy. You understand?"

"I think so," Moonflower said, her lips rubbing against the hard fabric.

"If I take that spit hood off, you won't bite me, right? If you hurt me, I'll hurt you worse. Understand?"

Moonflower nodded again.

He pulled her up into a sitting position and reached behind her head. The nylon straps pulled at her hair as he worked it free. The inside of his wrist came close to her mouth, and she smelled his lifeblood through the odors of his sweat and fear. Her stomach growled, resonating between the walls of the building, and he jerked back his hands, falling onto his rear, and scrabbling away.

It would have been so easy to seize the skin of his wrist between her teeth, open his veins before he had a chance to recoil. She could taste it on her lips, the salty, metallic heat of it. Her stomach growled once more at the thought. She dropped her head, closed her eyes, willed the hunger to sink back down to the depths of her, where it belonged. If she let it free now, let it take control, she knew that would be the end of her. The end of everything.

When she opened her eyes again, he stood over her, a cell phone in his hand. She heard the whirr of an artificial shutter, and a light flashed hard and bright, making her flinch. He cursed under his breath, goddammit, then took a second photograph, and a third. She could have told him that cameras never seemed to work around her, the images always over-bright and distorted.

"Fuck it," he said, then he thumbed at the screen.

She heard the click-clack of pretend keys as he typed, then a whoosh as he sent the images to someone.

Who could want to see a blurred picture of her? Before she could summon a guess, he pulled the stun gun from his pocket and touched the prongs to the skin beneath her ear. She saw a blinding flash of lightning, then all was pain.

File #: 89-49911-58
Subject: Rebecca Carter
OO: Flagstaff
Desc: Journal Entry, Handwritten
Date: Unknown

It's been ten years. Ten years last week, in fact. I didn't realize until this morning. It's not as if I've been counting the days like it was an anniversary to be celebrated. But we've survived this long, and I guess that's something to be glad about.

I think about my mother a lot. I wonder how age has changed her. I wish I could call her and tell her how much I love her and miss her. I wish she could take me in her arms and tell me everything will be all right. I wish.

We passed through Scottsdale a few days ago, getting into town around dawn. I drove around while Moonflower slept in the back of the van. She'd fed only two days before, so she slept hard and well. I passed the places that Peter had liked. His favorite burger joint, the mystery bookstore he loved, and finally I drove by his old house.

I say "old house" but, really, I had no idea if he still lived there or not. I imagine the police must have grilled him pretty hard after I disappeared to see if he knew anything. I'd be surprised if they hadn't kept him under surveillance for a while in case I showed up on his doorstep. I never so much as called him. I wouldn't put that on him. He didn't deserve it.

It was still pretty early when I pulled up across the road from his house. Good and warm out, but not the blistering heat that would come later in the day. Grackles gathered on the watered lawns, fluttering back and forth between the trees, cawing the way they do. Peter told me they're considered pests, but I always liked them.

I watched the house awhile, wondering if he still lived there, if he was home or out on the road. I wondered if he ever thought of me and Moonflower. I thought how happy we could've been. Just as I put the key back in the ignition, a little girl came out of the house. Maybe seven years old. She had a pair of roller-skates. The kind built into the boots, not the kind I had when I was a kid, that strapped over your shoes. She wore a helmet with elbow and knee pads, and she skated up and down the concrete driveway, unsteady, arms outstretched, one hesitant foot in front of the other.

She could've been Moonflower's little sister. That could've been our house. Our life.

I cried a little. I hadn't done that for a long time, but I couldn't help it. If this was Peter's home, his daughter, then part of me was glad for him. Happy for his happiness. But part of me resented it too, and I thought for a moment I was a bad person. My happiness for him should be unconditional.

But it's not. It can't be, and that's okay. Because, I realized, I don't begrudge him anything. It's just that I wanted it for myself as well, and I can't have it, and that hurts. I'm glad for him and sad for me. Both things are true, and I have to forgive myself for that.

The little girl fell, and my first instinct was to get out of the van and go to her. Thank God, I stopped myself. A woman came out of the house, summoned by the little girl's cries. She came walking with the weary concern of a parent who knows it's both nothing at all and also the worst thing in the world ever. As she gathered up her little girl, she glanced across the road.

Our eyes met, and I wanted to wave to her. But then I saw the expression on her face. A deep fear. I knew why. He must have told her about me. They must know I'm out there somewhere. They must realize the possibility that I could turn up someday, just like this.

She grabbed the girl and carried her, running, back to the house. I heard the door slam from inside the van.

I turned the key in the ignition and sped away. I drove for eleven hours straight, heading northwest, stopping only for gas. When Moonflower asked me what was wrong, I told her nothing. I wept again before I went to sleep that night. She didn't ask me why, and I'm glad of it.

It doesn't matter now. I stole a glimpse of a life that might have been mine, and what good did it do me? All that matters is that we keep going. Ten years. The Nurse told me it'd be a miracle if we made it six or seven years, but here we are, still alive after a decade.

We'll keep going. We'll keep fighting. We'll keep surviving, because that's all we have left. Life for its own sake.

It's not much, but I'll fight for it until my last breath.

5 5

Rebecca could barely see as she drove, shifting her focus between the phone in her hand and the road ahead. She blinked constantly, snatching moments of clarity before her vision clouded again. Her skin prickled and stung, and every breath brought raw pain to her throat and lungs. She spat into the footwell and wiped her nose on her sleeve.

It had taken all she had to get out of the park and reach the van, stumbling through the yards of newly built houses, tripping and falling more than once. It had seemed to take forever in the lowering dusk to find the driveway where she'd parked. The saline solution Donner had left her eased the burn somewhat, but her eyes still streamed, her vision a confusion of light and shade. Inside the van, she'd poured more into her eyes, took a mouthful, rinsed it round her teeth and tongue, and spat it out, not caring that it soaked her clothes. The bottle now lay on the passenger seat, the remnants sloshing as she navigated toward the scrapyard.

As Rebecca blinked again, her vision stayed clear longer. She squinted at the phone's display. The scrapyard was only a couple of minutes away. A car horn blared somewhere behind her. She looked up and saw she had drifted onto the wrong side of the road. Jerking the wheel, she corrected her course. The driver who had sounded his horn passed, his hand out the window, giving her the finger. She ignored him and kept driving, blinking tears from her eyes.

The phone told her to take the next right. Rebecca slowed, peering into the dark, looking for the turn. She almost missed it, and the passenger-side wheels mounted the dirt shoulder before finding the cracked asphalt again. The van's brakes whined as she brought it to a halt. The phone said the salvage yard was a hundred yards or so along this road. He'd expect her to drive right in. Instead, she would walk. But not empty-handed.

Rebecca shut off the engine and grabbed the bottle from the passenger seat. She poured the last of the saline into each eye, crying out at the searing pain, then she took a mouthful, spat it out. Blinking the water from her eyes, she looked around, saw there was no street lighting out here on the frayed edges of the city. In the dimness, she saw signs for salvage yards, auto shops, repair centers, an RV dealer. She couldn't see the place Donner had named, but she knew it wasn't far.

Rebecca opened the driver's door and climbed out. She didn't close it fully, mindful of the noise. At the side of the van, she opened the sliding door, and reached inside, feeling through the detritus until her fingertips found what she sought: the hard outline of the semi-automatic rifle she had taken from Guthrie Chambers. That, and the spare clip of ammunition. She shoved the clip into the pocket of her hoodie and hoisted up the rifle, placing the butt against her shoulder, her finger inside the trigger guard.

As she began her march toward the scrapyard, she heard sirens in the far distance. She looked back toward the city, saw a hint of blue and red light. Cops, coming here? Let them come. She didn't care.

Rebecca focused on the road ahead, the weight of the rifle in her hands, and what she planned to do with it.

5 6

Donner answered the phone on the first ring.

"Jesus Christ, Marc, what are you doing?" McGrath said, her voice razor-sharp in his ear.

"I got her," Donner said. "The photo wasn't clear, but it's her. I got her."

"Let her go," McGrath said.

"What?"

Donner paced the length of the room, limping back and forth.

"You have to let her go before anyone gets hurt."

"Too late for that," he said.

"Marc, I don't know who you've got there, I can't tell from the photo, but it's just a kid. Let her go, for God's sake, while there's still time."

He was about to reply, tell her no, he was all out of time, but a distant sound distracted him. Sirens, far off, but growing louder.

"Cops?" he asked. "Did you call the cops?"

"Of course I did," McGrath said.

He felt the world rock beneath his feet, and he fought the urge to let gravity pull him to the floor. Why did she do that?

"I told you to call the El Paso field office. I told you to get them to send their people. Not the fucking cops."

"The local police can respond quicker," McGrath said. "You've taken a child, for Christ's sake. Jesus, Marc, what did you expect me to do?"

"I expected you to call our people, like I asked you. Rebecca Carter's coming here. I can hand them both over, and they'll know I'm not crazy. But I need it to be our people."

"Marc, we're not your people anymore."

"Call the cops back, tell them not to come in here."

"I can't do that."

"McGrath," he said. "Sarah. I need this. Call them off. Tell them to send the local feds instead."

"No, Marc. Let the kid go."

"She has to stay with me."

"No, she doesn't. It doesn't have to be like this, Marc. Marc, are you listening? Whatever happens, stay on the line with me, okay?"

"Goddammit, Sarah, I needed you to do this one thing for me. Just this one thing."

"I know, Marc. I want to help you, I do, but you have to stay on the line and listen to me. First thing is, let the kid go. Then we can—"

Donner felt rage bloom inside of him, a fireball of it, and he threw the phone at the concrete floor. It bounced away, striking the wall, spraying glass fragments in its path. He roared at the empty space around him.

As the last reverberations of his voice faded, he approached the almost human form huddled on the floor. The creature's body still twitched as it recovered from the shock of the stun gun. It looked back up at him, blinking, pained confusion on its face. He aimed the revolver at its head and cocked the hammer. The creature stared for a few seconds before realizing what it saw. Then it curled into a ball and tried to tuck its head between its knees.

Just get it over with, he thought. Put a bullet in the monster's head. Then one in your own. Give in to the black nothing.

No, he thought. Not good enough.

They had to know what that thing is. They had to know he wasn't crazy, that he hadn't just dreamt it all up.

He uncocked the revolver and hunkered down over the creature. It looked so human, like a little girl. But he knew different. All he needed was for the others to see. That was all. Just let them see this thing for what it was, then he could start to put his life back together.

Donner heard something from outside. Faint, but it was there. A foot crunching on gravel.

He grabbed the creature's collar and dragged it back against the wall. It fought him, twisting and jerking its body as he struggled upright, bringing it with him. He pressed the revolver's muzzle against its head, and it became still.

"Be quiet," he whispered.

"It's her," the creature said.

"I know. Shut up."

"She's going to kill you."

"I know." He jabbed the muzzle against her temple. "Now be quiet."

The creature obeyed, the only sound now their hard breathing, and the thunderous rushing in his ears. Sweat trickled from his brow, stinging his eyes as he blinked it away. He watched the door, waiting, waiting, waiting . . .

57

Moonflower felt the terror flow from him, coming in pulsing waves like a lighthouse beacon. The gun's muzzle pressed into her temple, the hard edge biting into her scalp. She could sense his finger on the trigger, tightening.

She wished then that the stories were true. That she couldn't die. But the storytellers lied. She could and would die if he squeezed that trigger. There had been times when she would gladly have surrendered to it, but here and now, she wanted to live.

A metallic sound from the front of the workshop startled the man who held her. He removed the pistol from her temple and aimed it at the door. She saw his outstretched arm, his bare wrist. She ran her tongue around her teeth.

The door opened inward a few inches. The long black barrel of a rifle appeared there. The rifle Mom had taken from the Nurse. Mom followed, opening the door farther with her shoulder. She stepped inside, and Moonflower saw the bright burning red of her eyes, the tears on her cheeks, felt the searing pain radiating from her.

"Mom," she said.

"It's okay, baby," she said, her voice coarse as sand. "I'm here now."

"Don't come any closer," Donner said, returning the pistol to her temple. "I'll blow its brains out. I'll kill it, I swear to God."

"It?" Mom echoed. "*It*? Her name is Moonflower. Monica. She's just a little girl. Look at her. She's terrified."

"Shut up," he said. "Stay there."

"Look at her, Donner," Mom said. She came closer, blinking fiery tears from her eyes. "She is not a thing. She is human. She's my baby girl. You told me you have children. Two girls, you said. She's a person, a human being, just like them. She is not an animal."

The wail of sirens grew louder.

"Stop there," Donner said. "The cops are coming. They'll be here any minute. When they get here, we're going to put our weapons down, and we're going to let them take us in. Right?"

"No," Mom said. "That's not how this is going to work out. You know it won't."

"Stop!" Donner shouted.

He pulled back the hammer with his thumb. Moonflower felt the mechanical snick-snick through her scalp, and she imagined the explosion tearing through her skull. Mom paused halfway across the room. She kept the rifle aimed somewhere above Moonflower's head.

"Just let her go," Mom said.

"No. Not till the cops get here. Not till I show them what this fucking monster really is."

Something moved behind Mom's reddened eyes, a decision made. She knew she wasn't going to talk him down. Instead, she turned her attention to Moonflower.

"Baby, are you okay?"

Moonflower nodded.

"Listen to me, now. You have to let the other thing take control. Can you do that?"

Moonflower felt real fear rise in her for the first time.

"But what if I hurt you?"

"You won't, baby, I know you won't."

"But what if I do?"

"You won't because you're my good girl and I love you with all my heart. You know that, right?"

"Yeah," Moonflower said.

"Okay," Mom said. "You let it take control, and then you come back to me. Okay?"

"Okay," Moonflower said.

The sirens howled, close now. Moonflower saw the haze of red and blue lights through the greased-over windows. Police. They couldn't help. Not now.

"I love you, baby," Mom said.

"I love you, Mom."

Mom breathed in and out once then raised the rifle to aim at the single fluorescent light above. She pulled the trigger and the light exploded into a shower of sparks, glass, and plastic, and then all was night.

File #: 89-49911-81
Subject: Rebecca Carter
OO: El Paso
Desc: Interview Transcript (Excerpt), Interviewee:
Officer Amita Mehta, El Paso PD, Interviewer: Special
Agent Francis Visconti
Date: 01-27-2023

FV: Your conduct has not been called into question at all, so please, don't concern yourself with that.

AM: So why am I here? I've gone through all this already.

FV: We need to hear it one more time.

AM: Who's we?

FV: The Federal Bureau of Investigations.

AM: Which division?

FV: Officer Mehta, it was your—

AM: Which division? You're not CID, I'm pretty sure of—

FV: It was your weapon that fired the shots, correct?

AM: That's correct, yes.

FV: We don't need this to get any more complicated than it already is, do we?

AM: What's that supposed to mean? Are you threatening me? You know I had no choice but to fire.

FV: Please, just answer the questions.

AM: Goddammit. Go ahead and ask them, get this bullshit over with.

FV: You were at Limestone Ranch Park when the call came in, correct?

AM: That's right. Someone had called in a disturbance, said they'd heard a woman screaming from somewhere around the old park. We were cruising the new housing development there, looking for any signs of trouble. We were about to leave the area when the call came, said there was a possible hostage situation involving a child. We were less than two miles away, closest patrol to the reported location.

FV: And you drove straight there?

AM: Correct.

FV: The hostage situation was reported at ABC Auto Center, Mohair Drive. How long did it take you to get there?

AM: Less than ten minutes. Just as we turned into Mohair Drive from Dyer Street, we came upon a GMC van. We paused briefly to confirm that it had been abandoned, then we proceeded along Mohair Drive until we reached the gates of ABC Auto Center.

FV: And that's, what, an auto repair place?

AM: A small salvage yard with an office and a workshop. I think they went out of business during the pandemic, the site hadn't been occupied in a while. As we entered the property, we observed that chains securing the gates had been cut and entry forced.

FV: So you had probable cause to enter?

AM: Absolutely. The report of the hostage situation was cause enough.

FV: Did you know at that time it was an agent of the Bureau who called it in?

AM: We did not.

FV: So, you arrive at the scene . . .

AM: Yes. Both my partner and I immediately exited our vehicle and tried to establish where exactly the reported hostage situation was taking place. There were two buildings, one at either side of the yard, plus whatever scrap vehicles were abandoned at the site. It could've been anywhere. Then we heard the shots, and we knew it was in the workshop.

FV: Then, instead of waiting for backup or a trained nego-tiator, you took it upon yourselves to enter the building.

AM: Shots were fired. A child was at risk. You're goddamn right we entered the building.

5 8

Rebecca dropped to the floor and heard Donner's revolver fire, saw the muzzle flash in the darkness, knew that he had aimed in her direction before he pulled the trigger. She got up on one knee and raised the rifle, peering into the darkness. Through the electric crackle that sparked from the remains of the light, she heard struggling, grunting, hissing. Then a high, agonized howl cutting through the sirens' wail. Donner's voice.

Weak blue and red light dimly illuminated the room, and Rebecca saw Moonflower spill to the floor and roll away while Donner held his right forearm with his left. She had bitten him. Rebecca leveled the rifle's sights at Donner's chest and applied pressure to the trigger. As she squeezed, he ducked away, the muzzle flash illuminating his panicked expression. The bullet pierced the wall inches above his head.

Before Rebecca could adjust her aim, Donner threw himself at Moonflower, straddled her back, and pressed the pistol to the base of her skull. He grabbed a handful of hair with his left hand, pulled the revolver's hammer back with his right thumb. Leaning down, his chest against Moonflower's back, he looked up at the rifle's muzzle.

"How good a shot are you?" he asked.

"Good enough," Rebecca said, her finger on the trigger, the sight on his forehead.

"You sure you can hit me and not hit her? You sure if you get me, my finger won't pull on this trigger? You sure of that?"

Rebecca eased her finger away from the rifle's trigger because she wasn't sure at all. Not with so little light, not with her vision still blurred, her eyes still burning.

"Moonflower," she said. "Baby, it's time."

Moonflower didn't reply as she kept her eyes locked on Rebecca's. Her breathing deepened, quickened, her teeth bared.

"Don't," Donner said. "Don't make me—"

Her body bucked, her back arching, and Donner tumbled away. The pistol discharged as he fell, and Rebecca felt something tug at her left shoulder, followed by a searing heat. She watched as Moonflower strained at the cable ties that bound her wrists, heard the plastic snap. Moonflower rolled onto her back and prized the bonds from her ankles. She growled and turned to face Donner as he backed across the floor, the pistol raised.

Donner fired once, and Moonflower turned her body, the bullet passing as if she had never been in its path. Rebecca felt it cut the air a foot above her head. She went to raise the rifle again, but it seemed so heavy now, her left hand unable to lift it. The handguard slipped from her fingers, too slick with blood to hold. The muzzle rattled on the floor.

Moonflower advanced toward Donner, slow and deliberate steps, her hands out to her sides, ready to take him. Donner fired again, and again Moonflower moved aside. The bullet ricocheted off the concrete floor, sending up dust and stone chips.

Rebecca wiped her left hand on her thigh and tried once more to raise the rifle. Pain called from her shoulder, and she felt warmth spread down her flank and back. She tried to aim, but Moonflower was in the way, growling now, a bestial sound from deep inside her.

Donner cocked the revolver, aimed, and shouted, "Stay back!"

Moonflower moved closer, her body seeming to shift and change, the thing inside ready to breach her skin.

Donner roared and squeezed the trigger. Moonflower turned at the waist, raised one arm, let the bullet pass between it and her torso.

Something punched Rebecca hard in the chest.

She fell back, the rifle's grip still in her right hand. The ceiling glowed blue and red above her, the siren wail cutting into her ears. She gasped and something bubbled inside her chest, like blowing through a straw into a glass of warm milk.

"Moonflower," she said.

5 9

Donner watched as the creature changed, altered by the call of its own name.

It turned and said, "Mom?"

Time spun out like a silken thread, and Donner became aware of every hair on his head, every straining beat of his heart, every mote of dust in the dim air. The blue and red lights arcing across the ceiling and walls, bursts of radio static, hurried footsteps from beyond the doors.

"Mom?"

The creature moved toward its mother, slowly at first, then quickening its step. He knew with all certainty that he had to stop it. If he didn't, it would tear into whoever came through that door, rip them to shreds. They couldn't know what they faced.

He lunged after it, grabbed the back of its collar, allowed his momentum to throw them both to the floor. It screamed as it fell, reaching back for him, seeking his face, his eyes. He landed hard on its back, scrambled forward, placed his knee there and grabbed a fistful of its night-black hair.

Two cops entered, a man and a woman silhouetted in blue and red, their pistols drawn and aimed. One of them, the man, carried a flashlight, the searing beam cutting into Donner's eyes. They yelled at him to drop his weapon as he pressed the revolver's muzzle to the creature's head.

"No, listen to me," he shouted, squinting against the light.

"Drop the weapon, now!" the woman commanded.

"Please, listen. This thing isn't human. This thing—"

"Drop the weapon or I *will* shoot you!"

"—and its mother have murdered dozens of people. My name is Marc Donner, Special Agent Marc Donner, FBI, you can verify with the local field office, just please—"

"Final warning, drop the weapon!"

"—listen to me, just list—"

He saw the lightning flashes, felt a punch to his shoulder, another to his chest, then a hammer blow to his forehead, and then . . .

Then he saw Liz and his girls, the flickering Christmas tree lights, heard their laughter all around him. And then they were gone, the lights growing and flashing, exploding in dazzling constellations, and then he was falling into nothing.

Nothing at all.

60

Moonflower felt Donner's life and weight fall away, and she scrambled from beneath him, crawled toward her mother, crying, "Mom? Mom!"

The police officers shouted something, but she couldn't hear them, she could only hear the gurgle of blood flooding into the space between Mom's lungs and her diaphragm, drowning her.

"Mom, please, Mom, no . . ."

She reached her mother, knelt over her, cupped her face in her hands. Mom's eyes returned from some faraway place and focused on her, glinting under the beam of the flashlight.

"Hey, baby," she said, the vowels rattling in her chest and throat.

"Please, Mom, no, don't go, don't leave me, Mom, please."

Tears fell heavy like a summer shower, pattering on Mom's pearlescent skin. The police officers roared at her, threats, move away, do it now, but their calls were no more than murmurs to Moonflower's ears. Mom raised her left hand, touched Moonflower's cheek, left something wet behind.

"My good girl," she said, her voice wet and weak, her eyelids flickering.

I can save her, Moonflower thought. I can bring her back.

She brought her own wrist to her mouth. The veins glowed beneath her skin. She bit down hard, felt brilliant pain as her teeth separated skin and collagen and she tasted the metallic tang of her own essence. The police officers told her to stop, stop, move away, but she would not. Holding her wrist over Mom's lips, she let the blood drip.

Mom's eyes widened, and she spat it away, shaking her head.

"Mom, take it, please."

"No," Mom said, spitting. "No, I don't want it."

"Please, Mom, take it, please, don't leave me, please . . ."

Mom spat again and tried to take a breath, but only managed a gurgling rasp.

"I'm sorry, baby, I'm sorry. I love you . . . always . . . love . . ."

"Mom, please, take it, please, please, Mom . . ."

"Let me go."

"Mom, please . . ."

And then she was gone.

Like a light turned out, not even an afterglow to show she'd ever been there.

Moonflower lowered her forehead to rest against Mom's,

still warm, and she wept, racking convulsions that felt like they might turn her inside out.

"Move away," the woman cop shouted, her voice less urgent than it had been.

"Move away from the rifle," the man said.

Moonflower heard their footsteps come close, scraping on the concrete, but she ignored them. She kissed her mother's cheek, wrapped her arms around her neck, held her close, rocking her like Mom had rocked Moonflower so many times, telling her everything was going to be all right.

"Sweetheart, I need you to move away," the woman cop said, her voice soft now, and warm.

Fingers wrapped around Moonflower's upper arm.

"Come on, now, honey, you have to—"

The other thing, the hunger, took over. Moonflower could only watch.

File #: 89-49911-82
Subject: Rebecca Carter
OO: El Paso
Desc: Interview Transcript (Excerpt), Interviewee:
Officer Jackson Wylie, El Paso PD, Interviewer: Special
Agent Francis Visconte
Date: 01-29-2023

FV: I need you to go over this one more time.

JW: All right. But it's going to be same as last time. And the time before that.

FV: Officer Mehta fired on Agent Donner.

JW: That's right. He was given plenty of warning. You saw it on the bodycam footage.

FV: That's not in dispute. Nobody's questioning yours or Officer Mehta's judgement in that regard. It's what happens next that concerns me.

JW: (audible sigh) All right. The girl crawled to the woman, who was still alive at that time. She was obviously seriously injured. We could hear her struggling to breathe. There was an exchange between them.

FV: An exchange? Elaborate, please.

JW: Do I really have to go over this again?

FV: I'd appreciate it.

JW: She—the girl, I mean—bit herself on the wrist. Hard enough to draw blood. I'm a little vague on what was said between them, but the girl was clearly in distress. Then the woman ceased breathing. Her death was called later by the paramedics, but that was the moment she passed, as far as I'm concerned. The girl's distress intensified, and she was holding on to the woman, crying her heart out.

My colleague, Officer Mehta, she approached the child. There was a rifle within her reach, but at that stage, we didn't consider the child a threat. Officer Mehta touched the child's arm, told her we needed her to move away. (eight seconds silence)

FV: Then what happened?

JW: I . . . uh . . .

FV: Take your time.

JW: She changed.

FV: In what way?

JW: I don't know how to describe it.

FV: Try.

JW: She just . . . became something else. She looked up at us and growled. Like a dog or something. Then she grabbed Officer Mehta's wrist and threw her like she was nothing. I mean, Amita's not a small woman, you know? And that girl just tossed her aside like she was a doll. Before I could react, she launched herself at me, and Jesus, it was like getting hit by a truck. I mean, she lifted me right off my feet. I don't know how far she threw me, exactly, but I wound up not far from the door and I was able to see her run outside. But she didn't run like a regular person. It was on all fours, like an animal. Last I remember was seeing her climb onto the top of our cruiser. You have the dashcam footage, right?

FV: We do, but the image quality's poor. Overexposed.

JW: Overexposed. Is that what you call it? Same as the bodycams.

FV: That's right. Anyway, you saw the child climb over the top of the vehicle.

JW: Yeah. She paused there, and she looked back at me.

I remember the lights on her skin. Blue and red. And her eyes, staring at me. I thought for a second she was going to come back for me, but she didn't.

FV: What did she do?

JW: She looked up at the sky and she howled. I never heard anything like it. A girl that size can't make a noise like that. And then they answered, from all around, near and far. Damnedest thing I ever heard.

FV: Who answered?

JW: The dogs. The dogs called back to her. And then she was gone.

BEGINNING

The world slams into place with all the force of a freight train. A moment before, she was a single point of light in an infinite black universe. Now, she feels everything, every molecule, every atom of her being.

Cold steel pressing against the back of her head, her naked shoulders, her thighs, her heels, the immense weight of gravity pressing down on her. She can feel it, the spinning of the Earth, the moon, the sun, gravity pushing and pulling maddeningly in all directions.

And light, artificial as it is, needling through her eyelids.

Noise. Sound. Air rushing through ducts, the echo of cold tile, dripping of water somewhere deep in the skeleton of wherever she is. A shroud across her face and body, held there by this hulking gravity. She opens her eyes, sees pinpoints of light through the weave of the sheet's fabric.

She gasps, a rush of cold, cold air flooding her lungs, filling them until they might burst. Then out again. She wants more, so she takes it, sweet and cool on her tongue and in her throat.

Thrum.

In her chest, it pulses.

Thrum.

Her heart. It stutters, skips, then finds its rhythm.

Thrum. Th-Rum.

The muscles in her limbs, her shoulders, her chest, her abdomen, they all come alive at once, an instant of blinding pain, followed by tremors that ripple through her from head to toe, shouting something, insisting.

Move, they say.

First, her fingers. Then her toes. Then she draws up her legs, her knees tenting the sheet that covers her. Her hands press against the steel upon which she rests. She pushes herself upright, and the sheet falls away.

The light, hard and unnatural, sears its way into her skull. A few moments pass before she can fully open her eyes.

A room. Cold. Tiled walls and floor.

She sits on a steel table.

There are two others in here. One is empty. The last holds a shrouded form. A man beneath the sheet. She feels like she should know his name.

But does she know her own?

She thinks for a moment and realizes, yes, she does.

Her stomach clenches and groans.

She brings a hand to her naked belly.

Rebecca is hungry.

ACKNOWLEDGMENTS

Every book brings its own challenges, and as ever, I must wholeheartedly thank those people who helped bring this one to life:

First and foremost, my agents Nat Sobel, Judith Weber, and all at Sobel Weber Associates; Caspian Dennis and all at Abner Stein Ltd.

The good people at Soho Press who have continued to support me throughout my career, particularly Bronwen Hruska, Juliet Grames, and Paul Oliver; Katherine Armstrong at Simon & Schuster, who went well beyond the call of duty; and a special thank you to Ben Willis for his kindness and understanding under difficult circumstances.

In recent years, my sanity has largely been kept thanks to my fellow Fun Lovin' Crime Writers, all of whom make cameo appearances within these pages: Mark Billingham, Chris Brookmyre, Doug Johnstone, Val McDermid, and Luca Veste.

And most of all, Jo, Issy, and Ezra, for everything.